ARPERNOVELOFSUSPENSE
HARPERNOVELOFSUSPENSE
PERNOVELOFSUSPENSE
ERNOVELOFSUSPENSEAHARPE
RNOVELOFSUSPENSEAHARPE
NOVELOFSUSPENSEAHARPE
OVELOFSUSPENSEAHARPER
ELOFSUSPENSEAHARPERN
LOFSUSPENSEAHARPERNO
OFSUSPENSEAHARPERNOVE
FSUSPENSEAHARPERNOVEL
SUSPENSEAHARPERNOVELO
SPENSEAHARPERNOVELOF
PENSEAHARPERNOVELOFSU
NSEAHARPERNOVELOFSU
SEAHARPERNOVELOFSUSPE
EAHARPERNOVELOFSUSPENS
AHARPERNOVELOFSUSPENS
HARPERNOVELOFSUSPENSE
ARPERNOVELOFSUSPENSE

Enter
Certain
Murderers

Enter Certain Murderers

By SARA WOODS

✦━━✦

Enter certain Murderers, *hastily.*

(STAGE DIRECTION)

King Henry VI, Part 2, III, ii

✦━━➤

Harper & Row, Publishers
New York

Enter
Certain
Murderers

PROLOGUE

THE TELEPHONE BOX WHICH THE AUTOMOBILE ASSOCIA-
tion so thoughtfully provides for its members on the Scranton-
Mountalban road stands at perhaps the loneliest point of the twenty
miles that separate the two towns—a long, straight stretch of road,
with fields on either side. Beyond them, on the left as you go
toward Mountalban, the river is hidden by a straggle of bushes; on
the right, about a hundred yards away, is a belt of trees.

Even in winter the weekend traffic is heavy, and at midsummer
there is a steady stream during the week as well. But on this particular Tuesday afternoon in May there were few cars about, and
only an occasional lorry; a farm tractor went by, with a trailer
load of nitro-chalk. After that, the road was deserted until, just before three o'clock, a blue Mini Minor came into sight from the
direction of Scranton.

The little car seemed to be running well. There was no apparent
reason for the driver to draw up opposite the A.A. box, pick up
her handbag from the seat beside her and fumble for her key. A
moment later she was out of the car and crossing the grass verge,
her bag tucked under her arm and the key in her hand. A slim,
dark woman in a black suit, with a black hat worn at the wrong
angle. But there was no one in sight, certainly no one near enough
to appreciate the details of her costume. After one quick glance
round she made for the A.A. box in a purposeful way.

She was inside only a moment, surely not long enough for the briefest telephone call. As she came out she was snapping the clasp of her handbag. This time she didn't look about her, but made straight for the car; though—very properly—she glanced in the rear mirror before she drove away.

Not more than two minutes after she was out of sight a sleek, gray Jensen came round the corner, also from the direction of Scranton, and pulled over to the side of the road. The driver got out and opened the hood; the engine seemed to be causing him some anxiety. As there was an A.A. badge on the bumper, a passer-by might have been surprised at his independence; but, after all, some men hate to ask for help, or it could be that he hadn't noticed the box so short a distance ahead.

The third car approached from Mountalban, and drew up well short of the A.A. box while the driver consulted a map. At almost the same moment the owner of the Jensen stopped brooding over his difficulties, closed the hood and drove off. The engine purred to itself in a gratified way; it seemed unlikely that anything serious could have been amiss. In fact, one would think the driver's time might have been better spent in putting down the top on so surprisingly mellow a day. But the car remained closed.

As soon as the Jensen had gone, the driver of the third car folded his map and drove on until he was opposite the A.A. box. This time there was no insignia on the bumper, but an inconspicuous notice just above the number plate announced that the car—a Vauxhall—was the property of the Apex Hire Company. In spite of this, the driver had a key in his hand as he alighted.

He, too, disappeared into the box for no more than a moment, and when he emerged again he was tucking something away in an inner pocket. There was still nobody at all in sight. No need to hurry, he could stand for a moment savoring the pleasure of a perfect spring day. Sunshine, and a blue sky with some silly little clouds like cotton wool; meadows on the left, lush already with the promise of a good hay crop; ploughland on the right, and beyond that the wood—not in full leaf yet, but at the height of its beauty, before the fresh green was darkened by the summer dust.

The driver of the Vauxhall was not individually conscious of all

2

these things; his pleasure was purely instinctive and was not lessened by the thought that his errand was accomplished. He stood there only a moment, but it was more than enough for the marksman who had been watching for him, patient and invisible in the belt of trees. The man by the car never heard the shot that killed him, though the panic flight of the birds might have warned him if it had not already been too late. His thoughts were completely self-satisfied until the final moment when the world blackened in an instant of pain.

THE COURT HAD SAT LATE, AND AFTERWARD HE HAD A conference in chambers. It was after seven-thirty when Antony Maitland arrived home and paused before going into the house to frown at the rakish-looking sports car standing at the curb. He was tired, and hungry, and not in the best of tempers, and somehow he didn't think the car belonged to one of his uncle's friends. He went up the steps rather slowly, and swore when he couldn't immediately find his key.

The house in Kempenfeldt Square belonged to Sir Nicholas Harding, Q.C., and had been Antony's home for many years; now —by an arrangement no one any longer referred to as "temporary" —he and his wife, Jenny, occupied the two top floors. In name, a separate establishment; in fact, the barriers had never been very rigidly preserved. The study door was open when he went in, so it didn't look as if the car's owner was visiting his uncle. But when he reached his own quarters and let himself into the narrow hall there was no sound of voices; he took heart and pushed open the door opposite. A moment later the silence was explained: there were three people in the living room, but there isn't much to be said in face of a woman's tears.

It was years since anyone had seen Meg Hamilton cry, except on the stage, where she seemed to be able to produce the effect

4

at will. Antony found it quite unnerving, and though he was aware, vaguely, of the other visitor—a man he didn't know—for the moment he had no attention to spare.

"No, I say, Meg," he protested. "You can't do this sort of thing."

"Oh, yes, I can," said Meg, sitting up and dabbing at her eyes with an inadequate scrap of linen, so that he was moved to sacrifice the clean handkerchief from his breast pocket. "I'm sorry," she added. "I don't seem to be able to stop." She blew her nose in a determined way.

Over her head, Antony's eyes met his wife's with a frantic question. Jenny shook her head at him, which wasn't exactly reassuring, and then looked across at the stranger, who had risen from the wing chair at the other side of the hearth. "This is my husband," she said. "Roger Farrell, Antony. He's a friend of Meg's."

Turning, Antony saw a sturdily built man of about his own age, give or take a year or two, with thick, straight, sandy-colored hair, eyes that were vividly blue and a mouth and chin for which the description "firm" would have been blatantly an understatement. He also saw that Farrell was ill at ease, and he didn't think he was very familiar with the emotion.

"To be unchivalrous, you must blame Meg for this intrusion." Farrell had a deep voice and a pleasant way of speaking; but though he smiled as he spoke, there was no amusement in his eyes.

"Should I blame anyone?" said Antony vaguely.

"You may, when you know why we're here."

"Well, meanwhile, let me give you a refill." He was puzzled, and beginning to be worried; and some instinct made him reluctant to face whatever revelation might be coming.

When he returned to the group round the fireplace a few moments later, Meg was eyeing her reflection in the mirror of her compact in a despondent way. "I can't think how it is," she said. "On the stage I can cry for hours and it doesn't show." She dusted some powder unenthusiastically on her nose, and looked at him with a gleam of amusement in her eye. "Poor darling," she said. "What a damp homecoming." As he handed her the glass, he thought how little she had changed since her first ap-

5

pearance in London. She wouldn't have called him "darling" then, and he would probably have given her ginger ale instead of a Dubonnet. But she'd have been just as forthright as—he feared—she was going to be any minute now.

Meg was small and slightly built, not exactly pretty, but a woman who caught your attention and held it. And in spite of the unobtrusive elegance of her clothes and the old-fashioned way she did her hair in a long plait twisted round her head, she succeeded in looking very like the girl he had first met . . . how long ago was it, ten years, or more? It was hard to remember that she could chill your blood as Lady Macbeth; or that when she played the Queen in Hamlet nobody even thought of blaming Claudius for what had happened. She had a deep voice and wasn't above dramatizing . . . herself or the occasion, as she felt inclined. But at the moment she was unquestionably in earnest, and Farrell had implied —hadn't he?—that their errand wasn't a pleasant one. To each of them at the moment Antony was to some extent the focus of attention, but their awareness of each other was unmistakable, and for some reason it added to his uneasiness. He had seen Meg, over the years, with many different escorts, but he rather thought Roger Farrell was a new departure, someone as alien to her own circle as he and Jenny were; though, come to think of it, they were probably her closest friends. He stood on the hearthrug and looked down at Meg, and thought wearily that he might as well find out. . . .

"Well, now, what's the trouble?"

Meg put away the compact and snapped her handbag shut again. But when she looked up at him he realized that her calmness was assumed, a fragile thing that could be shattered with a word. "Roger's quite right," she told him, "I made him come here. And I'm sorry you're tired, darling, but it really is desperately important."

"Tell me, then," he invited.

"It's Roger's story. He'll have to tell you himself."

Maitland turned his head and found that Farrell was looking at him steadily. "I've been trying to think things out," he said, with an air of caution that was probably as foreign to his nature as the initial uneasiness had been.

6

"I see." He paused a moment before he amplified the statement. "Meg's enthusiastic, but perhaps not a good salesman?" Antony suggested, and saw by the other man's startled look that he had summed up the situation accurately enough. He smiled, a little ruefully. "There's no need at all to confide in me. Why should you want to?"

"I think I should like to." Farrell spoke slowly, but he was obviously used to making up his mind and there was no longer any doubt in his voice. He was, in fact, surprised by his own reaction. He had come at Meg's insistence but without very much confidence in what she had told him. "Intelligence during the war," she had said, "but don't mention that or he'll freeze us both out. Now he's a barrister, and as he's always busy I expect he's a good one. But he's . . . he's perceptive—" She had stopped there to consider the word, and nodded as though she approved it. "I'm sure if anyone can help us—" His own thoughts had not echoed her certainly, and now he studied Maitland and did not realize how open his interest was. An amused look, he thought, as though he finds something a little comical in the situation; younger that I expected; intelligent, undoubtedly. He said aloud, "The only thing is, I realize it's an imposition—"

"If that's all that's worrying you, go ahead." Antony took his glass from the mantelpiece and went to sit beside Meg on the sofa; she turned her head to look at him, and thought, a little fancifully, that his mind was closed against her. He was a tall man with a casual air, and he achieved what he considered the required standard of professional elegance only at some trouble to himself. Even so, his dark hair was generally untidy, and though he hadn't, of course, had time to change when he came in, he had already pulled his tie askew. His eyes were fixed on Roger, intent, and a little worried; she thought, perhaps they're too much alike to get on well together, and then wondered at herself because—on the surface at least—she had never known two men in sharper contrast.

Jenny had the wing chair which stood with its back to the window. She didn't offer to leave them to their discussion; she had already heard so much of the story from Meg that it would have been nonsensical to attempt a tactful withdrawal. But because it was natural for her to do so she sat very quietly listening, and imagined that in this way she would be disregarded. Antony was tired, she had seen that as soon as he came in; and Meg had noticed it too, and mentioned it, which hadn't pleased him. He was holding himself stiffly, which meant that his shoulder was painful . . . and thank goodness Meg hadn't mentioned *that*.

Roger Farrell hadn't immediately accepted the invitation to proceed. He was holding his glass cradled in both his hands, staring down into it as intently as if he were crystal-gazing, and when he looked up at last he seemed quite unaware of the silence that had spread itself uneasily through the room. "It won't take very long," he promised; and as he spoke Antony realized fully for the first time the strain he was under, the difficulty with which he restrained his gestures, kept his voice to an even pitch. And hard on this thought came its confirmation. "The main thing is that I've involved Meg in my affairs," Roger said, choosing his words with a sort of cold precision that couldn't possibly be natural. "I hope you can persuade her to be sensible."

"I shouldn't count on it," said Maitland. He leaned back then and stretched his legs, but his eyes remained fixed on Farrell's face. He was finding Meg's friend an interesting personality.

"It's a bit difficult to know where to begin," said Roger, "so perhaps I'd better explain first of all that my mother died two weeks ago, nearly . . . a week last Friday, to be exact. The inquest was last week."

The fellow seemed to have a tiresome knack of making unanswerable statements, but this one, at least, must be acknowledged. "I'm sorry," said Antony. "I take it she died suddenly—"

"She killed herself. 'An overdose of one of the barbiturates,'" quoted Farrell bitterly; and overthrew all Maitland's preconceived ideas by adding, "That was the verdict, and there's no doubt it was the right one."

"I see," said Antony carefully. Which was a lie.

"There wasn't any difficulty about it. She left a note for the coroner and one for me. Mine was just . . . her love . . . and she hoped I'd forgive her. The other . . . she said it was a year since my father died, and she found her grief grew no less; that

8

part was probably true enough. And she said she felt she couldn't go on any longer, and that I *didn't* believe." He was speaking harshly, with an obvious determination not to spare himself in the telling; against his will, Antony felt the first stirrings of sympathy.

"Why not?" he asked. "Why didn't you believe it?"

"Because she isn't . . . she wasn't that sort of person. A bit idealistic," said Roger indulgently, as though making allowances for one of the weaker sex, "but she could accept life as it was—however hard it was—when she had to."

"What can't be cured must be endured," said Maitland unoriginally.

"That's exactly what she used to say. But, of course—I'm telling this very badly—I'd a better reason than that for thinking there was something else to account for what she did."

"Go back a little, then. Was her death a surprise to you?"

"That's too small a word. But I've got to go back to the day before—Thursday, the week before last—when I picked up the extension phone in my room to make a call and found her already on the line." Having made up his mind, he was telling the story as quickly and concisely as possible and without the apologies that might have made the recital tedious. "I was just putting the receiver down again when I heard her say, 'Have you no pity?' That sounds foolish, doesn't it? But I assure you, the answer was life and death to her . . . and probably hell too. So I listened; it never occurred to me not to, and I don't think I could have put the phone down if I'd tried." Again the explanation held no hint of apology. Maitland made no comment, but said only:

"Go on."

"It was a man's voice that answered her; not an unpleasant voice, a little high-pitched, perhaps. It said, 'You know my terms already. If you don't comply—' and she gave a sob and interrupted in an agitated way, 'Six months ago you said it was just that once.' And the man laughed and said, 'I shall telephone you again next week at the same time,' and rang off; and I just stood there like a fool with the receiver in my hand and couldn't say a word."

"You think, then, that someone was blackmailing her?"

"Believe me, I tried to explain that scrap of conversation every way, but I always came back to that in the end. And I couldn't make up my mind what to do; it's difficult to explain, but how *could* I go to her and say . . . and say—"

"It may be difficult to explain," said Antony. "It's easy enough to understand."

"Yes, perhaps. But now I blame myself. I'd have had to talk to her sooner or later, and if I hadn't waited . . . it was that night she took the overdose, you see, some stuff she got from the chemist. She was dead by morning." Farrell was still speaking forcefully, almost belligerently, as though daring any of his companions to make an open expression of sympathy.

"Did you tell the police about this conversation?"

"No, I didn't. Why should I? Why should I tell them the letter she left was a lie? That there was something she'd done . . . because that's what I thought then. And there wasn't any need; as far as they were concerned the letters cleared everything up. They looked through her desk, and there was nothing they thought unusual. But over the weekend I had a look at her papers myself."

"And what did you find?"

"One queer thing—no, two. I was looking at her bank statements, of course, because if she'd had some dealings with this chap six months ago there ought to be some sort of record. But there wasn't anything out of the way . . . nothing I didn't know about, or at least understand. No substantial withdrawal, anyway. But there was a letter from the jewelers who always looked after her things, quoting a price for a pendant—sapphire and diamonds— with a pin and earrings to match. And she must have accepted the offer, because there was another letter from them a week later saying they had obtained a single diamond, according to her instructions. The price was one thousand and fifty pounds, and they enclosed their check for the balance (which wasn't much), and the stone was ready for collection at any time, as she'd said she'd prefer to call for it in person. It only gradually dawned on me that perhaps she got it to give to . . . this man."

"Not a bad idea," said Antony slowly. "I suppose the jewelers who sold it could identify a given stone . . . but who's to produce it for their inspection?"

"This one wasn't among her things, or at the bank," said Roger, taking the question literally. "The other queer thing—though I didn't think about it at the time—was that the A.A. book was in her bedroom."

"Shouldn't it have been?"

"She might have taken it in to look at; she'd never have left it there in the ordinary way . . . if for no other reason, because she always said the binding was *most* inartistic," said Roger, again with that air of affectionate mimicry. "But it was only later . . . I'm getting out of order again. It was at that stage I thought about Meg." He paused and looked across at her, and again Antony was aware of bewilderment. An ugly little story, and he could understand Farrell's carefully concealed distress. But he couldn't see where it was leading.

He said, "Well?" and his voice was sharper than he intended. Roger's eyes came back to meet his with an oddly challenging look.

"He'd said he'd phone again, and it wasn't very likely he'd have seen the bit in the papers. They weren't very interested. If he had, we'd be no worse off, but I thought the call might be illuminating. And he couldn't know Mother's voice all that well."

"So you asked Meg to impersonate her?" Something in his tone seemed to sting Farrell into the justification of his actions which he had so carefully avoided up to now.

"I had no right . . . you don't need to tell me that. But I didn't know then what was going to happen." He looked at Meg again, for the first time with an air of helplessness, and she said quickly:

"I couldn't impersonate her, of course, I didn't know her. But I can do 'English gentlewoman' when I like, and Roger said if I sounded upset the man would never know."

To Antony's mind this was a clear attempt to confuse the issue. He said coldly, "So you took the call?"

"Yes. He wasn't a nice man," she said, and unconsciously her voice dropped to its deepest and most dramatic register.

"I don't suppose he was."

"He said, had I made up my mind? And Roger had told me to agree to everything, so, of course, I said yes." Her eyes met

Antony's in a direct look, and he saw, to his discomfort, that she was again very near to tears. "So then he said, 'Put the diamond in an envelope and bring it to the A.A. box, eight miles out of Scranton on the Mountalban road. Be there at exactly three o'clock on Tuesday afternoon and mark the envelope: Mr. Jones, to be called for. Leave it in the box, propped up on the ledge, and then drive away.' And he repeated it all and asked if I understood, and then he laughed and said, 'Don't fail me.' " She paused and sniffed with a quite heart-rending pathos, and added defiantly, "I know it doesn't sound very bad, but it was *horrible*. I felt just as if . . . as if he was threatening me."

"I didn't realize—" Roger began, and broke off when he found Maitland's eye fixed on him.

"What exactly was the object of the exercise?"

"I wanted to know . . . of course I wanted to know who the chap was."

"Why?"

"Wouldn't you have felt the same?"

"Perhaps," Antony admitted. "But the police can be very discreet."

"If I'd known why he was threatening Mother . . . don't you see, I couldn't tell them when I didn't know what they'd find out?"

"You think I shall be less curious . . . or less efficient?"

"No, but . . . the situation has deteriorated," Farrell told him. "Anyway, I meant to go to the police eventually, if I could. I didn't want to think of other people being victimized."

"A very affecting sentiment. And how did you propose— Meg, you little fool," he added, turning quickly as the thought struck him, "you didn't go to meet this man?" As he spoke her eyes filled with tears, she stopped twisting his handkerchief between her fingers and raised it to her eyes again. From behind its folds her voice was muffled and indignant.

"I never saw him . . . I did just as he said. And it isn't any use being cross about it."

That was true enough. After a moment, "Come off it, Mrs. Siddons," he pleaded, carefully restraining his impulse to leave Meg to her tears while he expressed to Roger Farrell a little—

only a little—of the anger that was taking possession of him.

"Sometimes," said Meg, still indistinctly, "I *enjoy* crying." Whether this was true or not in this instance, she certainly didn't stop. Antony looked at Jenny and said, exasperated:

"It doesn't help matters, does it?"

"No, but . . . you're not really being sympathetic, are you?"

"I don't feel sympathetic," Antony pointed out. He turned again to Farrell. "You asked her to keep the appointment," he said. "Go on from there."

Roger was looking at Meg Hamilton, and his expression was hard to read. "She didn't know Mother, you see, so I didn't realize she'd be so upset."

"Good heavens, man, she's an actress! That means she has *some* imagination."

It may have been the bite in his tone, and a humanitarian desire to prevent bloodshed, that brought Meg out from behind the handkerchief again, in sufficient command of her emotions to say, "I don't think you're in a nice mood at all." So might Desdemona have spoken to Othello, and with such a look of bitter reproach.

"He's quite right, Meg," said Farrell. His glance at Maitland might be a little wary, but his tone remained hard and uncompromising. "Suppose we postpone the recriminations . . . that is, if you want to hear the rest."

"I want to hear it," said Antony grimly.

"I think perhaps you'd better look at the newspaper. Where is it, Meg?" But it was Jenny who produced the *Evening Chronicle* from under a cushion and passed it to her husband.

"*That* paragraph," she said as he took it from her. "Just by your thumb."

Antony looked down at the folded page, at all the diverse and disagreeable information upon which literate man daily sups full of horrors. Wars and rumors of wars, the bickering of Parliament, the guard shot dead in bullion robbery, the film star whose heart was broken by a delay in obtaining her fourth divorce. "Man found shot on the Mountalban road," he read, and looked at Roger with a question in his eyes.

"Read it," said Meg tragically.

13

"The man who was found dead outside an A.A. box, shortly after three o'clock yesterday afternoon, has been identified as Martin Grainger (47), of Copthall Court, E.C.2. Mr. Grainger was the proprietor of Galloway's Chop House and was well known in the City. He had been shot at a range of about one hundred yards and died instantly. Local inquiries are being made into the possibility of an accident, but meanwhile it is understood that Scotland Yard have been called into consultation. . . ." He finished reading and raised his eyes to Farrell's face. "So that's the end of the story," he commented. "Is that why you wanted to identify the blackmailer?"

"Do you think . . . do you really think I'd have let Meg go anywhere near the place if I'd intended murder?"

"I don't know. Suppose you tell me?"

"Well, I wouldn't," said Farrell shortly.

"An accident, then?"

"I don't know. I found him dead. But I can't help thinking it was a bit of a coincidence if someone was out with a gun just then."

"So do I. But if you're postulating murder . . . who else could have known he would be there?"

"If he made a habit of blackmail, there must have been plenty of people who'd be glad to see him dead."

"That wasn't what I asked you. He wouldn't have made a second assignation for the same time and place; he wouldn't have told anyone where he was going, either. A blackmailer's trade is essentially a lonely one, and he'd have had sense enough to keep his own counsel. Which brings us back to my question: who else could have known he'd be there?"

"I didn't tell anyone. I'm sure Meg didn't."

"What about it, Meg?" said Antony, without looking round.

"It wasn't my secret. Of course I didn't." Oddly, her indignation seemed to have left her, though her denial was vehement enough.

"Difficult, isn't it?" said Antony. He watched Farrell struggling between embarrassment and anger, and wondered why he bothered; why he didn't answer in kind, as instinct must surely have dictated.

14

"I quite realize how it must sound . . . now you point it out to me." His tone was a little strained, but otherwise Roger had himself well under control. "That doesn't matter, really, but Meg seems to value your opinion. I want you to tell her she mustn't mix herself up in all this."

"As things stand now—" Antony indicated the folded newspaper, which he had dropped when he finished reading—"if this is right, neither of you is mixed up in anything . . . so far."

"I am," said Roger steadily. "I found him."

"And told the police?"

"Of course. And now the paper says that Scotland Yard—"

"That might mean anything, or nothing. But if there's any indication in his papers of what he was doing . . . motive and opportunity . . . yes, I see."

"I rather thought you would," said Farrell. "Difficult, isn't it?" he added, throwing the question back at Maitland with a sort of gloomy satisfaction.

Antony did not answer immediately; he got up and began to move restlessly about the room, pausing for a moment to look out of the window and then coming back to stand behind Meg Hamilton. "And what was *your* idea, my precious," he asked, "in coming here today?"

Meg leaned back, found herself looking at him upside down, and twisted round far enough to face him directly. There were no tears now. He realized as their eyes met that she had known all the time what he had just pointed out to Farrell; that she had known, too, that sooner or later he would ask her that question, and when he did it would have to be answered.

"I hoped you'd believe what Roger told you," she said, meeting his look evenly. "And then I thought you'd help us."

"In what way?" His voice was very gentle.

"By finding out what really happened."

He glanced at Farrell. The question was on the tip of his tongue: do you really want to know? But instead of asking it, he turned back to Meg again. "If it was an accident, I doubt if it can be proved, unless someone comes forward."

"But if it wasn't . . . if somebody killed him deliberately?"

"If the police find any evidence of motive, they're liable to jump to conclusions . . . don't you think?"

"That's why I made Roger come here," said Meg, as triumphantly as if she had just gained her point. Antony glanced at Jenny, but she was looking straight ahead of her and seemed to have dissociated herself from the conversation. He said unhappily: "I'm no hand at miracles, Meg."

"Aren't you, darling? What you really mean is, you think Roger killed him, don't you?"

"That would be theorizing ahead of my data; quite unforgivable." This was not altogether honest; he thought he had heard enough. "What about it, Farrell? It's up to you, really, whether I take a hand."

"I've no right to ask it," said Roger stiffly.

"No, but Meg has."

"But I'm not in trouble," said Meg. "That's not what I meant at all. Roger is . . . or may be."

"I'm offering to do what you want, Meg. Do my reasons matter?" He wondered as he spoke if she was genuinely blind to her own situation. In spite of his anxiety, he found something almost amusing about what was happening, though the joke was a sour one and definitely against himself.

Farrell caught the look. He was still angry and not making a very good job of hiding the fact; and he didn't know which was worse, Maitland's amusement or the position—the quite intolerable position—into which Meg had maneuvered him. He didn't like asking favors. And then, as their eyes met, Maitland grinned at him . . . a companionable grin, not at all sardonic, or superior, or any of the things he had been thinking a moment before. His resentment vanished. "Meg seems to think you can do anything," he said. The statement, perhaps, was addressed more to himself than to the other man, but it served to break the silence that had been building up between them.

"You'd do much better to talk to your solicitor, you know."

"Not unless I have to. Armstrong would be shattered—"

"Armstrong, Horton and Holbrook?" said Antony; and laughed disconcertingly as Roger nodded, but this time the sound was one of pure amusement. "It only needed that," he said, and felt Meg tugging at his sleeve.

"What do you mean? What difference does that make?"

Maitland divided a smile between them. "Armstrong may be shattered," he said, "though I doubt it. What he will do is pass the thing over to his partner, Geoffrey Horton, who has plenty of experience in criminal practice."

"But Geoffrey's a friend of yours," Meg objected. "That makes it easier, not more difficult."

"It means I've no hope at all of bowing out if things get serious," said Antony, "as otherwise I might have been forced to do." It was only too clear that he would have given in to the compulsion gracefully.

"But that's a good thing," said Meg, with a serious look.

"That, my child, depends on your point of view. And there's another thing I should warn you about, Farrell . . . if we embark on an investigation you won't enjoy the process much. Personal questions, and some of them damned awkward. As bad as if you'd talked to the police in the first place."

"That can't be helped."

"All right, then. Are you free tomorrow?"

"I can be."

"I'll phone you, as soon as I'm through in Court. Right?"

"Right." Faced with the sudden and apparently uncharacteristic decision of Maitland's tone Roger sounded helpless, out of his depth. "I'll be at the office all day—Reade and Farrell—and my home address is Leinster Court."

"Did your mother live with you?"

"Yes. Or rather, I moved back with her after my father died. The flat was too big for her alone, but she didn't want to move just then."

"I see. Well, if the police get in touch with you in the meantime, you've no need to say anything to them until you've talked to your solicitor. Which being translated means, until we've found out how much they know. And that goes for you too, Meg," he added. "Understand?"

"If you're asking me to tell lies—" said Meg, suddenly pulling out all the stops and speaking with an intensity that would have occasioned remark even in the last act of one of Webster's tragedies.

"Heaven forbid!" He turned to give her his full attention. "I'm asking you to be discreet," he explained. "And if you don't know the meaning of the word, my dear, we'll look it up . . . after dinner."

Perhaps not surprisingly, a constraint had grown up between Meg and Roger now. Neither of them needed much persuasion to stay for the meal, and Antony was pretty sure this was because of a sudden diffidence about being alone together. He was rather afraid this might result in their staying forever; but good manners overcame whatever reluctance they felt, and they left soon after ten o'clock.

He went downstairs to see them out and stood on the top step to savor the freshness of the evening and admire the purr of the gray car as she drew away with her two passengers. When at last he moved he did so with an air of resolution, closing the front door firmly, and making for the study without any further hesitation.

The room was almost dark when he went in; Sir Nicholas was writing, and the only light was from the desk lamp. Antony stood looking down at him, and said in half-hearted apology: "Am I disturbing you, Uncle Nick?"

Sir Nicholas was fair-haired, and it was the practice among the Sunday newspapers to refer to him as "handsome," a habit which so infuriated him that it had led Jenny to institute a system of censorship when one of his cases was making the headlines. The description, however, was probably as well deserved as in most instances of its use in the press. He was a tall man, rather more heavily built than his nephew, and with a much more authoritative manner. Antony could not see his expression; only his hands lay within the circle of lamplight. He stopped writing and dropped his pen on the blotter, and after a moment leaned back in his chair and removed his glasses. "It's time I stopped," he said, but there was no conviction in his voice.

Thus encouraged, Antony sat down, and tilted the lamp a little so that they could see each other in a shadowy way. "Have you any experience of blackmail?" he asked.

"Neither as operator nor victim." On reflection, this seemed rather a bald statement, and he added helpfully, "The 1916 Act provides for severe penalties—"

"It's too late for that, the chap's dead."

"Then I don't quite see how his affairs can concern us."

"He was shot. It may have been murder."

"Even so—" There was an unusual air of vagueness about Sir Nicholas, his mind seemed to be slipping away from the subject, back to the problem represented by the documents on his desk.

"Jenny's just been giving supper to a man who had very good reason to kill him, and opportunity as well."

"My dear boy, you really should be more careful of her associates. Tell her," said Sir Nicholas, his eyes straying to the papers which were lying about him in confusion, "tell her to think of Saint Paul."

That sounded like an alluring byway, but heaven knew where it would lead them. Antony said very clearly, "A man called Farrell. Meg Hamilton brought him. I'm afraid—"

"If Meg is mixed up with a crook you must get her out of his clutches," said Sir Nicholas with sudden energy. "But, of course, you understand that as well as I do." He pushed aside the foolscap pad, picked up a pencil and began to draw on the green expanse of the blotter. Antony watched, fascinated . . . not the usual troop of ducks this time, but a solitary and lively-looking bird with a box of matches and a fiendish expression. The rapidly moving pencil seemed to have a mesmerizing effect.

"That arson case?" he asked.

Sir Nicholas nodded. "The brief," he said, "is eighteen inches high, or should it be 'thick'? The papers—" he gestured widely, but there was no need to do so, the papers were all over the room. "My instructing solicitor knows everything and can explain nothing. The lay client, on the other hand, is only too willing to explain everything—at length." He sat back a little to admire his sketch. "Did you want something, Antony?" he asked, almost lucidly.

19

"Well, you see, sir, I more or less promised Meg—"

"That's quite right, I'm very glad to hear it. It is, of course, possible," said Sir Nicholas, "that the lighted candle which in each case caused the fire was part of a religious ceremony, as my client avers. But do you really think it is likely?" He put the question earnestly, but it was only too obviously a rhetorical one. Antony gave it up and went away.

Upstairs, he found that Jenny had kicked off her shoes and was curled up in her usual corner of the sofa. She had run her fingers through her brown curls, so that they were tumbled wildly, and he thought she looked, for the moment, even younger than Meg. He fetched the decanter, poured Madeira for them both, and sat down in the chair she had vacated. "Excellent and most discreet of wives," he said, "what do you make of that?"

"I don't like it. I'm worried about Meg."

"So am I. If it comes to a trial it won't sound well, that story."

"It isn't just that." There was something almost secretive about her smile, he thought, something quite unlike her usual candor.

"You mean she's bound to be hurt if anything happens to this fellow."

"Yes, of course."

"There's nothing to be done about that, Jenny."

"Nothing, I suppose, if he's guilty. But I do think . . . he must be a little fond of Meg to have talked to her like that about his mother. And if he is, he wouldn't have involved her deliberately in a murder."

"I think he's more than 'a little fond,'" said Antony soberly. "But he's not exactly lacking in self-confidence, is he? He might have been sure he'd get away with it."

"Self-confident even to the extent of going to the police?"

"Yes, I think so. And we don't know the circumstances; someone may have seen him, his car's a pretty distinctive one."

"Well, would he have come here?"

"If I know Meg, he may not have had much choice."

"I thought you liked him, Antony."

"I did . . . I do. That doesn't make him a sea-green incorruptible. If what he says is true . . . but we don't even know that, do we?"

"What does Uncle Nick think?"

"He's immersed in that brief from Wattersons."

"Didn't you tell him—?"

"Little enough; I didn't get the chance. He told me I must take care of Meg's interests . . . oh, and make sure you didn't get into bad company. I'm not even certain he knew which one of you I'm married to."

"I don't think you can have done a very good job of explaining," said Jenny severely.

"I was also to tell you to think of Saint Paul," Antony told her.

"I never do if I can help it. But at least it means he knows who I am."

Antony's mind had already moved to the next problem. "Why wasn't Meg at the theater?" he demanded.

"She's rehearsing, don't you remember? That new play of Quentin's."

"Very Tragical Mirth?"

"That's the one. It sounds perfectly ghastly to me, but Meg says it's 'got something.' The dress rehearsal's tomorrow," she added, sounding worried. "And they open the day after."

"Well, let's hope they're not in for some unexpected publicity. I wonder what the chances really are that Grainger's death was accidental."

"Poor Meg. I suppose," said Jenny thoughtfully, "that anyone might fall in love with a murderer. But she wouldn't like Roger if he was really selfish."

"You don't know that. During the years we've known her she's had any number of suitors, but if she cared for any of them it's news to me." Jenny smiled at him again, and he added, with sudden amusement, "Don't tell me she's been pining in secret for someone I don't know about."

"It isn't really at all funny," said Jenny almost crossly.

"It can't have been Denis Dowling," said Antony, drawing his own conclusions from this rather oblique remark.

"Of course it wasn't Denis! She lost interest in him at almost exactly the same time he started taking an interest in her. And anyway, it wouldn't have done."

He didn't remind her that at one time he'd accused her of match-making in that quarter, and—he still thought—with justice. He said slowly, "I wouldn't hang a dog on the evidence of Meg's likes and dislikes. Or acquit him, either."

"But you're a man," said Jenny unanswerably. "I know you can't be sure of anything at this stage, but I wish you'd remember Roger may not have done anything wrong."

"I'm not his judge, love." He saw she wasn't going to persist with the subject, and leaned back, sipping his wine, relaxing for the first time. He was still tired, and for some reason his shoulder was aching abominably, and he loved Meg like a brother but he couldn't help welcoming this respite before he plunged himself into her affairs. And Farrell's . . . that was the snag, really; he'd tried to warn him of the difficulties, but probably without much success. So that tomorrow's session promised to be lively, but he didn't see how it could be helped.

Jenny, for her part, looked at her husband and thought it was one of the nicest things about him, that he could be so clever about some things and so utterly stupid about others.

2

As he penetrated for the first time into the opulent portals of Leinster Court, it became only too apparent to Antony that whatever Farrell's background might be, there was money in it. In the lobby he was ankle-deep before he knew it in a sea of blue Axminster, and the quiet luxury of the appointments—modern but stopping short of the bizarre—would alone have convinced him that he was moving well outside his own financial sphere. The doorman greeted and directed him in tones deferential enough for visiting royalty.

Seen on his own ground, Roger Farrell seemed to have undergone a subtle transformation. He was at once more assured and less aggressive, even though—having just returned from the City in response to Antony's phone call—he had removed coat and tie and came to the door in this state of partial undress.

The flat itself was feminine; charmingly so. Antony had a mental picture of the late Mrs. Farrell reclining on a sofa (that Empire piece in the corner of the room) clothed in flowing draperies in various sweet-pea shades; though his imagination stopped short of specifying the fabric. A gently spoken, rather fragile lady, who probably held the male members of her family in complete and willing subjection.

The drawing room overlooked the park, and the heating (wherever it came from) was adequate and discreet. Farrell waved

23

to two chairs he had set by the window, in defiance of what had clearly been a carefully symmetrical arrangement, and went over to the bar he had established on a nearby table, which again, Antony felt, had been no part of the original scheme of things. He realized now that he had been visualizing the flat as lonely and rather desolate, not filled, as it was, with the bereaved man's lively and rather turbulent personality.

"There's this to be said for your being later than you expected," said Roger, catching his guest's eye. "You can't possibly tell me it's too early for a drink."

"The judge had rather a lot to say," Antony explained. "And by the time he'd finished he'd got the jury as confused as he was."

"Pity," said Roger politely.

"Oh, no. At least, it was the only thing that could have got my client off," Antony corrected him. Farrell laughed and came across the room with a glass in each hand.

"I need this," he said a moment later. (Even the way he sits down, thought Antony a little resentfully, somehow conveys the impression of a vast store of energy.) "I've been thinking, Maitland," Roger added. His meaning was obvious: he hadn't liked the subject matter of his meditation.

Antony smiled at him and sipped his sherry. Until an hour before he had been furiously concentrated on the affairs of the client who even now was rejoicing in an unexpected acquittal, and the adjustment wasn't an easy one to make. He wondered even, in this moment of detachment, whether Farrell had any real cause for worry, whether he himself might not have been stampeded, the evening before, into taking seriously a problem that didn't exist.

Roger didn't seem to notice the silence; for once, his attention seemed to be turned inward, on himself. "It's very good of you," he said formally, "to take me on trust like this."

Antony shifted his glass to his left hand and held it up to catch the sunlight. "I don't think anything was said about trust," he remarked, almost apologetically. "It's no concern of mine who you kill." His attention might have been completely taken by the play of color in the crystal.

There was a moment of complete silence before Roger said, "I see," rather doubtfully. "For the record," he added, "I didn't shoot Grainger. Though I might have done, you know, if the idea had happened to occur to me." He looked up, found Maitland's eyes on him, and went on with a spurt of anger: "You've established your point . . . you're only concerned with Meg's welfare. Shall we go on from there?"

"I wasn't trying to establish anything," said Antony, still mildly. "My primary concern is for Meg, of course, so I prefer to believe you. But—leaving her out of it—I don't know that I'd blame you overmuch."

"I can't tell you," said Roger sarcastically, "how that relieves my mind."

"You still don't understand me," Maitland complained. He drank some of his sherry and put down the glass on the table beside him. "I want to know how you'll plead if you're charged with Grainger's murder, and I'm asking you that as a friend of Meg Hamilton, not as a lawyer."

Farrell was frowning at him. "Not guilty, of course," he said.

"It's not quite so simple. Your solicitor might feel it better to plead extreme provocation, and try to get the charge reduced to one of manslaughter."

"I won't do it."

"All right. I don't think it would stand up, anyway; I mean, you couldn't claim it wasn't premeditated. I just wanted you to know the position."

"It will be rotten for Meg either way." There was no rancor in Farrell's tone now. "I suppose you mean," he added, thinking it out, "that the jury and . . . and public opinion, I suppose, might be sympathetic to me and still never forgive Meg her part in it."

"That's exactly what I mean. But in fairness to yourself—"

"You can take it I'm not interested in getting out by the side door," said Roger shortly. He got up and refilled both glasses, and —still standing—raised his in an ironic toast. "To our alliance," he said. "Our reluctant alliance." Antony followed his example and grinned at his companion as both glasses were lowered together. Rather unwillingly, Farrell smiled back. "I suppose," he said, "that's why you wanted to see me alone."

"Precisely. And to get an idea of your background," he added, looking around him with deliberation.

"The place," said Roger, frowning again, "is hardly looking its best."

"You're on your own here?"

"Yes. There was just Mother's maid, and I let her go last week. The cleaning is part of the service, anyway, and I go out for most of my meals. I shan't stay here, of course."

"I suppose it's convenient," said Antony vaguely. "Tell me about your father; what was his occupation?"

"A stockbroker."

"Affluent?"

"Reasonably so."

"And your mother's financial position?"

"A trust fund. Plenty to live on, very comfortably. Not too big a surplus." (He had evidently taken the point of the questions, and what a comfort that was, thought Antony with gratitude.)

"She'd have found it difficult to meet a sudden demand for money?"

"If the amount of the first transaction is anything to go on, another thousand pounds would certainly have been beyond her. Dad has only been dead a year, as I think I told you; she wouldn't have had time to accumulate anything from income."

"No more jewelry?"

"Funnily enough, she wasn't particularly fond of it. I think it was really because she could remember being hard up and used to worry about the extravagance. Anyway, the things she disposed of six months ago were practically all she had."

"Could you have helped her?"

"Easily . . . if she'd trusted me."

"Are you on the Stock Exchange, too?" Antony supposed hazily that this explained the evidences of wealth. The whole business of dealing in stocks and shares was a mystery and might just as well be governed by black magic for all he knew to the contrary. He wasn't at all surprised to find these financial wizards well off . . . though, of course, there was always the minority, the chaps who ended in the dock, or jumped out of the office window, or something like that.

"Yes, my father's firm. And I'm not at all hard up, which I suppose is the next question; Grainger might quite reasonably have tried to get at me through Mother . . . if that's what you mean."

It was exactly what Antony had meant, and he was beginning to have a suspicion—entertained for the first time, briefly, the previous evening— that Farrell was by no means as insensitive as he would like to appear. "I suppose your mother belonged to the A.A.?" he asked, turning his line of questioning slightly, and aware as he did so that he was hedging.

"My father was a member, I think she kept it on. She always had her own little car and used it quite a lot."

"The one Meg borrowed?"

"Yes." He didn't like the reminder.

"What happened that afternoon, when you got to the A.A. box?"

"Meg left the envelope there, as directed. It wasn't really a diamond, just paste; I didn't think that mattered. I mean, if I managed to trail him, that was all right; if I didn't, that was all right too. Whatever he did, it couldn't hurt Mother . . . now."

"That was what you meant to do, was it . . . follow him?"

"Yes."

"And then go to the police?"

"Perhaps. I've admitted my actions were . . . stupid," said Farrell, in the tone of one goaded beyond endurance. "Before I did that I wanted to know the reason . . . why he was blackmailing her, why she'd rather die than tell me—"

"Yes, I see."

"But if I didn't do something I'd always remember how he laughed . . . and that she died because I did nothing to help her." For a moment he looked at Maitland, scowling; then he added abruptly, "Couldn't we take it from there?"

"Very well; you were telling me—"

"We both approached the place from Scranton. I assumed the

blackmailer would come that way, too, if he was driving out from town. I timed myself to arrive about four minutes after Meg, I didn't know how long a gap he'd be likely to leave, but when I turned the corner there was nobody in sight at all. It's a long, straight stretch of road, you know. I stopped about four hundred yards before I reached the A.A. box and got out and had a look at the engine. And then another car came into sight, from the direction of Mountalban. Funnily, I hadn't expected that, and it wasn't until he drew up at the roadside that I realized it might be the man I was after, and that he was waiting for me to go away. So I thought I'd better chance it, and I drove on, straight past him. He had a map out, I couldn't see his face; but the car was a Vauxhall, I made a note of the number and wrote it down as soon as I was out of sight."

"A hired car, I bet."

"Do you think so?" But he was taken up with his story now, not really interested in the speculation. "I found a place to turn, and then drove back towards Scranton. He hadn't been watching me when I went past, and I'd kept the top up; I thought the Jensen would be less noticeable that way. But when I came cautiously round the corner, the Vauxhall was standing by the A.A. box and I couldn't see the driver at all. I pulled up and waited, and after a bit I drove on, and he was lying on the grass verge by his car. So of course I got out to see what had happened, and he was very dead."

"How long had he been out of your sight?"

"About three minutes, I should say. Possibly four."

"You didn't hear a shot . . . no, of course, you wouldn't with your engine running. Did you get any impression of the direction from which it had been fired?"

"It must have been from the wood; that's on the right of the road as you go toward Mountalban. Otherwise, his car would have been between him and the marksman."

"Anything else?"

"Just a bloody great hole in his chest . . . and that's the *mot juste,* my friend. I had to get the envelope, you see, so I was rather conscious of it."

"You took—? Yes, of course, you would do that. And then you phoned the police?"

"From the A.A. box. And they told me to wait, so I waited. And a few cars came by, and they all stopped and waited too. It was quite a circus by the time the constabulary arrived."

"I see. And you told them, I suppose, that you just happened to be driving by—"

"I don't see," said Roger with spirit, "what else I could be expected to say."

"Nor I. It's absolutely infuriating," he added, "not knowing what sort of records Grainger would be likely to keep."

In spite of himself, Roger laughed. "A gap in our education," he agreed.

"Well, I ought to know, and I don't," said Maitland. He paused and then added as though he had reached a decision, "The next thing is, have you any idea why—?" He saw Roger's lips tighten, and broke off to add, with sudden irritation, "I'm not doing this for fun, you know. It's no pleasure to me to sit here asking questions and watch you squirm."

"I didn't think it was." Ridiculously, in the circumstances, Farrell sounded sulky. "But I can't give you the answer. Mother has lived such a sheltered life for years now. I suppose that's what made her so vulnerable."

"Could it have been on your account?"

"I almost wish I could think that, only then I suppose I'd feel even more responsible. I've thought about it, of course, but I honestly don't believe . . . Society has the habit of condoning so many of our sins today," he added reflectively. "And that makes what I'm going to say worse, if anything. I think it must have been . . . something to do with my father."

"But he was already dead."

"Yes, of course. What I think is that he was being blackmailed, and afterwards Grainger transferred his attentions to Mother. She adored Dad, and would have done anything to protect his memory, especially to keep me from knowing if there was anything . . . well . . . discreditable in his past."

"Is this just an idea, or do you know something to support it?"

"I admit, it wouldn't have occurred to me if I hadn't remembered a rather queer conversation I had with Armstrong after Dad died. He was the executor, you know. He asked me one day if my father had ever mentioned putting some of his money into jewels; a very portable form of investment, he said, and quite a lot of people were favoring it in these uncertain days. I didn't know about anything like that, and I didn't know if Dad had a safe-deposit box anywhere . . . except at the bank, of course, which Armstrong already knew about. And, thinking back, I suppose he shut up rather quickly after that; but it didn't occur to me at the time."

"You think he'd found some evidence in your father's papers that he'd been buying diamonds?"

"I know he had. When I looked through Mother's desk last week there was a bundle of jewelers' receipts in one of the pigeon-holes."

"She'd known all the time?"

"What I think is, she'd looked through Dad's stuff at the time of Grainger's first demand, and when she found the receipts they served to confirm the threat. Anyway, they showed quite a clear picture of regular purchases during the four years before Dad died."

"How often? And how much?"

"Two or three times a year. Always something around a thousand pounds. I could see what Armstrong had thought, of course, and why he'd been so tactful. I'd have jumped to the same conclusion myself, if it hadn't been for the coincidence of Mother's transaction on the same lines. Even as it is, I'm not sure there's too much logic about my deductions."

"There was nothing in his will, I suppose . . . no unexplained legacies?"

"Two or three fairly substantial sums to charity; the trust fund for Mother; the residue divided between Isabel and me."

"Isabel?"

"My sister." For a moment it seemed that he was going to leave it there, but then he added, as though reluctantly, "Isabel Wilson.

Her husband's with Bramley's . . . manager of their Fenchurch Street Branch."

"And the charities you mentioned, were they well known?"

"Very well known."

"And no personal request to you—"

"To make provision for a mistress? Nothing like that."

"Did he die suddenly?"

"He had a stroke. He lived for a month after that, but he couldn't move or speak." He paused and added thoughtfully, "I see what you mean, of course, he might have intended to make some provision. But I don't honestly think there was anyone. He might have paid to keep the affair from Mother, but I don't think even she would have been fat-headed enough to go to such lengths to keep it from me."

"I think you're right. The diamonds were for Grainger, but you still haven't told me . . . why?" Farrell's expression froze back into a stubborn immobility.

"I left it there; I thought that was good enough. If you must have it, I don't really want to know—"

"I daresay you don't. The trouble is, if you're accused of murder we shall need the truth."

"And we may have to wade through some pretty dirty water to get to it. Is that what you're telling me?"

"I'm afraid it is." He sounded almost diffident. Farrell eyed him for a moment and then said in his abrupt way:

"Well, nothing came of the other line I tried."

"What was that?"

"I remembered Dad's diaries, so I had a look round for them—" Antony could visualize only too clearly the trail of devastation the search had left in its wake—"and I ran them to earth at last in the drawer of Mother's dressing table. I don't mean he *kept* them," Roger added. "Just notes of appointments, things like that."

The meaning was obvious. "But he retained them?" said Antony, with no more than a passing thought for the difficulties into which the English language could lead you.

"There's the one he was using when he had the stroke, and five for the previous years. I've only glanced through them, really, but there's one thing that will interest you." Again, having made up his mind, Farrell was going ahead whole-heartedly with his revelations. "Every so often I noticed he'd drawn a diamond sign—like the diamonds on a pack of cards, I mean. So I checked the dates on the jewelers' receipts, and in each case the mark in the diary was a day or two later, sometimes as much as a week. I think they must have denoted the day he was to make payment, don't you?"

"It looks rather like it."

"I suppose you'd like to have a look at them."

"It's hardly likely," said Antony reluctantly, "that he made any more overt mention of what was going on. But still—"

Farrell got up. "I put them in here to be safe," he said, crossing the room and pulling open a drawer. "Here you are."

Six little books, varying in color, and bound in a soft-grained morocco. "The first diamond is in this one," said Roger, with the diary for 1958 in his hand. "Look."

Antony obeyed. The month was September, the day was Wednesday, the roughly drawn ♦ was the only entry in the space provided. The whole thing conveyed—as he had feared—nothing at all to him. He began to flip back through the earlier pages. "Watch Ticonderoga Mines," he read. "Lunch with Manning (Pimm's) . . . General Aircraft down . . . lunch with H.D. . . . remember to check Purcell's account with Reade . . . lunch, Cooper (Savoy) . . . dine at St. Albans (remind W.) . . . lunch with H.D." He looked up at Farrell, but held the diary still open on his knee. "Expound," he demanded.

"If you mean the people . . . Manning is one of the Head Office chaps from Bramley's (we've always banked with them); H.D. is my godfather, Hubert Denning." He stretched out a hand, and Maitland put the book into it, and he began to turn the pages more slowly. "Reade is the senior partner in the firm now, though he was junior to Dad; dinner at St. Albans would be with the Blakeleys—he's my former headmaster, long since retired, and she's a poetic sort of female, but otherwise harmless; W. is Mother, of course—Winifred—they'd go there together; Cooper . . . that's funny, I don't know the name. Not business, I'm sure of that. Oh, here's the name again . . . Vaughan T. Cooper, sounds

32

like an American . . . and a telephone number. H.D. again . . .
I told you about him—"

"The initials recur rather frequently."

"They lunched together once a week as long as I remember."

"An intimate friend? Your father might have confided in him."

"If he confided in anyone," said Roger doubtfully. "Uncle Hubert—" He broke off, frowning, and added irrelevantly, "He's no relation really."

"Could you ask him about this?"

"Well—"

"Think about it."

Farrell made no immediate reply, but after a while he said, in a dissatisfied tone, "I suppose I must. I can't think of anybody else."

"Your partner, for instance. Was he a close friend?"

"I wouldn't say they were really intimate."

"Could the cause of the blackmail be anything to do with the business?"

"I don't think so. But it's all so unlikely . . . how can I know? If Dad had cut any corners, I think I'd have known about it; that's the most I can say."

"Do you remember anything special about that summer, the one when the payments started?"

"Nothing, really; though Dad took Mother to Teneriffe for May, and that was earlier than they normally took their holiday." He held out the diary again for Antony's inspection. "There are no entries at all—see?—all that month. That's what reminded me."

"And the only name you don't know that occurs in the diary during those months is this chap Cooper?"

"That's right. But does it matter? We know who the blackmailer was."

"We still don't know how Grainger found out—or what he found out, for that matter."

"But even so—"

"Nothing to do with the case? I expect you're right. Tell me, then, what were your father's hobbies?"

"Sailing . . . swimming."

"What sort of people did he mix with outside his business circle?"

"He used to go down to Grunning's Hole every chance he got. We have a cottage there, and a yawl."

"Any friends who shared his tastes?" Melodramatically, his mind tossed up the picture of a stormy sea, and two men clinging to an upturned boat, exchanging confessions in the imminent expectation of death. Perhaps Roger's thoughts were running on something the same lines, at any rate he showed no surprise at the question, and even smiled a little as he replied:

"Hardly any of them who went more than once. Mostly I used to crew for him, or some of my friends."

"Not even Mr. Denning?"

"Not on your life. He has a large motor yacht, the *Susannah,* which he much prefers."

"How large?'

"Around a hundred and ten foot, twin-screw diesel, very well found." Roger paused, as though considering the adequacy of this description. "He has moorings up the Blackwater, and I think he sometimes brings her round to lie at Chelsea," he added, "and occasionally he invites some of his cronies to take a decorous cruise. I've never been, so I'm not sure if they actually dress for dinner every night . . . but I wouldn't put it past him."

"But, surely—"

"Oh, he takes off for a longer trip at least once a year . . . a couple of months or so in the Med. And I have known him charter her, with his own crew, of course."

"Not your idea of fun?"

"Not really."

There was a pause. Antony put the diaries down on the table at his elbow and picked up his glass again. "There's just one more thing—"

"One?" said Farrell. He sounded skeptical.

"I don't mean just one question," Antony told him. "One series of questions, is that more credible?" But before Roger could reply they heard, from the hall, the mellow notes of the chime that served to announce visitors.

"If that isn't Aunt Lucy," said Farrell, exasperated, "I'll eat my hat." And suddenly he laughed, with what was obviously quite genuine amusement. "My top hat," he said. "I don't think Mrs. Maitland would consider anything else quite suitable." He made for the door, paused to look critically round the room, added, "Oh, hell!" dispassionately, and disappeared.

Antony barely had time to wonder what Roger's headgear could possibly have to do with Jenny, when he heard the sound of voices from the hall. Not "Aunt Lucy" after all; a man . . . no, two men, and something in the tones of one of them that seemed familiar.

He ought to have expected it, of course; it had been foolish not to when there had been so much talk of the police and what they might have discovered. The two men who followed Roger Farrell into the room a moment later were very well known to Antony indeed: Superintendent Briggs and Detective-Inspector Sykes, both of the Criminal Investigation Department at New Scotland Yard.

It was surprising enough that Briggs should be there at all; but that could wait. Antony wasn't pleased to see him . . . or even Sykes, with whom he was on friendly terms enough. And he had the uncomfortable feeling that his own presence at Leinster Court wasn't going to do Farrell any good at all.

3

SUPERINTENDENT BRIGGS WAS A HEAVY MAN, BIG-BONED, with reddish hair growing now well back from a bulging forehead, and cold blue eyes which did not in the least reflect his somewhat choleric disposition. Following sedately in his wake, Inspector Sykes might have looked almost insignificant to a casual observer: a square-built, fresh-faced man, with a comfortable, country look about him and an unusual placidity of temperament. Roger Farrell, waiting to close the door behind the two newcomers, thought them both formidable. He turned to Maitland with the beginnings of an introduction, but let the words trail into silence when he saw that they would be superfluous.

In the course of his life, Antony had known a number of men whom he had disliked for one reason or another; and one, at least, he had feared. Even among his acquaintance at Scotland Yard there was a certain Inspector Conway for whose acid tongue he would have admitted—in his more candid moments—a degree of respect. But with Briggs it was different; his original antagonism toward the detective had been instinctive and wholly unreasonable, though later events had done nothing to decrease it; and the trouble was, of course, the feeling was by no means one-sided.

Superintendent Briggs, for his part, would have allowed instinct no part in his feelings; he would have said, quite simply, that his dislike of Maitland was based on distrust, though he might also have admitted to himself that other, lesser items contributed to the emotion. His casual air, for instance, his flippancy in the face of serious matters and—perhaps above all—the look of faint amusement which all too frequently crept into his eyes.

Inspector Sykes smiled grimly and resigned himself to the thankless role of peacemaker. He knew well enough the abrasive effect the encounter would have on his colleague's feelings, and he felt it was no more than he should have expected when Maitland, seizing the initiative, remarked innocently:

"You didn't tell me you were expecting friends, Roger." And then, to the newcomers, "This is a surprise, gentlemen."

"A pleasant surprise, I hope, Mr. Maitland," said Sykes primly.

"Cela va sans dire," Antony told him, making an extravagant gesture in the certain knowledge that it would annoy the superintendent. Briggs gave him a hostile look and said only:

"Good evening."

Roger Farrell looked at Antony, and then back at the detectives. He couldn't see Maitland's expression clearly, because he was standing with his back to the window; but he thought there was an alertness about him now. "This seems to be an official visit," he said. And added awkwardly, "I'm not sure why."

"But it can't be," said Antony. He waved a hand in Briggs's direction. "Superintendents of the Criminal Investigation Department don't go round calling on just anybody," he protested.

If a compliment was implied, Briggs didn't seem to appreciate it. He said harshly, "Mr. Farrell is right, we have official business with him."

"But, Superintendent–"

"There are circumstances," said Briggs awfully, "that made my presence desirable."

"Well, of course, it's none of my business, after all. Perhaps I shall see you later, Roger? I'd better leave you to it now."

"No!" Farrell was surprised himself by the violence of his reaction to this suggestion.

"No?" said Antony, with a humorous inflection in his voice.

"No. I don't know what all this is about, but there can be no reason—"

"Let's ask them," Antony suggested. His eyes moved back to Sykes, and then to Briggs; but it was the inspector who answered him.

"We have a few questions to put to Mr. Farrell about the death of Martin Grainger."

"Oh, *that!*" said Antony. "I thought you'd made a statement, Roger."

"So I did, to the police at Scranton." But Briggs didn't seem to be listening to him, his eyes were fixed on Maitland's face.

"*That,* Mr. Maitland," he said with heavy irony, "happens to be a little matter of murder."

"The papers said it was an accident."

"Then they were more than usually inaccurate."

"Were they now? I find that very interesting." He was looking at Briggs expectantly. Inspector Sykes started to say something, but before he could do so the superintendent went on:

"I find it impossible to believe in an 'accident' involving a .470 rifle. A farmer carrying his gun across the fields would hardly be expecting to meet big game."

"Particularly not at three in the afternoon," agreed Antony idiotically, and added more slowly, "Yes, I see what you mean." He glanced at Farrell, and was relieved to see that he looked cool now and in control of the situation.

"As the matter seems to be more serious than I thought," Roger said, "we'd better all sit down." He trundled forward the sofa from the corner until it stood opposite the window and formed a group with the two chairs they had been using. The disorganization of the drawing room was now complete. He waved a hand invitingly and returned to his former place. "Well, Superintendent?" he said.

"If you're going to make a statement, it might be as well to talk to Armstrong first," Antony objected. But Roger shook his head.

"I don't see that at all. I've nothing to add to what I said before." He wasn't allowing himself to be rattled; but I wish I could

38

say aloud, "Don't let them bluff you," Antony thought, watching him. "Well, Superintendent?" Roger said again.

Briggs waved a hand toward his colleague. On the fragile-seeming sofa he looked supremely uncomfortable, but the inspector had perched himself on it happily enough. He had a notebook on his knee and was studying it, unhurried. There was a perceptible pause before he looked up and said:

"You told Sergeant Moffatt, I believe, that you did not know the dead man."

"That's quite correct."

"You wouldn't like to amplify that statement, Mr. Farrell?"

"If you like. I didn't know him. I never saw him until I found him dead. I never knew his name until I saw it in the evening paper."

"But you had, perhaps, some business dealings with him?"

"I don't quite understand that, Inspector. With a man I didn't know?"

"I am looking for an explanation of the fact that your telephone number was written down on Grainger's desk pad," said Sykes, unmoved.

Farrell turned his head until his eyes met Antony's. "If that's true—" he began.

"You can take it from me that it is," Sykes told him.

"Still, I can't explain."

"At this stage," said Antony, watching Briggs as he spoke, "you don't need to."

Sykes ignored the interruption. He had a great gift, thought Antony, half amused and half exasperated, for these steam-roller tactics. "Had he ever telephoned you . . . with some proposition, perhaps?"

"No."

"I think," said Maitland gently, "I really think you must be more explicit." The inspector looked at him gravely.

"Will it content you, Mr. Maitland, if I ask your friend whether he was being blackmailed by Martin Grainger?"

"Blackmail's an ugly word. I take it you've some grounds for offering the suggestion."

"Sufficient grounds," agreed Sykes equably.

"Aren't you stepping rather outside your part?" The superintendent rejoined the conversation suddenly, and his tone was not placatory. "You have been at some pains to convey to us that your presence here is accidental—"

That could be dangerous ground. "If I were a strong swimmer," said Antony tartly, "I wouldn't make the fact an excuse for leaving a man to drown."

Sykes had a sedate smile for this retort. Briggs said angrily, "This interference—" and broke off as he caught Maitland's eye.

"C-common humanity, Superintendent." His tone was still gentle, but the slight stammer betrayed the fact that his temper was suffering under the strain. "Shall we leave it at that?" he added, and turned back to Inspector Sykes. "You were going to tell us—weren't you?—your grounds for that suggestion. Which, so far, I find rather implausible."

"Blackmail," said Sykes reflectively, and exchanged a glance with his colleague. To Antony, who knew them both, the implication was clearer than words: a motive for murder that even the most strait-laced might regard sympathetically . . . and closeted with their suspect they found a man whose unorthodox ways had led him, before now, into apparent conflict with the police. "No harm in putting Mr. Maitland in the picture," Sykes suggested.

"No harm at all," said Briggs heavily.

"Well then, this man Grainger, as you know, was the owner of a city Chop House in Copthall Court, close to the Stock Exchange. He owned the house in which the restaurant was situated, and his office and living quarters were upstairs. So, naturally enough, when we were asked to give a hand, we got in touch with the City police and went to have a look round."

"With your customary efficiency. But not with the superintendent at that stage . . . surely?"

"Not then," Sykes agreed. "We weren't too interested, you know, until we found his files." It was, perhaps, fortunate that his attention was fixed on the man he was addressing. Maitland, whose interest was divided, saw Roger Farrell's expression and wondered for a moment whether he was actually going to be sick or not. He said quickly:

"Stop being enigmatic, Inspector. It isn't really your style. You found his files, and they gave evidence—I must suppose—that his interests weren't absolutely confined to the running of his restaurant."

"That's right, Mr. Maitland," said Sykes, at his most amiable.

"And at that point the superintendent began to take an active interest. I see."

"I thought you might," Sykes nodded. "So I'm asking you again, Mr. Farrell, were you being threatened in any way by this man Grainger?"

"No," said Roger. His air of indifference was brittle and unreal.

"Perhaps your connection with him was at second hand, through some other person?"

"I—" said Roger, and at the same moment Antony snapped, "Be quiet!" and turned back to Sykes with a show of indignation. "I've asked you before, Inspector, not to wrap things up. I'm sure if you can show reason—"

"If you really want plain speaking, Mr. Maitland, I was referring to the late Mrs. Winifred Farrell."

"What about her?" He hadn't time to look at Roger again; it might be cruel to drag all this into the open, but he had to find out. . . .

"There is—I am sorry to bring the matter up, Mr. Farrell— there is the undoubted fact that she died by her own hand."

"Not enough, Inspector. Not nearly enough."

"Added to the fact that certain things in Grainger's files led us to suppose—"

"Then you're in a position to answer your own question. Aren't you?" he added, as the detective hesitated.

"You're going too fast for me, Mr. Maitland. I was about to say, Grainger's files were of such a nature as to create a strong presumption that he had been extorting money by threats."

"But there was nothing about Mrs. Farrell?" If there had been it was a safe bet Sykes would have told him straight out. "Just the

41

telephone number, which he might have written down in mistake for another?"

"That's not quite all, Mr. Maitland. The office had been ransacked—"

"When?"

"Probably after he left home the day he was killed. Certainly before we searched the place, which was late yesterday afternoon."

"That's odd . . . isn't it?"

"You may think this even stranger. There was an empty file folder among the others; it was marked 'J.G.F.' "

"You're assuming the contents were stolen? I take it all the files weren't empty."

"They were not."

"You'll be seeing the people concerned?"

"Certainly."

"And at least one of them is a V.I.P.? That's what the superintendent came along for, isn't it? But these accusations against Mrs. Farrell are guesswork, and you know it."

That brought Briggs back into the conversation again. He said with emphasis, "What we found in Grainger's office, added to Mrs. Farrell's suicide and the fact that Mr. Roger Farrell was present when Grainger was shot—"

"Now *you're* going too fast, Superintendent. Perhaps you would care to substitute the phrase 'in the vicinity'?"

"If you prefer. It won't alter the facts, you know," said Briggs contemptuously.

"N-no. And there's another fact that's beginning to bother me. If this is one of those c-cases that have to be cleared up quickly—"

"Don't you think you've said too much, Mr. Maitland?" Sykes interrupted him, forestalling the superintendent, who seemed to be about to erupt.

"I'm not at all s-sure," said Antony grimly, "whether I've said enough."

"You're losing your temper," Briggs pointed out, more mildly than would have seemed possible a moment before but without any pacific intent.

"S-so I am," said Antony, surprised. "Now, isn't that odd?"

42

"Perhaps we could go back a little. We are only trying to point out to Mr. Farrell that it is quite reasonable for us to ask for a further statement."

"Eminently reasonable, Inspector." For some reason, this bland agreement seemed to infuriate Briggs; he came to his feet with something ridiculously like a flounce, and said in an overwrought way:

"This is a sheer waste of time!"

"Oh, do you think so? I was going to ask whether you would prefer to wait while Mr. Farrell gets in touch with his solicitor; or . . . you could go to Scotland Yard tomorrow, couldn't you, Roger?"

"If that's what they want," said Roger, without any great show of enthusiasm.

"I think perhaps tomorrow . . . do you agree, sir?" asked Sykes, cautiously.

"Tomorrow, by all means," said Briggs, with feeling. He was no doubt thinking that in his own office he would have some control over who was present, and need admit only the principals. Antony grinned sympathetically.

"At ten-thirty then, Mr. Farrell, if that is convenient to you," Sykes was saying. Roger nodded, and they all moved towards the door. Briggs was already on the landing and ringing for the lift when the inspector turned in the doorway for a final word. "There's one thing I'd like to ask you, Mr. Farrell, but as Mr. Maitland so rightly points out these questions should wait until your solicitor can be present." There was so much meaning in his tone that it seemed to have an almost hypnotic effect on Roger, who asked, as though he had no choice in the matter:

"What is your question?"

"A very simple one really. Do you happen to know who took your mother's car out on the afternoon of the murder?" He smiled benevolently from Roger to Antony, and stepped onto the landing, pulling the door shut behind him.

Roger Farrell went straight back into the drawing room, and—ignoring the sherry altogether—poured Scotch into two glasses with a liberal hand. "I said before that I needed a drink," he remarked a moment later. "Now I really do." He eyed his companion morosely, and seemed to be searching for words. "Do you think that means they know it was Meg?"

"If I know Sykes . . . yes, I think so. Where is the car kept?"

"There's a basement garage. I told the man she'd be calling for it; I gave him her name."

"Of course, you *would* do that," said Antony unreasonably. "What are you going to tell the police . . . and your solicitor, of course?"

"Just what I've told you." Roger had taken out a cigarette and was tapping it on his case and scowling frightfully; he looked up now and caught Maitland's eye, and grinned as though in apology.

"That's all right then, only you mustn't change your story later on."

"Why should I do that?"

"For something more convenient. I'm trying to point out that I can back out now, and forget everything you've told me."

"So that I could have a free hand to tell what lies I like?"

"That's one way of putting it."

"Would it be better for Meg?"

"I'm not quite sure." He smiled suddenly. "Better for her, perhaps, if you could make up a really good tale *and* keep her muzzled. But certainly not better for that Presbyterian conscience of hers."

"Presbyterian?" said Roger, apparently forgetting the problem in face of this novel idea. "Perhaps I've got a conscience too," he added reflectively. "On the whole, I prefer to stick to the truth."

"You don't have to say anything at this stage," Antony pointed out.

"I was rather thinking it would have been better if I'd told them straight away."

"Good heavens, no. You couldn't have played it better."

"Why?" asked Roger a little sourly. "Because I let you take all the difficult shots?" Antony grinned at him.

"Do you realize," he said, "how much information they gave us?" He raised his glass in a parody of Farrell's earlier gesture.

44

"To our alliance," he said. And added, gently, "You will notice that I did not qualify the noun."

"What does that mean?"

"It means I don't like blackmailers. It also means I don't like Superintendent Briggs," he added with unwilling honesty; and saw the shadow of disappointment in his companion's eyes.

"I suppose that's as much as I've a right to expect," said Roger slowly. "About tomorrow—"

"You'd better phone Armstrong, hadn't you?"

"Yes. But I meant, do you think they'll arrest me?" His tone was commendably matter-of-fact now; he might have been wondering what the chances were for a fine day.

"They haven't questioned Meg yet or they'd have cautioned you just now. When they've heard her story and yours . . . yes, I do think they'll arrest you."

"And all this blackmail business—"

"Will be adduced by the prosecution to prove motive. I'm afraid you must accept that, however disagreeable you find it." He watched Farrell struggling with this for a moment, and then added quietly, "Were your father's initials J.G.F.?"

"They were. James Gerard. It's a bit of a facer, isn't it?"

"Not too good. And did you notice what they said about the gun?"

"Yes." His tone was reserved, and Antony added quickly:

"Another point for the prosecution?"

"It could be. I'm not interested in hunting, but Dad was. And he has a friend in Kenya he used to visit."

"Are his guns still around?"

"Not here, at the cottage. They could say—couldn't they?— I'd used one and disposed of it."

"If one had been taken, would you know?"

"That's rather far-fetched, isn't it?" Antony shrugged. "Well, I couldn't tell you if anything was missing, unless it was one of the duck guns I use sometimes. I don't know what Dad had for big game."

"And you are—don't tell me!—a good shot. Why the hell did you have to report finding the body?"

Surprisingly, Farrell laughed. "My civic duty," he said. "And that reminds me, what were you getting so hot under the collar about? Something to do with the other people who were being blackmailed?"

Antony finished his drink, and put down the glass, and walked to the window before he replied. "I doubt if I can answer that without slandering the good superintendent," he said. "If there's someone important involved—and there must be, or Briggs wouldn't have been here at all—it would undoubtedly be a convenience to get the matter cleared up quickly. By arresting you, for instance."

"Where's the slander?"

"I seem to be implying that Briggs would let that weigh with him." As he spoke, Maitland seemed to be asking himself a question. "Well, I think he would . . . but not consciously. Sykes knows that as well as I do, that's why he shut me up so quickly. But to do the superintendent justice, I think he'd be horrified at the very idea."

"But they've got a pretty good case, haven't they? I mean, they'd be justified—"

"That's true. I don't want them to miss any angles, that's all. About Meg, now; we ought to see her, but do you suppose she'll still be at the theater?"

"I should think so. I'll phone her flat if you like, and if nobody answers we'll go and see. After all, she's got to eat sometime."

"And so have we," said Antony. He found an envelope in his pocket and began to note down the questions he hadn't had time to ask. But he looked up before Roger reached the door. "Those diaries," he said. "May I borrow them?"

4

MEG DID NOT ANSWER THE PHONE, THOUGH ROGER dialed her number twice and waited each time a little longer than Antony thought reasonable. He put down the receiver at last with an air of discontent. "The theater it is," he said, and then grinned. "I hope your nerves are good."

Antony had followed him into the hall and was stowing the diaries away in his brief case when the bell rang. Farrell muttered something and pulled open the door. "Oh, come in, Uncle," he said. There was a measure of cordiality in his tone, and something else besides. "A friend of mine, Antony Maitland," he added, backing away to let the newcomer enter. "My godfather, Mr. Denning."

An elderly man of middle height, and very erect bearing, with a round, pink face and fluffy, white hair; a childlike effect until you met a disconcertingly bright and inquiring look. He had an amiable greeting for Antony, but there was a faint air of reproach in his tone as he turned back to his godson. "You were going out?" he said. "I came early, because yesterday evening—"

"I'm afraid we were. You see, I was alone and—"

"Yes, yes, it is quite natural you should wish for company. I just wanted to ask you if you would care to come down to Petersfield for the weekend. Isabel and Leonard will be coming, and as

I'm hoping to get away next week—" He paused, as though he had already offered sufficient inducement to warrant a reply, and Antony took the opportunity to suggest that he should go ahead and look for a taxi. But before he could move Farrell had made up his mind.

"No, wait," he said. And then, "You might be able to help me, Uncle, if you would."

"Anything at all I can do . . . you know that."

"Yes, but this is rather difficult." He paused, and Antony had time to wonder how he would handle the explanations. Not an easy matter, nor was it readily apparent what degree of affection and understanding there was between his two companions. "I've reason to believe Dad was being blackmailed," Roger said bluntly. "I want to find out why."

Perhaps there was something to be said for this bald approach, though as an explanation it lacked something of detail. Mr. Denning looked thoughtfully at his godson for a moment; then he moved, and seated himself deliberately on one of the hard chairs that stood one at each end of the hall table. "I'm a little out of touch with your affairs, my boy," he remarked. "Mr. Maitland, I must suppose, is an intimate friend?"

"Yes . . . of course," said Roger. He sounded a little taken aback by the question, perhaps he had expected some more violent reaction to the word "blackmail"; but there was also in his tone a sort of underlying amusement, as though the aptness of the description appealed to him.

"And this statement of yours . . . I can take your word for the fact that you are suspicious, at least. You don't mean that some sort of an approach has been made to you?"

"Good God, no!"

"I see." The hard, blue eyes moved until he was looking directly at Maitland. "How do you think I can help you?" he inquired, in a tone of gentle perplexity.

"We believe Mr. Farrell received the first demand five years ago," said Antony. This wasn't quite the approach he had envisaged, but it was too late to worry about that now. "As his closest friend—"

"I cannot believe," said Denning, "that there could be anything in James's life that he wished to hide." His tone had taken on a certain unction, and Antony wasn't altogether surprised when Roger interrupted impatiently:

"If you'd rather think that Mother—"

"What are you saying?" The old man looked a little bewildered, but his tone was sharply questioning. "Your mother—God rest her!—was one of the best women I ever knew. To suggest that she . . . to make such a terrible suggestion—"

"Terrible or not," said Farrell, "she was being blackmailed."

"But who—?"

"A man named Grainger. He was murdered the day before yesterday. The police think I killed him," said Roger, whose decisiveness—sufficiently noticeable before—had now become almost alarming. In some obscure way, he seemed to enjoy making these revelations.

"But—" said Denning helplessly. "But—"

"The situation is a little involved," said Antony, feeling some note of regret, if not of apology, was called for. "I'm sure Farrell will wish to explain it to you, but in the meantime perhaps you could just accept that it really is serious."

"I see. And your own part in this—er—situation?"

"An advisory one, sir." He held Denning's look steadily, and wondered what sort of an impression he was making. Roger was silent for the moment, which perhaps was just as well.

"And I am to take your word for the fact that my old friends . . . that someone was blackmailing them," said Denning incredulously.

"I think you may take Roger's word for that. There doesn't seem to be much room for doubt."

"And this man, you say, was murdered?"

"He was shot on Tuesday afternoon, on a country road in Essex." Roger came forcefully back into the conversation. "I was there. I found him. And the police are in a position to prove I had a motive."

"Now, really, Roger—"

"Don't you think I had cause enough?" asked Farrell, in a hard tone. "After all, it was because of him that Mother killed herself."

Denning brought his hand down sharply on the table beside him. "Did you kill him?" he demanded.

"No, I didn't," said Roger shortly. After what he had been saying it was perhaps unreasonable that he should resent even so blunt a question. The old man sat looking up at him for a moment, but there was nothing in Mr. Denning's expression that reflected either doubt or credulity.

"In any event, your defense must be looked to," he said at last. "I will arrange—"

"I'm seeing Armstrong in the morning," Farrell told him.

"I assure you, my boy, in this matter it would be wise to be guided by me."

"It's all fixed," said Roger brusquely. Only too plainly, he didn't like taking direction. "I can manage my own affairs."

"So much seems obvious." In the circumstances he might be forgiven the dryness of his tone. "You will take your own way, I suppose, but if I can help you—" He came to his feet as he spoke and stood looking at his godson with a curious expression, almost as if he understood and sympathized with Roger's feelings.

"You may be able to," said Farrell, "if you'll have a talk with Maitland tomorrow." Antony was beginning to feel more than ever as though he were being swept along in the eye of a hurricane. There was a deceptive calm about the process, which was, none the less, quite inexorable.

"Ah, yes, Mr. Maitland." He turned a little, to give Antony his attention. "I seem to have heard your name," he said.

"Very likely you have, Uncle. He's a barrister."

"I see," said Hubert Denning, and could not have expressed his bewilderment more clearly.

"But I'm not here in a professional capacity," Antony explained. "As a friend of Roger's I may be able to help a little."

"By asking questions?"

"That's the general idea."

"It all seems very irregular," Denning complained.

"It is . . . very," Antony agreed earnestly. "All the same—"

"Very well, then." Perhaps Roger's decisiveness was catching. "Tomorrow, at what time?"

"If you're going into the country—"

"That can wait."

"I shan't be free till evening, you see."

"Shall we say nine o'clock, then? I have a *pied-à-terre,* Roger will tell you. Will you call on me there, Mr. Maitland?" He began to move toward the door.

"I'll get you a taxi," said Roger, with an air of relief that went far beyond the bounds of politeness.

When they had found a cab themselves and were on their way to the Cornmarket Theatre, Antony said mildly, "You know, you make me giddy. I can't help feeling that your approach to Mr. Denning was lacking in finesse."

Roger had been looking out of the window, but now he turned with an anxious look. "You said you'd take a hand," he pointed out.

"I did. And I meant it."

"Well, then!"

There were a good many things Antony could have said to that, but what was the use, after all? First Meg, and now Roger; he was being drawn into their affairs, but he had said—hadn't he?—that he was no longer reluctant. That might be only half true, but for a moment, in there, he'd almost believed Roger's denials. "If only it wasn't impossible," he said aloud, and ignored his companion's questioning look and he stared out in his turn at the sunlit street and the crowds of people going home, or going to dinner, or hastening to a rendezvous.

The taxi left them at the front of the theater, which had every appearance of being deserted. There were posters already in place, and Antony stopped to study them: *Very Tragical Mirth,* a drama of today. What had Jenny said about it? Not a good part for Meg. And then, more outspokenly, it sounds altogether too elevated . . . too intense. But when he turned to the photographs of the cast, there was Meg laughing her head off. Not a characteristic pose; she had plenty of humor, but it didn't generally overflow. For some reason, these reflections cast a damper on his spirits, as if he'd consulted an oracle and the omens were all bad.

"Come *on,*" said Farrell impatiently. Antony turned to look at him, already finding it difficult to visualize him as a stranger. Roger seemed to be in no mood for dawdling, but that was apparently quite normal.

"Shouldn't we go round to the stage door or something?"

"Not if this one's open." The first door was locked, but the second yielded to the pressure of his hand. Antony followed him, and resisted an impulse to walk on tiptoe out of respect for the unbroken silence in the foyer. Roger strode across it, apparently untroubled by any misgivings; he went up three steps and across a wide expanse of carpet, turned sharply to the right, and pushed open another door. Beyond was a confusion of sound: hammering in the distance and an odd sort of noise—which recurred occasionally all the time they were in the theater, but which Antony never identified—as if a wicker laundry basket were being dragged down a wooden flight of stairs.

The stage was lighted, but the auditorium was in darkness except for such illumination as spilled over into the front of the stalls. As they penetrated farther they could see a sturdy figure hunched up in the second row, but there was no lack of movement on the stage to attract their attention. The scene was a living room, penny plain but not squalid, a room that had been furnished, perhaps, in the 1920's . . . a solid, lower-middle-class background. A middle-aged man in shirt sleeves moved across the stage as they watched, and started to wind the clock "on mantelpiece R," thought Antony to himself, trying to get into the spirit of the thing. A boy was sitting at the center table with his fingers stuffed in his ears and a pile of books spread in front of him. Meg herself, in a gown of incongruous splendor, was standing at the other side of the table laughing hysterically. And a beautiful young man, who had been sitting quietly reading a newspaper, got up and advanced on her, as graceful as a panther, but with a wary look that rendered the whole thing ridiculous. Then, after a moment's evident hesitation, he raised his hand and tapped her lightly on the cheek. And as he did so, the crouched figure in the stalls exploded into action.

"Stop! I cannot bear it!" He was waving his arms wildly, as though to emphasize his point; a little, round man, without jacket or tie, and as energetic as a rubber ball. "You . . . Meg . . . you are not Antigone, you are not Clytemnestra, you are not—"

Meg had already stopped laughing and assumed a look of astonishment, which deepened now to one of sheer outrage. "I ken that fine," she said coldly.

"And Ben . . . think, man, think of the situation, I implore you. You do not wish to listen to her laughter, but it maddens you, it tears your nerves; at last you stride across the room—"

"The fact is," said the shirt-sleeved man moodily, "it isn't true to life." He closed the clock face, and lumbered across the stage to stand with the others, near the table. He peered out into the stalls. "What," he said, "isn't Laurie here?" He sounded disappointed.

"No, he isn't," said Meg, this time in her normal voice, "so it's no use making cracks about the play. But Ossy—" She gestured toward the man in the stalls.

"It's no use blaming the play," asserted Ossy, "when Meg is playing tragedy and Ben is playing farce." At this point, the boy at the table unstoppered his ears and looked up vaguely.

"What's the matter?" he asked. And then, "I say, this is a jolly interesting book." Ossy raised his hands in silent appeal to heaven.

"We shall try again," he announced. "And this time, Ben, you hit her . . . so, I show you." He moved out into the aisle, and seemed to be ready to bounce up on to the stage.

"No," said Meg. She spoke quietly, but with enough venom in her tone to stop poor Ossy in his tracks.

"You see what I mean," he appealed to the others.

"Meg's all right," said the middle-aged man tolerantly. "But I do think, Ben, you should try not to look like a cat on hot bricks."

"I don't know what you expect." Ben sounded sulky. "When I try to put some feeling into the scene she goes for me like a tiger."

"I've got to react, haven't I?" Like Ossy, Meg seemed to be making a general plea for understanding.

"Surprise . . . oh, yes, surprise," Ossy conceded.

"If he clouts me the way you're telling him to," said Meg roundly, "I shall be furious!"

The boy at the table had gone back to his book again. "Did you know," he asked, "that when a Maori meets another Maori he has to recite his *whole* pedigree, right back to the canoe he landed from?"

Ossy said: "Canoe . . . canoe?" and looked round him wildly, while the shirt-sleeved man, with his first sign of emotion, exclaimed:

"Now it's Maoris!" in a voice that echoed despairingly through the empty theater.

Antony saw with regret that Roger, who had been standing halfway down the center aisle, had begun to move forward again. He halted when he was level with Ossy and said clearly, "I'm sorry to interrupt," so that the little man spun round with a cry of alarm.

"Hallo, Roger." Meg came quickly down to the front of the stage. "It would be awfully nice, Ossy, wouldn't it, if we stopped for half an hour?" she said, and now she spoke with blatant cajolery.

Ossy glanced at the newcomer and scowled as though in him he saw his worse fears realized. "And when you come back you will let Ben hit you," he said, not very hopefully.

"Perhaps," said Meg. She smiled impartially at her fellow actors and moved toward the side of the stage. "There's a door down there, darlings," she said, gesturing. Roger and Antony moved obediently toward it.

Backstage, Antony felt such shreds of sanity as he still possessed slipping away from him. They fell over a man who might have been the twin of the shirt-sleeved man on stage but who obviously believed in minding his own business; which was, apparently, to make as much noise as he possibly could with a large hammer, some nails and a number of oddly shaped pieces of wood. They collided with a yellow-haired girl in a dress very similar to the one Meg was wearing, though even in the half-light it had a tawdry look. They narrowly avoided a burly man in a brown suit who was leaning against a thing that looked like a flying buttress, with an evening paper folded open at the sports page. And before them flitted a little, black-clad figure, with gray hair dressed very neatly and unbecomingly, who fell upon Meg with the demand that she remove her dress instantly for alteration. Meg disappeared and came back surprisingly quickly in a blue suit with a severe-looking white blouse. With the make-up still plastered thickly on her face she looked incongruous in the extreme, and Antony eyed her critically.

"Don't say a word!" she told him. "I haven't time to take it off, and no one will notice anyway. We'll just go next door."

Next door was conveniently situated, though not quite so conveniently as Meg had implied. It provided them with sandwiches and coffee, which depressed Antony still further, though both were quite good. And Meg was right: her appearance occasioned no interest at all.

"You didn't tell me you were coming," she said. Her eyes flickered to Antony's face and then came to rest on Roger again.

"We thought we'd better see you," said Farrell. "You see, the police—" He was more at ease now, Antony noticed, than at any time since his godfather's arrival at Leinster Court; and Antony wondered, suddenly, what had passed between these two when they left Kempenfeldt Square last night. The constraint seemed to have vanished now . . . or, had it? Meg was drinking her coffee thirstily as she listened, but she didn't seem to want anything to eat. Her eyes were intent, as though she were trying to read into Farrell's unadorned statements something more than appeared on the surface. "What does that mean?" she said when he had finished.

Roger's hand came out to cover hers. "It means, my dear," he said, "that when you see the police you'll tell them exactly what happened."

"That's all very well," Meg objected. "What about you?"

"I . . . don't quite know." He glanced uneasily at Maitland as he spoke.

Antony was stirring his coffee as if the simple task absorbed him. "You may as well tell her," he said, not looking up. But when a dead silence followed he raised his eyes at last and added carefully, "They have a case, you know."

"And I'll be helping them!" Meg's voice rose dramatically on the assertion. "I'll not be doing it," she added firmly.

"You can refuse to answer questions at this stage, though I wouldn't advise it. I take it you're not prepared to perjure yourself when the matter comes to trial."

"No . . . no. Is that what I must do, tell them everything?"

"Yes." He didn't attempt to elaborate, and after a moment she said submissively:

"When?"

"They'll want to see you before they see Roger again. So, at a guess, early tomorrow morning."

"I . . . you couldn't be there, Antony, could you?"

"I'm sorry, Meg. I have to be in court." And suddenly, as he looked at her, he was angry; angry because, against his will, he was sorry for her; angry because she was so susceptible to hurt and not even troubling to hide her vulnerability. It took a real effort to keep his voice gentle. "Eat your sandwich, Meg, and I'll get you some more coffee. I've some questions to ask you first, myself."

When the coffee was brought and they were alone again, she looked at him questioningly over the rim of her cup. "I told you everything," she said.

"Except the answer to the most important question of all. Who could have known of the appointment with Grainger?"

Meg seemed to be taking her time to digest this. Antony glanced at Roger and saw again the look af sick dismay, as though he were realizing for the first time that if this question couldn't be answered there was no way out at all. "No one could have known," he said, and perhaps Meg's thoughts were following his because she interrupted fiercely:

"You've got to believe him, Antony, when he says he didn't shoot that man." And then her voice had the coaxing note he had heard in the theater. "It's so obvious, darling, really quite obvious—"

"Oh, for heaven's s-sake, Meg, I'm not c-clairvoyant!" he said, his anger suddenly boiling up again.

56

"Well, neither am I," said Meg crossly, "so how can I know who Grainger may have told?"

Antony compressed his lips. Every instinct told him that Grainger, whatever else he might or might not have done, hadn't confided in anybody else his plans for Tuesday afternoon. Nor was it likely that he had betrayed them accidentally; the very nature of the assignation made it imperative that caution should be observed. But didn't that apply to Farrell too? He ignored the creeping doubt and turned to Roger. "What time was it when Grainger was speaking to Mrs. Farrell?" he asked. "The call you overheard."

"About three o'clock."

"A Thursday afternoon, you said. What were you doing at home?"

"I'd been to a luncheon . . . at the Dorchester. I went home afterwards to get a book I'd promised to lend Sam Reade."

"So the call Meg took was last Thursday, at three o'clock?"

"It was."

"Were you at home?"

"No, I couldn't be there. I gave her a key."

"You were quite alone, Meg?"

"Of course."

"And afterwards, did you phone Roger at his office?"

"I wasn't there, either. It was the afternoon Mother was buried."

"I left a note for him," said Meg.

"I didn't know whether I'd be able to see her that night; there were all the relations—"

"Wait a bit. This note, Meg."

"I just wrote down the time and place. I didn't want to think about the rest of the conversation . . . ever again."

"I want to know exactly."

"Well, I suppose, 'A.A. box, eight miles from Scranton on the Mountalban road. Tuesday, the seventh of May, 3 P.M.' " said Meg doubtfully. "That's what he *said*."

"Is that right, Farrell?"

"Near enough."

"And you went back to the flat . . . when?"

"About five-thirty. We had to see some of the aunts off from Paddington."

"Were you alone?"

"No. My sister was with me, and her husband. And my partner, Sam Reade. And Uncle Hubert, whom you met just now."

"Where had Meg left the note?"

"In my bedroom. I told her to put it there. It was folded up on top of the tallboy, with my stud box on top of it."

"And what did you do when you'd read it?"

"I don't know." He spoke slowly, thinking it out. "I know I put it in my wallet, but that was later. Just then, I think, I left it there. Like Meg, I wanted the information; but I wanted to—to dissociate myself from it, too."

"So any of your guests might have seen it?"

"I suppose so. But—"

"If your father was being blackmailed," said Antony, "it's quite possible that one of his associates was also involved." He paused, eyeing the other man a little sardonically. "Hadn't you thought of that?"

"Oddly enough, no." He caught Maitland's eye, and added defensively, "that happens to be true."

"Think of it now. Mr. Denning was his closest friend—"

"But they didn't do business together."

"No? What is Denning's business?"

"Something to do with insurance. He has an office in Lombard Street, and he comes up once or twice a week. There is also the *pied-à-terre* he spoke of—which isn't as small as all that—in Piccadilly."

"Sam Reade was your father's junior partner, I think you said."

"I suppose you mean that makes him the most likely person." He seemed to be struggling with the idea. "The trouble is . . . I've always trusted him."

"And your brother-in-law?"

"Oh, Leonard! Somehow I don't think—"

"*Don't* think," said Antony. "Answer the question!"

"He was on quite good terms with Dad, but I can't see them getting together on any project; certainly not a . . . a shady one."

"Why not?" He paused, but when Farrell made no immediate reply he added, less abruptly, "Forget about the possible shadiness for the moment."

"Well, of course, you don't know Leonard."

"I don't even know his name," said Maitland, more tartly.

"Leonard Wilson. He's about forty-five, I should say; a good few years older than Isabel, anyway. And he's the manager of the Fenchurch Street Branch of Bramley's. But he's one of those people . . . well, I'll tell you," said Roger, putting his elbows on the table. "I can imagine him being as tough as you please with some poor devil of a clerk who needed an overdraft; but with anyone in any sort of a position he'd be much more conciliatory. And that's putting it mildly; I really mean he's a bit of a worm."

"But you said Bramley's was your bank, didn't you?"

"The firm's account is at Fenchurch Street, certainly, but I can't see that Leonard's cooperation would have been the slightest use to Dad in any sort of deal he might want to put through. He'd hardly have asked for an overdraft, for instance, to finance an illegal transaction."

"I was really wondering if the operation of the account might have given him some clue—?"

"If you mean the money Dad spent on diamonds, that was from his personal account, of course, which was at the Bayswater Branch."

"I see. But any of those three men might have seen Meg's note, and if they'd ever paid blackmail to Grainger, the first words would have been sufficient—"

"If, if, if," said Roger discontentedly.

"I'm afraid it's the best we can do at this stage. If we work from the fact of your innocence, two things follow: someone else had a motive for killing Grainger, and knew where he'd be on Tuesday afternoon."

"I know . . . we have to start somewhere." There was no resignation in the way he spoke, only a thinly veiled savagery. Meg glanced anxiously at Maitland and began to drink her coffee with a show of haste. "I suppose," Roger added in a grumbling tone, "you've got to get back to that madhouse."

"Well, darling, I did promise, you know."

If Antony had felt any resentment at Roger's tone a moment before, it wouldn't have survived Meg's desperate attempt to be natural, though he wondered for a moment if Farrell was deceived by it. But when she came to her feet and added, "Don't come with me," he decided that Roger knew very well what she was feeling. He would not otherwise have obeyed her. As it was, he contented himself with going to the door, but he was swearing under his breath as he came back to the table.

"I'd like to have been able to go to her first night," he said as he seated himself. And then restlessly, "I wish I knew what the police would ask her tomorrow."

"I hope it will be fairly straightforward."

Roger was absent-mindedly eating the sandwich that Meg had left untouched. He said between mouthfuls, "Let me ask you a question. Why do you want to know the reason my father was being blackmailed?"

"I've already explained—"

"That you think he may have had a partner in crime. Someone who didn't mind more or less framing me," he added thoughtfully.

"I doubt if that was intentional. I mean, someone saw the note, and obviously they didn't care if they involved you, but I don't think it could have been planned that way beforehand." I'm talking, he thought, as if I believe what he's told me, but unless I take that for granted . . .

"I suppose not." Roger had finished eating and was feeling for his cigarette case. "If it weren't for Meg," he said, "I wouldn't care." And added as he caught Maitland's eye, "I don't blame you for not believing that, though it happens to be true. You see, I'm beginning to think there's a sort of poetic justice about the whole thing."

"That doesn't sound very sensible," said Antony after considering the statement.

"My father killed my mother," said Roger. He had found the cigarette case now and was sitting looking down at it as though he couldn't remember its purpose. "You can put it less forcefully, if you like; say, that what he did was responsible for her death."

"It may be ironic that you should pay—indirectly—for his sins," said Antony, considerably startled, "but I wouldn't call it justice."

"Wouldn't you?" He sounded as though he was prepared to consider the question dispassionately, but Antony, meeting his eyes, decided that as far as Farrell was concerned, the issue was already judged. "It's just that I . . . oh, well!" He got up suddenly, as though he found inactivity intolerable. "There's one thing," he said. "I needn't see Meg again."

Antony followed him out and only just remembered to stop and pay the bill. He was conscious of a cold sense of foreboding. Farrell had been far more shaken by his mother's suicide than he would have ever admitted, centainly more than he realized himself. And the trouble about that was it didn't help convince you that he hadn't planned Grainger's death.

"But can you tell me, love," he said to Jenny later, "why I have to be such a fool?" Perhaps he was catching Farrell's habit of making unanswerable statements, or perhaps Jenny was just too wise to give him a reply.

5

THE NEXT DAY PROMISED TO BE A FULL ONE, AND AS IT turned out the promise was more than redeemed. Antony snatched five minutes to consult Sir Nicholas in chambers before he left for court but found him no less preoccupied than he had been on Wednesday evening. He showed a brief interest when Superintendent Briggs's name was mentioned, but a few moments later he was saying earnestly, "Now, if you could tell me the true value of six thousand packages of dried egg, that would be really helpful." He picked up a document, eyed it suspiciously, and dropped it back into the confusion on his desk. "The figure for which they were insured," he added severely, "seems to me to be out of all proportion, especially as I strongly suspect they were out of date and should have been used long ago."

Rightly surmising that it was his uncle's client who had done the insuring, Antony murmured his sympathy and withdrew. He had troubles of his own awaiting him, including a lay client who was too sad and a solicitor who was too hearty. But they had their point of view, after all, and, for the moment, deserved his attention.

Perhaps the judge was hungry; he adjourned in good time for the luncheon recess, and the reassembling of the court was fixed no earlier than usual. Antony found a telephone, and dialed

Meg's number, and listened to the bell shrilling through the empty flat. Illogically, the sound disturbed him; and it was illogical, too, that he felt no surprise when he put down the receiver at last and turned to find Willett at his elbow. "It's Miss Hamilton," the clerk explained. "I said I'd try to find you."

"Where is she?"

"I took her to Astroff's, Mr. Maitland, was that right?" He seemed to feel his action needed a little more explanation and added anxiously, "Well, I told her I didn't know if you'd have time to join her, only I could see she was upset—" But Antony was already on his way.

He found Meg in the bar with an empty glass in front of her, and because she did not immediately see him he had plenty of chance to study her as he crossed the room. She looked tired and nervous, as though she hadn't slept, and he mentally acquitted Willett of having succumbed to the blandishments of a siren; it seemed so much more likely that his sympathies had led him astray. And in this he did Willett more than justice and Meg considerably less, as he should have realized when she looked up and saw him and immediately began to glow. "I'm so glad you could get here, darling."

"So am I." He slid into a chair opposite her and signaled the waiter. "Do you never drink anything but that stuff?" he asked when the man had gone again. "And not so much of your theatrical jargon, Meg," he added. "They know me here, and I've a reputation to keep up."

"Have you, darling . . . er—*have* you?" said Meg. Antony grinned at her.

"Never mind," he told her. "Has anything happened?"

"If you mean, did the police come . . . yes, they did. Your friend Inspector Sykes and another man, Sergeant Somebody. And they came at nine o'clock and had to wait till I dressed because we didn't finish at the theater until terribly late, you see. But they were quite nice," she said, considering the word, and apparently finding it not altogether inappropriate.

"So I should hope. No awkward questions?"

"Not really. No . . . not really. Only it was like . . . when

63

somebody smiles at you and their eyes don't," said Meg. From her air of triumph it was obvious that she felt she had now made everything abundantly clear . . . as indeed she had. "But that wasn't what I wanted to talk about." She hesitated and then went on in a rush. "I wanted to know . . . Antony, what do you think of Roger?"

And if that wasn't like a woman, he thought, exasperated. But he only said, "I like him," cautiously.

"You know I meant more than that. I don't see why you can't give me a straight answer," she complained. But when he didn't reply immediately she laughed a little self-consciously. "I know I'm not being reasonable," she said. "I want him to trust me, and I don't know why he should. Because I don't . . . altogether . . . trust him."

And what was there to be said to that? He couldn't tell her that she should be thinking of herself, of what her story was going to sound like if she had to tell it in court. However innocent her motives, it seemed she had been instrumental in leading Martin Grainger to his death; and if Farrell's plot had been laid with that in mind . . . if he were guilty . . .

Her eyes were fixed on his face. She said, as though he had spoken, "I know, darling, I know. My feelings don't matter. I should be thinking of—of the more serious aspects of the situation. But I can't operate like that, I can't worry about things just because I *should*." She paused and lifted her head . . . an oddly defiant gesture he had seen her use on the stage, only now, he was sure, it was completely artless. "You see the kind of fool I am," she said. "But I've got to tell somebody, and there's only you."

"I'm listening, Meg."

"I know you are. And I expect you know what I mean without my putting it into words. I suppose you know I don't care if he killed that man . . . not really. But if he used me and didn't tell me, that would be . . . I just couldn't bear it."

"I see. Meg—"

"Yes?"

"I can't say, 'Don't worry.' I can't say, 'I think Farrell's innocent,' because I don't know. But if he did deceive you about his motives, it could have been to protect you. Don't you see?" And suddenly Meg smiled at him. It was rather an uncertain smile, but she seemed to be genuinely amused.

"I might have known you'd say that. You treat us as children and then have the gall to tell us it's for our own good." But Antony was thinking that what he had just put forward as a possibility could very well be true, and he thought of Roger Farrell's tormented look the evening before, when he had said—with such a drastic reversal of mood—"perhaps it's justice." But he couldn't tell Meg that, so he drained his glass and got to his feet.

"Come and have lunch," he invited.

She sat a moment longer, looking up at him. "At least . . . I can trust you, Antony, can't I?"

"Of course you can." But the question echoed in his head as he followed her into the dining room, and the answer twisted itself grotesquely into his thoughts: you can trust me, of course . . . for what it's worth.

Jenny was going to the first night of *Very Tragical Mirth* and had succeeded in finding a friend who would use Antony's ticket. So they had supper early, and that was a good thing, as it turned out. Because almost as soon as she had gone there was a knock on the door, and when he went to answer it he found Inspector Sykes on the landing.

"Well . . . come in, Inspector." He did his best, but his tone was resigned, rather than welcoming.

"I met Mrs. Maitland downstairs, and she told me to come straight up," said Sykes, coming into the hall. The statement might have been designed by way of apology. "I hope I'm not disturbing you," he added.

"I have to go out in half an hour. Until then . . . I'm just having coffee, Inspector. Will you join me?"

Sykes had a knack for making himself at home. "An unofficial visit, Mr. Maitland," he said a moment later, adding a fifth lump of sugar to the cup at his elbow.

"I'm relieved to hear it." It wasn't the first time Sykes had sat there, and sometimes they had been allies, and more often there had been a certain amount of sparring. This time . . . ? "Is Roger Farrell under arrest?" he asked abruptly.

"For the moment, no." He paused and seemed to be considering whether or not this statement was sufficiently precise. Antony hid his impatience; it wasn't the slightest use, as he well knew, trying to hurry Sykes. "That's why I'm here," the inspector added, and leaned back in his chair, as bland and inscrutable as a Chinese god.

"Is it?" Antony's tone was cautious.

"You see, there are certain things the defense will learn when Farrell is arrested," said Sykes.

"And as it's only a matter of time—" He didn't finish the sentence, because he had a sudden feeling he must be guessing wrong; but Sykes beamed at him, as though gratified by this evidence of intelligence, and said:

"That's just it, Mr. Maitland," in a pleased tone.

"Wait a bit. You're offering to help me, Inspector . . . what's the catch?"

"I thought you might like to know a little more about Martin Grainger. There are no strings to the offer," Sykes assured him.

Antony was frowning over this. "A line of defense," he said, "which Farrell has rejected."

"He may yet change his mind," said the detective placidly. "I've a shrewd idea that in this instance, Mr. Maitland, you've been sold a pup."

"It's happened before," said Antony. He was standing on the hearthrug and frowning down at the inspector, and it was very evident that, for the moment, his attention was completely caught. "Look here," he added, "why did you give me a chance to talk to Meg Hamilton before you did?"

"Because I was pretty sure you'd advise her to be frank with me, once you'd had your fun. Though I don't mind admitting I was fair put out when I found you with Mr. Farrell. That talk would have gone more smoothly—"

"I suppose it would. About Grainger, now. I suppose your offer doesn't extend to the contents of his files?"

"Now, there's something," Sykes told him, "that won't be available to the defense, and it may help both of us if I make it plain that it isn't relevant. It's no use you thinking it will help matters for you to come into headlong collision with the superintendent over it, because it won't."

This was plain speaking, indeed, from so cautious a man as Sykes. "What can you tell me, then?"

"Just what I told you, a little more about Grainger. Seems he'd decided to keep a sort of diary, though it's written in an ordinary notebook, not dated in any way. I see no reason why you can't take a look at it now."

"If you're going to add: on condition we don't ask for production of the other papers—"

"You know me better than that, Mr. Maitland." Sykes sounded hurt.

"Well, I'm sorry, but—"

"You can take it from me, you wouldn't have a hope of getting an Order."

"But you're not asking me to promise not to try."

"Nothing like that."

"Very well. I can't escape a feeling that one of us is mad, but . . . very well."

Sykes produced some typewritten sheets from his pocket without further comment. "An exact copy of the original," he remarked, and sat back to watch Antony's expression as he read.

When I left the Service, nearly ten years ago, I had, as they say, mixed feelings. Not that I was finding the work too much for me, I was as active as ever and I'd always enjoyed it; knowledge is power, someone said, and, brother, was he right! It wasn't the periods of activity I couldn't take any longer, it was the sheer boredom of the long, dreary days when there was nothing to do but watch and wait. There was an old man who said "sometimes I sits and thinks, and sometimes I just sits." And there can be quite a lot of "just sitting" about that job.

So I thought, you've got to get out someday, why not now? I'd an ambition to spend a bit of time in England, for a change, and I was ahead of the game financially; and if anybody asked me how that came about, I didn't have to tell him, did I?

Writing reports always bored me, though it had to be done sometimes. So it's odd to be sitting here with a pen in my hand and a real desire to get something down on paper. The truth is, a man needs someone to talk to; but that also means "someone to trust," and I'm not that much of a fool. I suppose I'm confiding in myself really (you know how to keep your mouth shut, Martin Grainger, I'll say that for you); the urge to communicate is there, and this seems the safest way to—what's the word—to sublimate it. If it weren't for that fool Official Secrets Act I might even rush into print with my reminiscences: *Confessions of a Secret Agent* would look well on the bookstalls, wouldn't it? The joke is, that was all good, clean fun, no one would blame me for a thing that happened all those years. Questionable methods—oh, well, regrettable of course, but in the circumstances—! Frightfully bad form to admit you enjoyed yourself—those sad, those distressing occasions, for instance, that ended with somebody dead. Bad luck, old boy; know how you hate that sort of thing. But there was the quick flare of fear to remember, in a man's eyes before he died; or, better still, in a woman's.

Perhaps it's as well I took to blackmail. It's more artistically satisfying than murder, of course, besides being more profitable. But I might never have found that out; and though I think I'm a pretty sane, level-headed sort of chap, really, it might—it just might be that the police would be investigating another Jack the Ripper if I hadn't. They'd have talked about Sex Maniacs, of course, in this day and age—at least, the newspapers would; and they'd have been all wrong. It's just that there's a beauty in fear, which only a few of us can appreciate.

But I made quite an innocent start in civil life, and with, as I said, a bit of money. And I knew quite well what I wanted to do. A fellow I knew in a Bank once told me, if he'd any money to invest (which he hadn't) he'd stick to one of the catering trades; people have got to eat, he said. And I took the idea and played with it, and after a bit I added an angle of my own: and that was to go where the money is. So when the time came I went prospecting in the City of London, and after a bit I found just what I was after: a nice little oldish building in Copthall Court, barely two minutes from the Stock Exchange. And in course of time it became Galloway's Chop House, at least, the ground floor did. I made my own quarters upstairs, not being one to find the stillness of the City at night an intimidating thing, which many people say they do. And when they did the reconstruction, I aimed for atmosphere. Paneled walls—the paneling came from a bombed-out tavern, the whole place had been declared unsafe but one end was hardly touched and I got it cheap. A few cartoons by Leech, and a quantity of brass—lacquer is good enough, if it's only to be seen at a distance, and saves a lot of work. Each table was a refectory table in miniature, smooth, well-polished oak; and at one time I thought that had been a waste of money because we always used cloths at lunchtime—good, heavy damask that I got at a sale in the country— but after a while the habit grew up in the neighboring offices of slipping in to Galloway's for coffee or tea. I didn't stint on anything, though I bought second hand; china and silver were the best I could get, and so was the crystal. And I found a chap who was making (new) those old-fashioned Windsor chairs; nothing matched anything else as far as period went, of course, but I didn't care about that. I was aiming for an effect, and you can be sure I got it. I hired a good chef, and the waiters knew their job, and the idea was to give our customers what they wanted—and see that they weren't undercharged for it.

So there I was, with a business that would pay for watching (and it did pay, almost from the start), but that gave me a good deal of leisure besides. No point in being open in the evening or at weekends; and if I wanted an occasional afternoon in the country, Jaime would always take over. But a good deal of the zest had gone out of life once things were running smoothly.

I soon began to know my customers, of course. They were mostly stockbrokers, with a sprinkling from the Banks and other offices in the immediate neighborhood, and—very occasionally—a group of youngsters celebrating the promotion, or marriage, or whatever-it-might-be of one of their number. That didn't happen too often, the prices weren't encouraging to anyone in a lower income bracket. It was the successful men I was aiming to attract, the sleek, well-dressed, well-fed tycoons, and it was obvious from the beginning that they liked the place. It was quiet, and discreet, and the tables were well-spaced so that there was little fear of being overheard. More and more they came to eat and stayed to talk over their affairs; and I noticed that there were two or three tables at the far end of the room that were particularly popular for these conferences. The feeling of isolation was an illusion, of course, but I know from experience there are worse places to exchange confidences than a well-filled restaurant.

At first I was merely gratified to see how well things were going, but after a while I began to wonder just what they were talking about so earnestly. It was mostly the Stock Exchange chaps who stayed to talk; the Bankers and other office workers (however exalted their position) couldn't—or at any rate didn't—spare so much of their time. There'd be tips to be picked up, worth far more than the financial papers could tell you. A man who could overhear the conversation of some of the richest men in the country would find it, literally, priceless.

Knowledge is power. I remember my form master used to insist "knowledge itself—" but perhaps I haven't much feeling for the English language, the shorter phrase always seems perfectly adequate to me. Mind you, the idea had always had a sort of fascination; and now that my mind was disengaged, as you might say, it began to occupy my thoughts more and more. Knowledge that a man could turn to his own profit . . .

. . . So over one Christmas, when the City was deserted, I "bugged" those three conference tables and installed a tape recorder in my room upstairs. The thing could be set in motion from below, of course, and I got quite cunning at directing the people I wanted to those tables and keeping the less interesting of my customers at bay.

By this time I was beginning to think I had a flair for money-making. I hadn't much to invest at first, and one or two things went wrong. But all in all my bank balance was growing, and I'll not deny it added an interest to life, all the more because my oracles weren't quite infallible. I suppose I went on for four or five years like that; still quite innocent, you see. (There's a word for you—innocence! I like to think of myself as I was in those days, how I've grown since then.) But one day I was playing back a conversation I'd reason to think might prove interesting—and I was listening to two highly respectable citizens arranging one of the brightest, neatest little swindles you can imagine.

Even then, it didn't occur to me right away the use I might make of the information. I just sat and hugged my knowledge to myself; "little do they know—" like any villain of melodrama. And then I thought—well, why not? Why shouldn't they pay me for my silence? But there was plenty of time, I wasn't in any hurry, I'd work out a foolproof scheme.

Money can be traced; so I wouldn't ask for cash, I'd tell them I wanted diamonds. And make it quite clear I knew something about precious stones, in case anyone thought of fobbing me off with paste. (That's true enough, as it happens; I picked up the knowledge years ago in Trieste.) That way, there'd be no unexplained payments into the bank; just a small package in my safety-deposit box, easily portable, easily negotiable—a good investment. And no tell-tale numbers or markings, as there would be on bank notes, however old.

I'd make my demands by telephone, of course; a nice, anonymous medium, nothing in writing. And I'd tell them—I'd tell them to go to an A.A. box, to wrap the diamond, or diamonds, in tissue paper and put them in an envelope, and leave the envelope there to be collected. I'd choose a box on an empty stretch of road, and I'd tell them just when to leave the diamonds there. That way, I could easily see if there was an ambush arranged; they'd realize that, I thought, they wouldn't risk it.

It worked like a charm. And it was so much more amusing, even than playing the stock markets. I began to record more and more conversations; not such a bore as you'd think, listening to them, even though I don't suppose I've hit the jackpot more than three—no four times in the past few years. I've always stuck to the same method of payment and collection; it makes for a little delay, but I'm in no hurry. It's surprising how much you can tell from a person's voice on the telephone, how fully it expresses their fear. But it's better still to see them the next day in the restaurant, attending to business as usual, but scared to death of showing that something is wrong. And they haven't a notion, of course, where the leakage occurred. If they're regulars, you can watch them for days before the payment's made and they breathe again—for a time.

I've lost a couple of clients, of course. One chap, a solicitor, dipped into his Clients' Account to pay me, which was foolish, because I've never made the mistake of putting my demands too high. Except for my one really big fish, whom I'd never thought of getting more than a few good tips from; and he was the easiest of all to deal with . . . why not? He wouldn't miss the money, and his position made him particularly vulnerable.

But to go back to the client I lost, he was stupid to go in for fraud to pay me because his original indiscretion was—just that. Nothing criminal. And it was even more stupid to get caught. Another of them died, but I took a chance and had a chat with the widow. An easy touch, she was—where one goes, another comes, as they say. And I've also found out who the second party to the original conversation was, quite by chance. Come to think of it, another big fish, though in a different way—nothing to do with the councils of the mighty, but a sort of financial whale. He may be a better bet than Mrs. F. in the long run—tricky creatures, women. I'll collect from her this once, and then we'll see.

I've bought a few diamonds myself since I started, lovely things, it would be easy to become obsessed by them. But it is the power they give me that is really significant—the power of movement, by the very fact that they are so easily negotiable—the power they represent over the people who donated them, so unwillingly, to my retirement fund.

Knowledge itself is power—but you have to work at it a bit, too. . . .

Antony read slowly and turned back several times, as though to remind himself of what had gone before. When he had finished he said nothing for a moment but folded the sheets of paper carefully and stood with them in his hands and stared across the room. Then he turned and held them out to the inspector with an abrupt gesture, and when Sykes had accepted them flung himself down in the chair at the other side of the hearth.

"So Grainger had been an agent?" he remarked.

"That part of the statement is quite true," said Sykes.

"And the rest of it?"

"I know nothing to suggest it's untrue," said the inspector carefully. "And so far as it can be verified—"

"I see. Four cases . . . how many files?"

"Three. And the empty folder I told you of."

"And he had the place bugged." He was frowning again. "What about the tapes?"

"Three remained, three recorded conversations. The files contained what you might call additional evidence, which his experience, no doubt, made him well suited to obtain. And to answer what I'm sure will be your next question . . . if there was ever a tape to go with the J.G.F. folder . . . it had gone."

"And the people concerned never knew who was threatening them. I don't see . . . you said the place had been ransacked, Inspector?"

"A professional job. You could get to Grainger's quarters through the restaurant, or there was a private door in the alley at the side; that's the way the thief got in."

"Was much taken?"

"So far as we can tell, only the contents of that file. The outer lock didn't present much of a problem, but the safe was a different matter, and that's where he kept his confidential papers."

"Well . . . look here, Inspector, you're not suggesting Farrell's an expert safe-blower?"

"Such people can be hired, Mr. Maitland."

"But only if you know where to look for them. Is that why you haven't made an arrest?" Sykes only shook his head at him. "Do you know who the expert was?"

"We have . . . a fair idea." The cautious side of Sykes's nature seemed to be uppermost again. "Unfortunately, the man can't be found at the moment."

"And if you can trace a connection with Farrell—" He stopped, to think that out. "The prosecution will say he set his trap, and shot Grainger, and then . . . yes, it would fit, after all . . . he phoned his accomplice from the A.A. box and gave him the address. Could he have done that?"

"If you mean, had Grainger any identifying papers, yes, he had." Antony sighed. "And there's one thing you may not have considered, Mr. Maitland, he wouldn't have had a hope of following Grainger home, which he says was the idea behind all this."

"*We* know that, Inspector. I don't suppose it ever occurred to Farrell there'd be any difficulty about it."

"Three cars at least," said Sykes, emphasizing his point.

"You don't have to convince me. But you're right about one thing, I seem to have lost interest in these other clients of Grainger's; except that I should have liked to see the superintendent being tactful with the biggest fish of all," he added, smiling.

"I can see I've something to be thankful for, Mr. Maitland . . . that you weren't there."

"Just one point, Inspector. I'm interested, as you can imagine, in the chap Grainger calls 'the second party to the original conversation' with James Farrell."

"And you want to know whether he might be one of the highly respectable citizens who first gave Grainger the idea of turning to blackmail."

"How well you understand me, Inspector."

"I think I've 'appen said too much already," said Sykes gloomily. "But there's a recording that fits in very well with what he says about those two, and neither of the men was James Farrell."

"So we're still no wiser as to what he'd been up to. But aren't you at all interested in the other man? After all, Grainger says he was bringing pressure to bear on him, too."

"Not really." It was only too obvious that Sykes was telling the truth. "I can see how your mind's working, you know . . . and you'll forgive me for saying it's not a good hypothesis to work on. You're treating Roger Farrell's innocence as a fact, and you know the superintendent well enough to realize he feels it's a disingenuous approach."

"Is that what you think?" Antony asked curiously.

"I believe it's an honest opinion, Mr. Maitland . . . and one that could well be dangerous."

"For Farrell? Yes, I realized my presence had probably put Briggs's back up." He paused, because he thought he saw a shade of disappointment in the inspector's eyes; and then decided he must have been mistaken, as Sykes got to his feet.

"I mustn't keep you any longer. You were saying you had to go out."

"Yes, a pity. We ought to celebrate, Inspector. Do you realize that for the first time on record you haven't asked me a single question since you arrived?"

"I told you why I came."

"Yes, but I can't help feeling you had a *reason*," Antony told him. He was on his feet, too, by this time, and following Sykes toward the door.

"That's not so easily explained." It seemed for a moment that the inspector wasn't even going to try, but at least he hadn't pretended not to understand. He didn't pause until he was in the hall and had picked up his hat and found his raincoat in the cupboard. Then he said, in rather an odd tone, "I believe Miss Margaret Hamilton is a friend of yours."

"She is." He kept his voice level; but he was anxious, and the inspector saw it.

"I went to see her today," said Sykes conversationally. "She'd a rather odd story to tell me, but I've no doubt you know that."

"Even so—"

"It hasn't occurred to you that when Farrell is charged her position may be difficult?"

"Of course it has!"

"I don't just mean public opinion, Mr. Maitland." He was watching Antony's expression as he spoke. "She may be charged as an accessory," he added.

"If you're trying to tell me you think it was a conspiracy—"

"No!" It wasn't often Sykes sounded so vehement. "But you must admit it sounds like a put-up job, and then there's this tale of the note she left for Farrell. An afterthought, that sounds like, to open the door a little wider—"

The frown was back between Antony's eyes again. He was basing all his calculations on that note, he had to, but what Sykes was implying could so easily be true. Not about Meg's story, she wouldn't lie to him; but everything Roger had said about the three men who might have seen the message could have been a fabrication. "I never thought . . . it doesn't seem possible," he said, and it occurred to the detective that in all the years of their acquaintance, he had never before seen his companion so completely at a loss for words.

"I thought I should warn you," he said again stolidly, but not altogether without sympathy.

"Briggs?" said Antony. "No, don't tell me; I know all about the final responsibility for framing a charge. But it's one of those fixed ideas of his, isn't it?"

"You must admit—"

"I admit I was a fool not to consider the possibility, especially once he knew of my concern. But there's something I'm wondering, Inspector. Suppose Farrell confessed?"

"That isn't my province, Mr. Maitland." The mildness of his tone was in itself a rebuke.

"No, I'm sorry, I shouldn't have asked you that." But it was true, for all that, he thought; if the police had a confession that cleared Meg, they'd be much less likely to press the charge against her. In fact, it was almost certain it would be quietly dropped. He hadn't time to think it out now, but dimly he was aware that this new knowledge opened up a most appalling dilemma. "You don't know Meg, Inspector. It's fantastic!" He caught Sykes's eye and added with an odd effect of formality, "I realize it's difficult . . . I'm very grateful."

"No need of that. All I ask is your discretion," said Sykes, with an unexpected gleam of humor.

"Yes, of course." But he spoke absently and only seemed to bring the detective's face into focus with a deliberate effort. "Heaven and earth!" he said softly. "Where do we go from here?"

6

THE ANSWER, OF COURSE, WAS TO HUBERT DENNING'S inappropriately styled *pied-à-terre*. He arrived there ten minutes late, but he was calm again by then and even capable of seeing a certain humor in his host's reaction to this tardiness, which was carefully calculated to abash the offender without laying the old man open to a charge of discourtesy. It seemed likely he wasn't used to being kept waiting.

If the Farrells' flat had been luxurious, this was equally so in a different, more masculine way; and it had the advantage of not having known the disruptive effect of Roger's presence. Antony took time to wonder, as he resigned himself to the embrace of a deep club chair and accepted a single malt whisky on Denning's recommendation, whether the rows of books were for use or for show. But perhaps it didn't matter; the bindings glowed mellowly in the lamplight, the whole room invited you to comfortable relaxation, an insidious atmosphere at the end of a long day. Only too easy to forget your problems and the people who relied on you. . . .

But if he had been really attracted by this lotus dream, he still had Hubert Denning to reckon with. "You were going to explain to me, Mr. Maitland, exactly what has been going on."

He couldn't deny the reasonableness of the request, but he had forgotten the necessity and now the reminder was sharply irritating.

"To be brief—" he said, and condensed the recital as much as he could. He raised his eyes when he had finished and found the old man watching him in a considering way.

"Naturally, I should wish to help Roger if I can. But he told me nothing of what was going on."

"We'll look elsewhere for evidence. Now, I want the background."

"I can't tell you why James Farrell was being blackmailed. I don't even understand why you should want to know. You say it is a fact, but I must admit my mind rejects it."

"Forget it, then. Just tell me about him as a person. You'd known him a long time?"

"Since . . . let me see . . . since 1920. He had just been demobilized, and a friend sent him to me for advice. That's a long time ago, Mr. Maitland. Were you in the Army in the last war?"

The blue eyes were intent, the question a little less than casual. It may have been imagination, but Antony felt that Denning had already noted the stiffness of his shoulder, the limited movement of which his right arm was capable. He said curtly, "I was."

"Then you will understand his state of mind. The restlessness, the difficulty he found in adjusting to everyday life. I was more fortunate, or less fortunate . . . I wonder which you would say?" He paused, rather as though he were seriously pondering the question. "I was twenty-four in 1914, but already it was felt my services could be more usefully employed at home, rather than in the trenches."

Antony thought, in "something to do with insurance"? Perhaps he looked doubtful; in any event Hubert Denning, suddenly benign again, answered as though he had spoken his thought aloud.

"I was working with one of the Ministries, but I still kept in touch with affairs in the City, I still kept in touch. So when James came to me—he was twenty then, twenty-one perhaps, and had been a year at the front before the Armistice—I was able to find him a position, a modest position, in a firm where I had some influence. And what was perhaps more important, I was able to persuade him to persevere in his employment in the years that followed. There were times when he felt frustrated—"

"You mean he wasn't altogether cut out for the City?"

"He had a rather fatiguing addiction to the outdoor life," said Denning reflectively, "but how better attain the things he wanted? I could put him on the path and he knew it."

"What did he want?"

"Money. And the things that it would buy."

"He wasn't married when first you knew him?"

Denning laughed. "If I follow your train of thought, Mr. Maitland, it's an extremely cynical one. I admit there wasn't so much talk of resigning after he married Winifred, but at that time he was still with the firm I spoke of; it wasn't until a year or two later that he branched out alone."

"Still with your help, sir?" As he put the question he saw the old man's eyes narrow, so that he had for a moment a look almost of calculation.

"With my advice, Mr. Maitland. My advice and encouragement." There could be no doubt about it, Hubert Denning was enjoying the interview; also, in some obscure way, he found the situation amusing. Antony said sharply, to hide a creeping embarrassment:

"Perhaps he married money," and then grinned to himself as he remembered one of Jenny's aunts who had told him roundly that the practice of the law had a very vulgarizing effect.

Oddly, Mr. Denning seemed to find no cause in the question for either surprise or resentment. He said in a reminiscent tone, "Winifred was a beauty, you know, and of a very old family, she liked to remember that. But she hadn't a penny when she married James. If you will forgive an old man a touch of sentiment, it was a love match." The amusement was very evident now, and Antony recognized in himself, without surprise, the first stirrings of anger.

"Then you've no idea where he got his capital?"

"No idea in the world. But in financial matters, you know, one lucky coup is enough to set a man on his feet."

This seemed to Antony an over-simplification. "And the 'things he wanted,' sir? When would you say he began to enjoy them?"

"I forget, really I forget."

"When did he get his yawl?"

"That was a fairly recent acquisition. But he'd had a sailing boat of one sort or another since before the war."

"And the cottage at Grunning's Hole?"

"That too." Denning paused again to contemplate the picture he was presenting. "A paradox, as you can see. In town, a sybaritic appreciation of the good things of life. In the country, a taste for simple pleasures."

Antony let his eyes wander round the room and come to rest thoughtfully on Denning's face. The old man said, as though he had spoken:

"You're right, of course. One of his tastes I share. The other I let him enjoy alone."

"Roger spoke of a motor yacht." He wondered as he put the question how much longer he could count on his host's forbearance.

"Hardly the simple life, Mr. Maitland." Denning took the point smoothly. "I was hoping to get away next week, as a matter of fact, but it doesn't look hopeful now, does it? Roger may not want my help—"

"Perhaps not just as you want to give it, sir."

"And I mustn't complain about that, I suppose. But I was telling you . . . in my younger days, of course, I enjoyed something smaller, more strenuous than the *Susannah;* and James was glad to accompany me, if only because I was kind enough to let him do all the work."

"And Roger grew up sharing his tastes, I imagine."

The old man looked at him sharply. "I suppose he's told you," he said. "He used to come along too, as a small boy, during the summer. And that reminds me, if you really want to know when James bought the cottage, it must have been 1934, because Roger was ten and went away to school for the first time." He seemed to be looking back down the years. "They didn't come out with me so much after that," he said. "I suppose it sounds odd, but James seemed to—to rely on Roger, you know, right up to the time he was called up. He was in the Navy from . . . it must have been from 1942. And afterwards—after Alice died—they were un-usually close companions."

"Alice?"

Denning's look was speculative, his tone gently mocking. "Not quite so intimate, Mr. Maitland? Roger was married before he was twenty, to a child his own age. She was killed in one of the later air raids, a flying bomb, while he was at sea."

Antony was frowning over the information. "He took it hard?" he said after a moment.

"I have no means of telling." There was a measure of asperity in Denning's voice now. "Roger doesn't confide in me, and for all his devotion to his parents, I shouldn't say he had lived precisely as a hermit."

"I don't suppose so." He would have liked to hear more of Alice, but the old man's antagonism made him uneasy. "You don't know of anything in James Farrell's life that might have provided a motive for blackmail?"

It was Hubert Denning's turn to frown. "I have thought of little else since I saw you," he admitted. "And while I can understand that Winifred would do anything to protect her husband's memory, I cannot conceive that James . . . I cannot think—"

"If you know anything at all, sir, I hope you'll tell me for Roger's sake," Antony told him bluntly. And thought, when he saw his companion's expression, that he had said exactly the wrong thing to persuade him into frankness. But the look was gone in an instant; perhaps it was no more than a dislike of Roger's deter-mined independence, an impatience with a personality as dominant as his own.

"If he would permit me to help him," said Denning, "I believe I could do so. But I think, if you will forgive my saying so, that his defense can best be undertaken on other lines than those you have in mind."

"He says he didn't shoot Grainger." Antony was tired suddenly and it sounded in his voice, but it was quite possible that Denning thought him skeptical.

"If the circumstances are as you have outlined them, it is diffi-cult to see who else could have done so," he pointed out.

81

This was true enough, and opened up besides the whole problem that Sykes's revelations had posed for him. "If you can't help me, sir, do you think his partner could?"

"Sam Reade? Sam's an excellent fellow, steady, reliable." And beneath my interest, his tone added, only too clearly.

"You don't think there might be anything—anything shady going on at the firm?" He had paused before adopting Roger's phrase, and now there was another and longer silence, and again he watched Denning's expression and wondered if the old man was more amused or annoyed by his insistence.

"You must remember I had the greatest respect for James Farrell, but it seems I must accept the fact that he . . . that there was something—" (Antony mastered an impulse to murmur, We're none of us perfect.) "And starting from there, I can imagine him giving his confidence to Roger. Not to Sam Reade."

"I see." Under his hand the soft leather of the chair arm was cool and pleasant to the touch. He was aware that he didn't like what he heard but was too weary for the moment to formulate any reply, even in his own mind. He said without subtlety, "There's a daughter, too."

"You are not implying—"

"I'm groping in the dark, that's all. Can't you see?"

"Well, Isabel, of course, has never been connected with any business matter in her life. And if you're thinking of Leonard Wilson . . . you haven't met him, I take it."

"Not yet."

"I can't vouch for his honesty, I don't know him well enough. They certainly live beyond a bank manager's salary, but James was always generous. However, I should say he tolerated his son-in-law . . . no more than that."

"Does Wilson get on well with Roger?"

"Well enough, I think." He paused and favored Antony with a decidedly appraising stare. "Roger is inclined to intolerance, as I'm sure you know."

"Do you remember the day of Mrs. Farrell's funeral?"

"A week ago? Yes, I remember quite well."

"I didn't mean—" But why try to explain himself, after all? "There was a note lying on top of the tallboy in Roger's bedroom when you went back to Leinster Court. Did you notice either of the other men pick it up?"

This time Denning sat and looked at him for so long that it seemed as if he wasn't going to answer. At last he said, "I know nothing of a note, so the rest of your question answers itself. But I should like to know why you ask it."

"The note contained details of the rendezvous with Grainger."

"I see. That sounds like a dangerous assumption, Mr. Maitland."

"I didn't say—"

"Your meaning, however, could not have been more clear. Tell me, do you really believe everything Roger tells you?"

"Let's say, a man's presumed innocent—"

"A very proper attitude," Denning applauded. "But don't you think you're carrying it a little too far?"

"In what way? I'm sorry if my questions offend you, but I want to know the answers, you see."

"And the next one, I suppose, will be concerned with motive. As you tell me the murdered man was a blackmailer, the field may be a wide one."

"But motive and opportunity in this case must be taken together. And by opportunity I mean, primarily, knowing where Grainger would be."

"Yes, I understand that. Do you know, Mr. Maitland, I find you rather a disconcerting companion?"

"If it comes to that, sir, I haven't found what you've told me exactly . . . comforting."

The amused look was back in Denning's eyes. "I'll do all I can to help Roger," he said deliberately. "But you mustn't try to pull the wool over my eyes, you know. You mustn't expect me to believe him."

There was a silence. Antony looked across at the old man and thought his attitude was eminently reasonable, but it would have helped if it had been more sympathetic. "Is it any good," he said, "asking you if you remember anything unusual happening to James Farrell five years ago?"

"If you mean, do I know of anything that might have laid him open to blackmail—"

"Just what I said, sir. Anything unusual." His tone was flat, discouraged. "If it helps at all, it was the year Mr. and Mrs. Farrell went to Teneriffe in May. That summer, for instance—"

"They seemed to have enjoyed their holiday," said Denning, a little dryly. "As for the rest, there was nothing out of the way."

Antony sat looking at him. He thought, if I knew the right questions . . . but now he seemed to have come to the end of his ideas. "I never saw too much of James during the summer months," said Denning suddenly. "He was forever going down to that cottage of his."

"I rather gather you're no fonder of Grunning's Hole than you are of sailing."

"My dear Mr. Maitland! Have you seen the place? Even an estate agent would need an unusually lively imagination to describe its conveniences." He thought for a moment and then added grudgingly, "James always said it was peaceful."

And probably that was true enough, and just about as helpful as what had gone before. "Do you know Galloway's Chop House?" he asked, and saw Denning's surprised look at the abrupt change of subject.

"In Copthall Court? Yes, I've been there." His tone made the words a question, so that Antony said, explaining:

"It belonged to Martin Grainger."

"The man who was shot? Well, it isn't near my office, but James lunched there regularly, so far as I recollect. And I've been there as his guest."

"Did you know Grainger, then?"

"I suppose I must have seen him. I have no precise recollection." He stopped, frowning again. "No, I am sorry. No recollection at all."

"Then it's no use asking if you noticed anything in his attitude to Mr. Farrell. No, I thought not." Antony's tone was despondent, he hardly waited for the quick shake of Denning's head. "Have

84

you been there recently—to Galloway's I mean—since James Farrell died?"

"Not that I recall; no, I am sure I have not."

"Then I think, sir, I needn't worry you any further. Not just now." He got up as he spoke and was aware as he did so of a deep dissatisfaction, because if Hubert Denning couldn't enlighten him, who else could? But it wasn't only that, of course, it was the old man's easy acceptance of Roger's guilt.

Denning accompanied him to the door, fussing gently now as though he would have been glad enough to leave him with a more favorable impression of his relations with his godson. As he reached the ground floor Antony was wondering whether the police would have any occasion to visit him and what Sykes, for instance, would think of the *pied-à-terre*. In spite of his depression he was grinning to himself as he looked about him for a taxi. The inspector would be unimpressed, of course, but his comments might well be worth hearing.

"I hope you don't mean to cut me dead," said a voice at his elbow. And as he turned Roger added rather sourly, "You seem to have been having an amusing time."

"I was just thinking—" He finished the sentence with a gesture, because it was quite impossible to explain.

"Well, come on!" said Farrell. "I'm parked just round the corner." He set off at a pace which would have precluded conversation, even if his companion hadn't been fully occupied dodging other equally determined pedestrians in an effort to keep up with him. 'The animals do order one about so,' said Antony to himself, and was quite relieved to see the rakish, gray car standing demurely by the curb. He got into the passenger seat without further invitation.

Roger maneuvered the Jensen out into the stream of traffic and drove in silence until he had accomplished a detour and was able to turn into the park. Then he ventured a look at his companion. "I hope you aren't in too much of a hurry," he remarked, his eyes on the road again.

"No hurry at all. It's very good of you."

"I was waiting for you," said Roger, "and not for any altruistic motive." He paused and might have been considering how best to word his question; if that were so, he obviously decided on bluntness. "I wanted to ask you why they didn't arrest me today."

Maitland twisted a little, to study the other man's profile as the street lights passed in procession. "I think because they'd like to find a connection between you and the chap who broke into Grainger's office. But I shouldn't count on continued immunity, if I were you."

"I won't." Roger's hands were steady on the wheel; it occurred to Antony for the first time that he was an extremely competent driver. It also occurred to him that Farrell seemed strangely uninterested in the statement he had just made. "Have you heard," he asked now, "how Meg got on with the police?"

"She said they were 'quite nice.'"

"They didn't upset her? Today of all days—"

"I don't think *they* worried her." As he spoke he was thinking of Meg's expression in that brief moment before she turned and saw him; but he couldn't betray her to Farrell any more than he could speak of Sykes's disclosures. Instead he asked, "You didn't go to the theater?" And it was a foolish question, because the answer was obviously "no."

"If I had," said Roger, "I'd have gone backstage to see her, and I didn't think that would be fair." He made the explanation in a matter-of-fact tone; perhaps it was only in Antony's imagination that his voice held a touch of desperation.

"Roger, what did you do after you left Scranton that afternoon?" he asked abruptly.

"After I'd finished talking to the police? I went home."

"What time was that?"

"I didn't notice exactly, but I met the rush-hour traffic coming out of town."

"Would the garage attendant at Leinster Court have noticed?"

"I doubt it. And I don't see—"

"No, of course you don't. I'm sorry. Were you alone at the flat when you got in?"

"For a while. Well, I went down to get some dinner about eight-thirty, and after that I went round to see Meg." He was driving more slowly now, and frowning at the road ahead. "I suppose you mean, could this burglar have come to see me? He didn't, but he could have done."

"I see." Nothing there to help matters, but perhaps it made no difference either way.

"What did Uncle Hubert have to say for himself?" asked Roger.

"Quite a lot, and none of it useful."

"Did he tell you about Alice?"

"He mentioned her."

"I thought he might. I don't think," he added thoughtfully, "he altogether approves of me."

"On that particular point—"

"Oh, well," said Roger, "lack of forethought, lack of considera-tion. And we didn't ask anyone's advice, that always makes you unpopular." He was silent for a moment and then added, "It's one thing I did that I've never regretted." But now it seemed as if he was speaking to himself.

In any case, there didn't seem to be any comment that could usefully be made. Antony waited a moment and then asked, "What about your interview with the police? Did Armstrong accompany you?"

Farrell seemed amused by the question. "I think he meant to, until I mentioned that I'd been talking to you. Then he gave a despairing cry and sent for Geoffrey Horton."

"It's a sad reflection," said Antony, "that the Lord Chancellor is probably the only man in London who is completely convinced of my respectability. Still," he added more cheerfully, "Geoffrey knows my ways."

"He's an unsympathetic blighter," said Roger. "Well, I told my story and they may have believed me but I'd bet they didn't. Which is reasonable enough, after all."

"Did you see your sister?"

"Yes, I had lunch with her. I told her you'd be going to see them."

"Does she know the whole story?"

"About the blackmail? I told her," said Roger. "And I told her you'd got Dad's diaries. *She* won't have hysterics when you talk to her; Leonard might."

"And Sam Reade?" Maitland asked, carefully avoiding discussion of this far-from-entrancing possibility.

"I didn't go to the office today, but I had a word with him on the phone. He's expecting to see you, but I doubt if he can be helpful. I explained to him too . . . in a way."

"Well, we'll see what they have to say. Meanwhile, if you were describing either of them—Reade or Wilson—would you be inclined to use the expression 'a financial whale'?"

Roger pondered this for a moment. "So now we're playing guessing games," he remarked with surprising mildness. "And I suppose I shan't be popular if I ask you why you want to know."

"I'd rather you answered my question."

"You've been talking to Uncle Hubert; it would fit him all right."

"Somehow," said Antony, "I guessed that by myself."

"Well, Leonard? Fenchurch Street is one of the plums, you know, and from what I know of the banking world it means he'll be moved to Head Office before very long. So I think . . . yes, the phrase would fit him very well. As for Sam—" he paused there, and something seemed to be amusing him—"he's a wealthier man than he'll ever admit, and a cautious one, too."

"Would that be generally known?"

"In the City, certainly. Money has a—a sort of smell of its own," said Roger reflectively. "You can't mistake it."

"So the description could apply to him, too."

Farrell made no answer; probably he thought it wasn't called for. The car had speeded up again now, and they had left the park; his whole attention seemed concentrated on his driving. He wasn't relaxed any more, his hands had tightened on the wheel; and Maitland noted for the first time, though without interest, that his right hand was bruised and the skin broken across the knuckles. He might have commented vaguely on this, but before he could do so they turned into Kempenfeldt Square.

"Come in for a while. Jenny won't be long, and she can tell us how the play went."

Roger hesitated and then shook his head. "I thought," he said, looking straight ahead of him, "I'd drive down to the cottage for the weekend."

"To Grunning's Hole? Tonight?"

"Why not? It's better than sitting here thinking. Only I thought I'd let you know where I'd gone."

"Does Geoffrey know?"

"Yes, and the police. I've no ambition to start a hue and cry."

"That's all right then." He pushed open the car door, and paused, half in and half out, for a final word. "Let me know, won't you, when you get back?"

But as he watched Roger drive away he was again aware that he was uneasy. He wished now he'd tried to detain him, told him his presence in town was vital, even though that wasn't true. It might even have been better . . .

The Jensen's rear lights disappeared round the corner. After a moment Antony shrugged and went into the house.

7

HE WONDERED LATER WHAT HAD AWAKENED HIM THAT night and came to the conclusion that it was just one of those things. Certainly he had heard no sound, but perhaps his subconscious was dealing more efficiently with the situation than was his conscious mind, recognizing as valid the fear he had so far denied. But however it might have been, he was wide awake on the instant; and when he realized that sleep was, for the moment, out of the question, he pulled himself up a little on the pillows so that he could look out through the window at the night sky. There was a good deal of cloud now, perhaps the spell of fine weather was going to break. The moon was about three-quarters full, but it had to struggle to get a look in.

Jenny had got home a little late and full of forebodings about the play, though Meg, she maintained—a little too vehemently—was *magnificent*. Antony thought she was probably right about that; he had a good deal of confidence in Meg's ability to rise to a situation. If Jenny was doubtful it was probably because she was expecting to see some signs of strain. But he found himself disinclined for conversation and they went to bed as soon as the teapot was empty.

Now he wished he had asked more questions, as Jenny's comments on *Very Tragical Mirth* would certainly have been more amusing than going over and over in his mind the conversation he had had with Inspector Sykes. Three o'clock in the morning is, of course, no time for optimism; he had both Roger and Meg convicted of murder within a few minutes of waking up. It was at this point that he became aware of a ghostly whispering from the room below.

The phenomenon was not altogether unfamiliar, though they had never noticed it until three years ago when Sir Nicholas had bronchitis. Then it became for the first time apparent that voices in his bedroom were faintly audible in theirs, and they put it down to the central heating, in which they were probably quite correct. Now there were voices, and Uncle Nick didn't talk in his sleep; so the problem was, why? Antony hadn't thought anything short of an earthquake would get Gibbs, the butler, out of bed in the middle of the night, and even then he'd have regarded the necessity as a source of personal grievance. He was an old man now, but they had all given up hope of his retiring . . . the trouble was, he enjoyed being a martyr. So Antony's mind was running on sudden illness when he slid cautiously out of bed, and the silence with which he moved was due merely to the feeling that it was no use waking Jenny unless he must. He was therefore unprepared for a clutching hand when he reached the landing below and a voice that hissed "Quiet!" unnecessarily in his ear.

Sir Nicholas pulled him unceremoniously into the bedroom and closed the door again. The only light was from the lamp at the head of the bed, and it was impossible to see his expression. Gibbs, majestic even in a dressing gown, stood stiffly near the wardrobe. "We're being burgled," Sir Nicholas announced, quite as dramatically as Meg might have done, though in a much less carrying tone.

"Well, then—" said Antony. But his uncle was between him and the door.

"That's just why I didn't call you," said Sir Nicholas. "Always rushing in, when everything's been taken care of."

"The police should be here any moment now," added Gibbs.

"Yes, but . . . are you sure—?"

"It is not my custom to act impulsively, Mr. Maitland," said Gibbs, at his most repressive. "Being at the back of the house I heard the sound of the garden door, which must have been forced because it was certainly locked when I came to bed. When I came onto the landing there was a man already in the hall below, and I watched while he looked into each room in turn with the aid of a flashlight. When he came to the study he went in and shut the door, and I came in here to use the telephone."

"The study? What the hell does he think he'll find in there?" asked Antony, momentarily diverted.

"Not the family jewels," said Sir Nicholas. "And as far as I'm concerned, he is very welcome to anything he thinks may come in useful . . . except, perhaps, my cigars."

"All the same, I think I'll just see—" This time Sir Nicholas, unwilling perhaps actually to skirmish for possession of the door-knob, moved a little to let him pass. Antony reached the head of the stairs and began to descend slowly. He could hear his uncle's breathing close behind him and was just about to whisper a reminder that the fifth step creaked when he heard a car draw up in the square outside.

So far there had been no indication that Gibbs wasn't dreaming. The hall was dark and there was no light from the study, no sound of movement. But in the silence the intruder must also have heard the car; the door flew open, and against the dim glow of the desk lamp they saw a dark figure move swiftly but silently into the hall, hesitate for a moment, and then turn right toward the back of the house. Antony abandoned caution and followed at a run.

Once through the service door it became obvious where the man had gone: not down to the kitchen quarters but straight along the passage and through the garden door, the way Gibbs said he had entered. The door was standing ajar when Antony reached it, and he was halfway down the path when he heard the sound of a shot, and someone cried out, and someone shouted what might have been a warning. And then there were two more shots.

As he reached the narrow lane beyond the little square of garden the moon made one of its brief appearances from behind a bank of cloud. But the high wall cast a shadow, and in his haste Antony did not notice the fallen man until he had almost reached him. Footsteps were thudding away toward Avery Street, and even as he abandoned the chase a man's figure was silhouetted briefly at the end of the alley as he left the shelter of the wall to turn left, away from the square. Antony knelt down beside the man on the ground, and at the same moment Sir Nicholas spoke at his shoulder.

"Is he badly hurt?"

There was a silence, and then Antony said in an expressionless voice, "A police constable. He's dead." And as he got to his feet he saw for the first time a hand that had groped out from the shadows into the moonlight, and the dark shape of another figure lying in the shelter of the wall.

Sir Nicholas had armed himself with a blackthorn stick, a singularly useless defense against gunfire, but now he used it for the purpose of gesticulation, being apparently at a loss for words. Then he stepped over the dead man's legs, and this time it was his nephew who brought up the rear.

The second man was also in uniform. Antony unbuttoned his tunic and brought away his hand sticky with blood. "A doctor," he said without looking up, and heard his uncle retreating toward the house, and—before his footsteps had died away—another but more distant fusillade. As if it had been a signal the man on the ground stirred and opened his eyes.

"Don't try to move. The doctor's coming, then you'll be all right."

"Jenkinson?" He had to bend his head to catch the word, but he didn't need to do that to hear the man's tortured breathing. "Is he dead?"

"I'm afraid he's hurt, too."

"Point-blank . . . the bastard!" For a moment the constable's voice was stronger, but then it faded again to a whisper. "Tried to hold him," he said. "Tore out his jacket pocket . . . something fell." He raised his hand a couple of inches, and then it dropped limply again. Antony saw that the fingers were clenched about a piece of dark material. He said:

"Take it easy!" and hoped that reinforcements wouldn't be too long delayed. The man on the ground was weak and growing weaker, and he thought one fatal casualty was enough for a night's work. He was in no doubt at all the man he had examined was dead, there'd been light enough to see the extent of his injuries.

It wasn't long before Sir Nicholas came padding back, and this time he was accompanied by Jenny, who was carrying a pillow and an armful of blankets, and another, taller figure, which materialized at close quarters into a third policeman. "The sergeant came in one of the cars that responded to Gibbs's message," Sir Nicholas explained. "His colleague is still—er—covering the front of the house."

The sergeant had been bending over the dead man. "Jenkinson's had it," he said now, straightening himself. There was a controlled viciousness in his voice. He turned to look down at the shadowy group near the wall. Jenny was on her knees in the dust beside the second constable, and he must have recognized her competence because he did not attempt to approach but said only, "Is there anything—?"

"Not till the doctor comes." She thought the man was unconscious now, and though she had slipped the pillow under his head and spread a blanket over him, she was aware that her actions were futile, except in so far as they satisfied her own urge to do something . . . anything. More practically, she handed a second blanket to her husband, who accepted it in silence and scrambled to his feet.

"The other shots?" he asked.

The sergeant was already moving down the alley toward Avery Street. He moved quickly, but silently for so large a man. Antony glanced at his uncle, who nodded his head and said testily, "There's nothing you can do here." He caught up with the policeman before he had passed old Miss Webber's house.

"Robbins and Jenner came by, cruising," said the sergeant, not slackening his pace. "I sent them to see what cars were parked nearby."

"It sounded like random shooting." Antony wanted to believe that; he didn't want to think that anyone else had been hit. But already he was afraid. . . .

There was more light in Avery Street—a lamp at the corner of the square and another farther down on the far side of the road—

but the tableau was quite as macabre as the one they had left behind in the darkness of the alley. There was the sprawled figure in the roadway and another man running back toward him from the opposite pavement. The sergeant said, "What the . . . Jenner!" and the man halted and said, panting:

"He got Robbins through the head. And now he's got away."

"Is Robbins dead?"

"Yes, he is. But that's what I didn't know, Sergeant, I thought there might be something I could do for him. And while I was looking the car drove off."

The sergeant was examining the fallen man. "I heard it," he said, not looking up. And then, "Are you hurt?"

"No, Sergeant, just—" He broke off and then added in a constrained tone, "There's a baby due any time, you see. Their first."

"You'd better tell me what happened." He was on his feet again now, and his voice and face were alike expressionless.

"Those cars down there"—he gesticulated—"we had a look at them, but the engines are cold. But across the way there was a big Austin which hadn't been parked for long, it was still quite warm. And just as we'd found it we heard the shots and started across the road; and then there was this man came hurtling out of the passage and there wasn't time to say nothing, nor to do nothing neither. He just started blazing away with his gun."

"And Robbins was hit." For the first time he seemed to remember Antony's presence. "The ambulance will be coming, sir. If you'd just go back to the house and tell them—"

"Of course."

"And . . . the car number, Jenner?"

"Here, Sergeant. I wrote it down."

"I'll phone it in, shall I?" Antony asked, taking the ragged sheet of paper that had obviously been torn from Jenner's notebook.

"If you'd be so good, sir. I'd like to stay here."

"Yes, of course. I'm . . . more than sorry." The sergeant's distress was as controlled as his anger had been, but people were beginning to congregate now, a little diffident in their curiosity, but still they'd need coping with. The fact that these were the first arrivals made him realize how quickly everything had happened since the first shots were fired. Antony, making his way back down the alley with the blanket clutched round his shoulders, could at first get no further than the profitless thought: if only Gibbs hadn't heard anything. The gunman could have ransacked the house at leisure and been welcome to what he found. Now there were two men dead, and perhaps a third still to follow. But at about the same time as he realized that the cobbles were cold to his feet because he had kicked off his slippers at the foot of the stairs to make better speed, he also began to wonder what on earth so desperate a criminal could have been seeking among Sir Nicholas's papers.

Their neighbor, Dr. Nelson, had arrived by the time he rejoined the group at the back of the house, and the police doctor came up at almost the same moment. Antony explained what had happened, and then took Jenny back into the house to watch for the ambulance.

They got to bed at last at about five-thirty, and Antony slept heavily for a few hours, but Jenny must have been restless. At any rate, she was already up when he awoke, and the smell of freshly made coffee got him out of bed far more quickly than any amount of exhortation would have done.

They sat at the table by the window, and after all it was another sunny morning. The garden in the center of the square was green and fresh-looking, just for a little while. Neither of them felt much like talking, and even less like eating, but the coffee was hot and comforting, and the amount they drank should have reduced them both to nervous wrecks for the rest of their lives.

They were washing up when the house phone rang, and Antony put down the tea towel and went into the hall to answer it. He was a little surprised, because Gibbs usually refused to use the instrument, preferring to deliver any messages in person and then complain of the bother.

"Two gentlemen from the police to see you, Mr. Maitland." The choice of words was even more indicative of his perturbed state of mind than the fact that he had willingly forgone a cause of grievance, and his quavering tone perhaps a surer sign of agitation than either. Antony couldn't recall that he had ever before honored a member of the force—however exalted—with any more complimentary description than "a person."

"I'll come down then. Have you told Sir Nicholas?"

"He went for a walk."

"Oh, well . . . put them in the study, anyway. I don't suppose he'll be long." He was reflecting as he replaced the receiver that it wasn't often anything happened that shook Gibbs as this had. It meant he was human after all, a fact which Antony sometimes doubted.

He had a word with Jenny and went to put on a tie, and when he came back she had dried her hands and was standing in the hall. She said, "Antony, I've been wondering . . . if only we knew *why.*"

"I wish we did, love. But there's nothing missing." He paused and then added with belated honesty, "Only Uncle Nick's engagement book, the one you bought him."

"But it's so silly," said Jenny. "It isn't as if he ever used it."

"Don't worry. Whatever the chap was looking for, he won't come back."

"That isn't it at all. It's just that he didn't care at all how much damage he did. And you know, Antony, there are those diaries you were looking at last night."

"So there are." But what was the use of hedging, after all. "I've been wondering about them myself," he admitted. "Though there's nothing important in them that I can see."

"Someone might think there was. But they belong to Roger's father, don't they? And that means—"

"It may mean something, love. Honestly, I don't know; it would take the whole affair onto a different plane."

"But you ought to tell Inspector Sykes," she insisted.

"All right, I'll have a word with him when I'm through with these chaps downstairs." And he'll feel just as bewildered as I do, he thought, but perhaps it will take his mind off Meg.

Jenny went back into the kitchen and stood for a long time

staring at the calendar on the wall—a highly sentimental representation of a large, woolly dog and a small, unnaturally clean child, which the local grocer had chosen last Christmas as a declaration of good will, if not to all men, at least to those who were his customers. Considered as a decoration, she particularly disliked it, but he always asked if she found it useful, and Jenny wasn't at all happy telling lies. This morning she didn't even see it. Her thoughts were in confusion: I didn't want Meg to get hurt, I wanted things to be . . . just right . . . this time; and I wish I were sure, quite sure, that Antony will be safe. But when I think of those two men, and the one who still may die . . .

After a while she roused herself and went resolutely back to the sink. And it didn't occur to her to wonder why the police had wanted to see Antony again.

Antony wasn't wondering, either, as he ran down the stairs; he assumed it was the divisional inspector and was quite prepared to believe they'd both forgotten a few things in the confusion the night before. Even when he went into the study and found Briggs and Sykes waiting for him, he wasn't particularly surprised. The killing of a member of the police force creates a situation in which all the ordinary rules are forgotten, and in spite of what he had just said to Jenny, he wasn't thinking of Roger Farrell's affairs as he closed the door and started to cross the room toward the desk. But then he heard Briggs's voice, cutting harshly through his own greeting and the decorous expression of his sympathy.

"Don't you think things are getting a little out of hand, Mr. Maitland? Surely *now* we can expect your cooperation."

The words, and still more the tone in which they were uttered, stopped Antony short halfway across the room. For a moment he looked blankly from one of the detectives to the other: at Inspector Sykes, whose face was as nearly expressionless as it is possible for the human countenance to be, and then again at Briggs, large and angry and undeniably formidable.

"I d-don't think I q-quite understand you, Superintendent. H-how have I failed—?"

"That's exactly what we want to find out," said Briggs. For whatever reason, he was so angry himself as to be almost past discretion. "I wasn't happy about the situation when I found you conferring with Farrell—"

Inspector Sykes, watching, wished for the twentieth time that he'd been able to make this call alone. Maitland was reacting exactly as he had expected, and had become—after the first startled resentment—dangerously quiet.

"Don't you think you'd better explain?" As he spoke, Antony completed his journey to the desk, pushed aside a pile of papers, and perched himself on one corner. "Won't you sit down, gentlemen?" His tone had an icy politeness; neither of the detectives moved.

"You won't deny you're in Farrell's confidence?" said Briggs. He seemed to be making some effort now to match Maitland's coolness, but his voice had a hectoring note.

"I believe so, certainly."

"And as a friend, not as his counsel?"

"Does he need my professional services?"

"He will," said the superintendent, grimly pleased at the thought.

"And you know the strength of the case against him." Sykes's interruption was unexpected, and Antony turned his head and looked at him reproachfully for a moment.

"Suppose I do?"

"But still you think you can help him?"

"I can try."

"This passion for lost causes!" sneered Briggs.

"I think that what you're complaining of is that some of the causes haven't been lost at all," Antony pointed out. The gleam in his eye might have been anger, and certainly wasn't amusement.

"We have some knowledge of your outlook, after all; and of your . . . well, your single-minded approach where your friends are concerned."

"Isn't this where we came in?" He'd known quite well what Briggs was thinking when they met at Leinster Court, and it occurred to him now that Sykes had tried to warn him of this, only he hadn't understood. He glanced at the inspector again, but his face told him nothing. "Are you under the impression you're being tactful, I wonder?"

"If you want it straight," said Briggs, "I think that story about the note three other men might have seen was your idea."

"Put it that it's easy to let loyalty outrun discretion," said the inspector, in his quiet way, but rather hurriedly for all that.

Antony laughed angrily. "I think, on the whole, I prefer the superintendent's frankness," he said. And then a rather startled look came into his eyes as he realized the suggestion wasn't altogether unreasonable; he couldn't have sworn it hadn't been his questions that put the idea into Roger's mind, and if that was true . . . "Very well!" he said. "You think Farrell murdered Martin Grainger, and that I'm prepared to manufacture evidence to clear him."

"You're going too fast, Mr. Maitland," said Sykes. He sounded as unmoved as ever.

"Don't spoil it, Inspector," Antony begged. "Just tell me, one of you, what brought you here this morning? I don't suppose it was only to insult me."

"Can you ask that?" said Briggs, suddenly furious again. "After what happened last night."

"But—"

"Perhaps, sir, if I explain to Mr. Maitland," Sykes suggested.

"Oh, very well!" Briggs began to move heavily up and down the room; and Antony, who had taken the same path so often himself, watched him reflectively for a moment before he turned to the inspector again.

"I suppose you mean there's a connection," he said.

"You wouldn't have any ideas yourself?"

"Ideas? Oh, yes. None of them reasonable."

"Then I'd better tell you what we know of the man who entered this house last night."

"You've caught him, Inspector?" For once, Sykes did not smile at his eagerness.

"Not yet." Just for a moment the sedate façade was broken by an angry look. "But we do know something about him."

"He didn't leave his prints in here?" said Antony, looking about him rather as if he expected to see some visible sign of the intruder's presence.

"You told Sergeant Matthews that Bates said he'd grabbed the pocket of the man who shot him," Sykes went on, ignoring the interruption. "The man's jacket pocket, that was; it had ripped right out. So Matthews had a look round in the alley and he found a little pocket calendar. You know the kind: advert on one side, good and clear; and all twelve months on the other, much too small to read. It had a plastic sort of finish, so it took prints a treat."

"Then you know who he was?"

"Not that, either." His slowness seemed to reprove Antony's impatience. "The first thing is that the advertisement was for Galloway's Chop House, and while your visitor may have been a patron . . . well, don't tell me it's a coincidence, that's all."

"I won't," Antony promised, and hoped his dismay wasn't apparent.

"The other thing," Sykes went on, "is even more startling, I believe. You may have noticed the account of a bullion robbery at London Airport in the papers a few days ago."

"I believe I did; what of it?"

"One of the guards was shot. There have been other, similar hold-ups over the last few years, and all with the same trademark, you might say: organized with extraordinary precision and executed with complete ruthlessness."

"Yes, but—"

"About six months ago a consignment was lifted coming up by road to one of the bullion brokers. And we got a set of prints from that job; one of the crates had been levered open and the lid left lying on the floor of the van. The first bit of carelessness they'd ever been guilty of, and it did us no good in the end . . . records had never heard of him."

"And this was the same man?" Antony sounded incredulous, and for the first time the smallest degree of satisfaction was evident in Sykes's manner.

"The very same," he said.

"But stick-up men don't commit burglary. It just isn't done!"

101

"It isn't reasonable," Sykes nodded. "That's why I'd like some of those ideas of yours . . . reasonable or not."

"I see."

"If the situation wasn't so serious," Sykes began, and was interrupted by the superintendent, who halted his pacing and said with emphasis:

"If you have learned anything at all that connects the two affairs, I think in view of what has happened we have a right to demand that you tell us."

"I haven't learned anything"—unexpectedly, he grinned with real amusement—"well, hardly anything, except what you've told me yourselves. But there's something I was going to phone you about anyway," he went on, and heard the superintendent give a skeptical snort. "The chap didn't get any farther than this room last night, and the only thing he took was my uncle's engagement book."

"So I understand."

"Well, he didn't go to all that trouble to get a book that was almost unused. Uncle Nick makes a point of never remembering anything unless Mallory reminds him—"

"Just what are you getting at, Mr. Maitland?"

Now that it came to the point, he didn't want to tell them. But there was a connection, there had to be, and so—as Briggs had pointed out so ungraciously—they had a right to know. "James Farrell's diaries for the last five years of his life are upstairs in my living room," he said. "There's damn-all in them, but I can't help wondering—"

"We'll make up our own minds about that," said Briggs. Antony looked at him unlovingly.

"I'll get them for you," he offered. "But there's nothing there."

"Never mind that! You've admitted you knew of the connection."

"I've d-done nothing of the kind. It only occurred to me this morning that there might be one, and then it was the wildest of guesses."

The superintendent ignored this. "It can be a very dangerous policy," he said didactically, "to attempt to conceal matters of this gravity."

"If you'd l-listen—" He broke off and turned again to Sykes with a rueful look. "It doesn't matter whether you believe me or not," he said, "but . . . gang warfare? Could that have been the motive for Grainger's death, do you think?" He expected the superintendent to break in again with a furious denial, and was surprised to see a look almost of smugness on his face.

"It seems," said Sykes in his careful way, "that we may not have to look any further for the reason James Farrell was being blackmailed."

"You're putting him as a member of the gang?" Even now, the idea seemed a ludicrous one.

"Or its leader."

"In that case . . . oh, I see," said Antony bitterly. "The king is dead, long live the king!" He paused, considering. "I don't think I like that idea at all," he said.

"I was afraid you might not." Sykes sounded regretful. "But I think I'd bear it in mind, if I were you."

"I'll admit the connection between Grainger's death and the bullion robberies . . . but why tie the Farrells in with either?"

"Think of the evidence," Briggs snapped.

"That's just what I am doing. What would the point of last night have been?"

"If Roger Farrell is involved with the gang in his turn, the fact that he had asked your help might well prove an embarrassment to his associates. You may be right that there's nothing incriminating in the diaries, but they may not have known that."

"You're not blaming *him* for what happened to your chaps, then?"

"Perhaps. Perhaps not." Briggs's temper seemed to have cooled now; he had a self-satisfied look. "But I do warn you very seriously, Mr. Maitland—"

"Good morning, gentlemen," said Sir Nicholas from the doorway.

Sykes was the only one who took this sudden entrance at all

calmly. The superintendent swung round with a startled look, and his greeting sounded ungracious. "We were about to take our leave," he added in his most pompous tone.

Antony was wondering just how much his uncle had overheard, and felt himself uneasily at a disadvantage. He slid off the corner of the desk and came up to Briggs's elbow. "I can quite understand," he said softly, "when you've something really slanderous to say it's always as well to avoid having an independent witness."

"I came here to ask your cooperation," said Briggs, swinging round to face him again.

"Which I have given you."

"Up to a point; I haven't said I'm satisfied."

"No. I thought it was rather rude of you," said Antony in a tone of gentle regret.

"I have also warned you about taking any further part in Roger Farrell's affairs—"

"And against the evils in store for me if I continue to follow the paths of deceit." Over Briggs's shoulder his eyes met his uncle's. "The superintendent's in a very moral mood," he assured him.

Briggs turned on his heel and swept out of the room, and Sykes shook his head sadly. "We're all a bit upset this morning."

"I like you so much better," said Antony savagely, "when you're being honest."

"I honestly wish I'd come alone." He was genuinely sorry, but there was amusement, too, in his tone. "Those diaries, now—"

"I'll get them." Sir Nicholas cleared his throat. "Or if you don't mind asking Jenny—"

"That'll be all right, then." In his turn, the inspector moved toward the door. "But I wouldn't disregard everything the superintendent said, Mr. Maitland. Not if I were you."

A moment later he was speaking to Sir Nicholas with all his usual placidity, and then he went out and closed the door firmly behind him. Antony took a step toward it, but his uncle said mildly, "Gibbs is there," and moved across in a leisurely way to his usual chair by the fireplace. "I thought," he went on, "you were on reasonable terms with the police just now."

"So did I. Briggs, of course—"

"Ah, yes. Briggs." Sir Nicholas had located his cigars, and was now patting his pockets in an ineffectual search for matches. Antony found a box on the desk and offered them in silence. "No doubt," said his uncle, still affably, "you're going to explain to me—"

"I suppose I must," said Antony, with no enthusiasm at all.

"Yes, I think so. And before you begin you can tell me, my dear boy . . . who is Roger Farrell?" asked Sir Nicholas. Obviously he was no longer completely absorbed in the arson brief, but Antony wasn't at all sure that he found much comfort in that.

8

IT WAS A LONG STORY BY NOW, AND A COMPLICATED ONE,
and because Sir Nicholas was in one of his more captious moods
it wasn't told without interruptions. When the narrative was finished, he eyed his nephew in silence for a while. "Why didn't you
tell me all this before?" he said at last, and still amiably enough
to make Antony glance at him uneasily.

"I did. At least, I tried to. And all you would do," he added,
his sense of grievance overcoming his discretion, "was draw incen-
diary-minded ducks on the blotter, and burble about dried eggs
and out-of-the-way religious ceremonies."

Sir Nicholas waved this aside. "Do I understand you? If an
arrest is made, Horton proposes to offer me the brief?"

"Yes." He did not add that Geoffrey had telephoned him in a
panic the previous day, after the session at Scotland Yard; or that
he had more or less guaranteed his learned relative's compliance.
But it is probable that Sir Nicholas found this simple agreement
sufficiently informative.

"And you intend to—er—associate yourself with the defense.
Am I expected to welcome your participation?" he asked.

"I know what you're thinking, sir."

"I doubt it." The dry tone had its effect. Antony grinned reluctantly.

"You've complained before of my meddling, Uncle Nick."

"On that point I find myself almost in sympathy with the police," Sir Nicholas admitted.

"Well, I can't help wondering if I've just made things worse."

"Something's got to be done about Meg," said his uncle, with authority.

"That's what I think, sir." He paused, and then added in a worried tone, "You see, I don't know what to do."

"You'd better tell me what the trouble is."

Antony looked at him warily, but the sympathy sounded genuine, and he badly needed advice. "Sykes said Meg might be charged as an accessory—"

"So you have informed me."

"Yes, but . . . don't you see, it's a thousand to one against their going as far as that if they had a confession—a full confession that exonerated her."

"You're probably right about that," said Sir Nicholas thoughtfully, "but as Farrell denies that he killed Grainger—"

"If I put it to him like that, I think he'd admit it. And even with the evidence of premeditation, he might get off fairly lightly when the full tale was told."

"Are you telling me he's guilty?"

"No, I . . . the thing is, I don't know. If he is, that'd be the best advice I could give him, both for his own sake and Meg's. But if he isn't—"

"He'll persist in his denial . . . surely?"

"I don't know if he would, sir. He's fond of Meg, I'm pretty sure of that; and there's this weird idea he's got about poetic justice. At the moment he thinks the only way to defend Meg is to defend himself, but if it weren't for that I don't know what he'd do."

"I see. And whatever you decide you run the risk of being unfair to one of them."

"What shall I do, Uncle Nick?"

"I think you must first make up your mind as to his guilt or innocence."

"How can I, for sure?"

"It isn't just Grainger's murder now," Sir Nicholas pointed out. "If it were, I might possibly agree to act. But the kind of callousness that results in last night's slaughter—"

"That's one thing I'm certain about, sir. Roger wasn't responsible for the deaths of those two policemen."

"But you agree there's some connection?"

"Yes. I've got to."

"And that James Farrell was implicated in some way in these bullion robberies?"

"That would have been a motive for blackmail, wouldn't it, if Grainger had found out? And I suppose it's the sort of thing he might have discussed with a confederate in a place he felt secure. And it *must* have been Farrell's diaries our burglar was looking for, however stupid it seems."

Sir Nicholas was eyeing him in silence, not a tranquil silence. *"My* study," he said at last, bitterly. *"My* engagement book. I suppose I must be thankful I'd made very little use of it."

"Well, someone who just knew my address," said Antony, "might easily have made the mistake."

"Yes, indeed. But I don't find the reflection at all comforting," his uncle told him. "You've looked at the diaries, I suppose. Do they tell you anything?"

"Nothing at all. I did wonder whether the months immediately before the blackmail started might give some clue. After all, Grainger must have got the goods on Farrell during that period. If anything at all unusual had happened—" He broke off to glance at his uncle, who had closed his eyes and seemed to be praying. "But it didn't," he added despondently.

Sir Nicholas opened his eyes. "I don't see how any of this convinces you of Roger Farrell's innocence," he said.

"If it's just a matter of shooting Grainger," Antony told him, wisely refraining from argument, "you couldn't possibly object to that."

"Perhaps not. Though I think you might have phrased it more happily. It wouldn't be at all difficult to frame a defense if he would admit what he has done, though how far it would be successful is another matter again. But if he persists in his denials—"

"I admit the case against him is . . . almost overwhelming, sir."

"Almost?" said Sir Nicholas scornfully. "He was the only person in a position to know where Grainger would be that afternoon. He obtained this information by means of a subterfuge, which won't sound well in court. He is known to have been at the scene of the murder; he could have searched the body for identifying papers and phoned an accomplice to arrange the burglary in Copthall Court, before he reported to the police. In fact, he admits having recovered the envelope with the diamond from Grainger's pocket. As for his motive—"

"I'm not arguing about the strength of the case, sir."

Sir Nicholas swept the interruption aside. "His motive is undeniable," he stated, "and completely convincing to any normal person. While if you attempt to demonstrate his innocence you are left with a murderer who must have known Grainger's identity already, as—on Farrell's own showing—he had no opportunity to search the body—"

"And who had at least one accomplice, an expert safe-blower."

"That applies, whoever committed the crime. But this hypothetical murderer of yours must also have been in a position to see Meg's note about the appointment, and to recognize it for what it was. From which we may make two further deductions: that he was one of the men who went home with Roger Farrell after his mother's funeral and that he had probably been blackmailed at least once by Grainger, and made payment by the same method as was demanded of Mrs. Farrell." He paused and fixed Antony with a cold eye. "Do you think it at all likely that such a man exists?" he demanded.

"Well, sir . . . since you ask me . . . yes, I do."

"Then all I can say—"

"I know, Uncle Nick, but . . . don't! You're going to tell me I want Roger to be innocent, and in a way that's true. But it isn't only that."

Sir Nicholas compressed his lips. "This . . . this creature of your imagination," he said, "must also have been ruthless enough to see his own safety in framing Roger Farrell." He sounded anything but convinced.

"That brings us round full circle, sir. If he's one of the gang, we know he's ruthless," said Antony, with an air of reasonableness that made his uncle's head spin. "But I've got a sort of feeling that wasn't the reason for the blackmail; I mean, if Grainger had known James Farrell had all the resources of a gang at his disposal, do you think he'd have risked it?"

"The connection has been demonstrated."

"Yes, but not necessarily *that* connection. Oh, I don't know, it doesn't make sense, any of it," he added in a dissatisfied tone. "It's getting on my nerves, and I'm not really thinking straight."

"But if you encourage Roger Farrell to confess, you'll always wonder if you did him an injustice," said Sir Nicholas shrewdly.

"And if I don't, I may be unfair to Meg. What would you do, sir?"

"A few more facts—" his uncle suggested.

"Yes, of course. But by the time I've got them it may be too late."

They were still arguing the matter at the luncheon table, and neither had succeeded in moving the other a jot from his original position when Jenny went out to fetch the car. Sir Nicholas accompanied his nephew to the front steps to wait for her, and was still delivering an impassioned speech to an invisible jury when Antony left him.

The depressing thing was, he seemed to have forgotten the role for which he was cast, and to be summing up for the prosecution.

Sam Reade lived in a rambling old house near the river at Twickenham, which took a bit of finding even though Jenny followed Roger's instructions (so far as Antony recalled them) to the letter. Obviously there was a large, disorderly family; Antony, remembering what he had been told of Reade's financial position, looked about him with interest. What the establishment lacked in elegance it gained, perhaps, in comfort; the differences might be due to personal taste, or simply to less ample funds than were at Denning's disposal.

He was admitted by a fair boy of about eighteen, who weaved his way in a practiced manner through a sort of obstacle course of golf clubs and tennis rackets to a door at the back of the hall. He flung this open, made a sweeping gesture of invitation, grinned, and disappeared. Antony went in, and found a man in his late fifties heaving himself up from a chair near the window. Two small girls, who bore him a strong resemblance, were arguing over a jigsaw puzzle at the table in the center of the room; but they disappeared obediently enough on the laconic command "Out!" Antony stood aside to let them pass. The taller of the two sidled by with an air of apology, but the little one gave him a stare of unabashed curiosity and a friendly grin.

It struck him as he turned back to the man again that he had an air of relief about him, as though he had just performed a trick he hadn't been quite sure would come off. Reade was a squarish, middle-sized man, whose fair hair was faded and thinning. Perhaps to compensate for this he had grown a fierce and unmistakably ginger mustache. He had gray eyes and an air of alertness which at first glance seemed at variance with his rather shabby tweeds. For some reason Antony again recalled Roger Farrell's remark about top hats, and made a mental note to remember to ask Jenny. . . .

"I've been worried to death," said Reade, "ever since Roger phoned me." And for the moment he looked as if this might quite literally be true. He waved a hand to a chair near his own and hospitably opened a box of cigarettes, which proved to be empty.

"He said he'd explained to you—" said Antony, seating himself and letting the sentence trail off hopefully.

"Yes, he did. In a way." The echo of Roger's own phrasing must have been unconscious. "I don't pretend I altogether understand the situation, but I gather it's serious."

"Very serious, I'm afraid." Beyond the window, the garden was as rambling and untidy as the house itself, but peaceful enough in spite of the clouds which had gathered as the day wore on. Antony thought of the dead man in the lane the night before, and the harsh breathing of his companion who might or might not still be alive. Perhaps his tone was more grim than he had intended. Sam Reade said:

"Oh, dear!" And then, even more helplessly, "I've always been afraid he'd get into trouble one day."

"Why?" asked Antony. The other man looked a little taken aback, and said vaguely:

"He's headstrong . . . reckless—"

"Not the best attributes for a stockbroker, surely?"

"Ah, but he has judgment. No, I assure you, Mr. Maitland, I couldn't wish for a more able partner, though sometimes I wonder whether his heart's really in the business," he added wistfully.

"He entered it, I suppose, to join his father."

"It was a good opening," said Reade, almost defensively. "And not too easy for a man who's been in the services to know what he wants to do when the war is over."

"I suppose, too, he was upset at that time by the death of his wife." (Now, why had he brought that up? Surely it was, of all things, the most irrelevant.)

"He told you about Alice?" Reade sounded surprised.

"Mr. Denning mentioned her to me."

"Oh, I see. Well, frankly, I don't know whether to agree with you or not. About his being upset, I mean." He paused, and seemed for the moment a long way away, and his thoughts unhappy. "You know she was my niece," he said at last. "I never thought . . . but then, Roger isn't one to let you know his feelings."

"I didn't know," said Antony. He was wishing, with some impatience, that the other man would make up his mind whether he wanted to attack his partner, or defend him.

"She lived with us," said Reade. "Like our own daughter, though we'd none of our own then. My wife always said Roger spoiled her, made her as stubborn as he is, as set on her own way. We didn't want her to go into the W.R.N.S., you see, but he was in the navy."

"They were very young," said Antony, because some sort of

comment seemed to be called for. And thought for a moment of Jenny, and that it was sometimes a good thing to be foolish.

"She wouldn't have been killed, you see, if she'd been at home with us." He paused again and nodded as Antony murmured something, and then said more strongly, "But you're not really interested in that."

He was, and he wasn't. If it helped him to understand Roger . . . "I was hoping to hear about James Farrell," Maitland told him. "When did you first get to know him?"

"James? Well . . . about 1930, I suppose." Though he had invited this change of subject he seemed to find it a little bewildering. "He was on his own by then, of course, and I was working for the same firm he started with. Later we went into partnership; that must have been 1935, because my grandfather died the year before."

A legacy, presumably. And why should the obvious questions be so hard to find words for? He'd been blunt enough with Denning, but after all *he* was a cynic, whereas Reade had an air of vulnerability, surprising in a businessman. Aloud he said (and the pause had been barely perceptible), "Do you know how Farrell originally financed his operations?"

"I think he once said he'd built up his capital, bit by bit."

"Not too easy, I should have thought."

For the first time Sam Reade smiled. "Just possible," he said, "for a man with a little money, a great deal of patience, and a real interest in what he was doing. He'd also need good advice in the beginning, and an instinct for the movements of the market . . . that's something I can't possibly explain."

"Black magic," said Antony, grinning in his turn. "I knew it!"

"Well, I know James had the qualities I've mentioned, which is why I always felt our association was a fortunate one for me. He had a lucky break over some mining stock a couple of years before we joined forces, and I think that's what finally secured his position. The difference between comfort and affluence, you know."

"I wonder . . . have you any particular reason for remembering that, Mr. Reade?"

113

"For one thing there was a lot of talk about it. Farrell's luck, they were saying; he got out just in time." He paused and sighed. "Instinct, really," he said, "not luck at all. But the other reason I remember is that I'd got a couple of hundred quid in it myself, which I couldn't afford to lose."

"You must have known him well."

"Yes, of course." He hesitated and then said slowly, "Not that we shared much social life; an exchange of dinners around the Christmas season would about sum it up. He had more taste for luxury than I have and was certainly better able to indulge it. And I had a great regard for Winifred, but she was rather . . . we didn't quite hit it off. On the other hand, I've been down to that place of his on the coast, and frankly, once was enough."

"Did you know he was being blackmailed?"

"Roger told me. Before that I had no idea."

"Now that you know of it, can you hazard a guess as to why?"

That brought a silence. At last Reade said stiffly, "If I knew I would tell you. It had nothing to do with the firm's activities, but I realize that's difficult to prove."

"Can you be sure of it? There must surely have been occasions when he acted on his own."

"Oh, yes, of course, but . . . I'm satisfied, Mr. Maitland."

"Could he have been carrying on any completely separate activity?"

"It would have been contrary to the terms of our agreement, but naturally not impossible."

Antony was frowning. Long before this, Reade should have been protesting the complete faith he had always had in James Farrell's probity. He said, feeling his way, "The opportunity for blackmail may have arisen from some deal in the past that wouldn't bear scrutiny." But Sam Reade must have been following his train of thought, because his answer cut across the careful phrasing of the question.

"In his dealings with me I always found him honest. But there was a streak of unscrupulousness as well; I can't say where it might have led him."

"That mining stock, for instance. You say it was worthless?"

"That's the way it turned out. The ore was there all right, nothing wrong with the survey; it was just that there was a problem of transportation which we'd none of us appreciated. Abukcheech Mine, I've never forgotten the name, even though it's such an odd one. It was up in Northern Quebec somewhere, and quite uneconomic to get the stuff out. Well, two hundred quid was a lot of money to me in those days, but James had made a sizable investment and the stock went up all right, and he sold out just about at the peak, I'd say. But there was nothing odd about that."

"No, I see. Some other project, then. And if he'd had a partner—"

"Roger, undoubtedly. At any time during the last ten years, that is." An unpleasant echo of Denning's opinion. Antony was just reflecting how best to word a further query when Reade added, "Roger had a great regard for his father," as though the words might in some way be an extenuation. But it wasn't quite clear what fault was being excused.

"Would you rule out criminal activities?" Reade's attitude might be puzzling, but at least it seemed that his scruples had been unnecessary. Antony even wondered, for a moment, if his companion had any interest in his partner's affairs except a financial one; and he thought of Roger saying "I've always trusted him." But his tone remained mild and friendly.

"I've never considered the possibility. Surely it's unlikely."

"The first blackmail demand was made nearly five years ago. September, 1958. Can you remember anything unusual happening during that summer? If it helps at all, it was the year Mr. and Mrs. Farrell went to Teneriffe in May."

Reade seemed to be reflecting. "Nothing at all," he said at length. And then, as though making up his mind, "Couldn't the diaries help you?"

"Unfortunately, no. A list of appointments, no more. Did Roger tell you—?"

"He said you thought they might furnish a clue to the reason for the blackmail. I don't think," he added, "that he was particularly keen on finding out." His smile was humorless.

"I hoped they might. I can't say I expected it. There was a chap called Cooper, for instance. Vaughan Cooper. Roger couldn't identify him, but there's nothing to suggest—"

"Vaughan Cooper. No, I don't know either. If they met socially, Isabel might remember. It's the kind of thing Winifred would have told her."

"I see." And I wish I thought it was important. It seemed only too likely that the bullion robberies sufficiently explained Martin Grainger's hold over James Farrell, without any wild theorizing about other possible causes. But there still was that little nagging uncertainty in his mind.

"Did you know Martin Grainger?" he asked, following this train of thought.

"Oh, yes. James was very fond of the Chop House; I often lunched there with him."

"And since his death?"

"I still go in occasionally. It's convenient to the office."

"What did you think of Grainger?"

"A good *restaurateur*. Watchful," said Reade, obviously seeking for the one perfect word to express his meaning.

"You weren't surprised to hear of his other activities?"

"I didn't know him well enough to be surprised."

"You know Hubert Denning, of course?"

"Slightly. He was a great friend of James's."

"And Roger's godfather."

"If you're looking for a partisan opinion, Mr. Maitland, don't go to Denning. He hasn't much time for Roger."

"Why not?"

"He likes to take his own way."

"I see. And when Winifred Farrell died, had you any suspicion there might be another reason for her suicide than the one she revealed in her letters?"

"She was devoted to James. I thought it reason enough."

"Do you remember the day of her funeral?"

"Of course I do."

"You went back to Leinster Court afterwards?"

"The least we could do, I should think."

"You and Mrs. Reade?"

"I was alone. My wife was unwell."

"Who else was there?"

"Roger, of course. Hubert Denning. Isabel and Leonard Wilson. But I don't quite see, if you'll forgive me, what this has to do—"

The protest seemed long overdue. "It may be relevant," said Antony hastily. "You'd been to the flat before, even if you didn't know it well?"

"Yes."

"Then you know which is Roger's bedroom."

"The one that used to be the spare room." He was speaking reluctantly now and frowning as he spoke.

"I'm just trying to confirm something Roger told me. That the men made use of his room and bathroom, while Isabel used her mother's."

"If it's important to check his veracity on a completely irrelevant point, the statement is quite correct," said Reade irritably.

"There was a note on top of the tallboy. Did you see anybody pick it up and read it?"

"No."

"Or even glance in that direction?"

"How can I say? I didn't know there was anything there, I wouldn't have noticed." He was angry now, and perhaps he was worried too; a complete reversal of mood. "I don't know what all this is about," he said again. "What are you trying to prove?"

"At this point, nothing at all." Perhaps, after all, it was the apparent irrelevance that bothered Reade, though that seemed odd when he had answered quite readily so much that was undeniably impertinent. Go back to James Farrell's affairs, then, and press the questions a little further. . . .

But it wasn't really very long before he went out to rejoin Jenny. She wasn't in the car, but he saw her a moment later walking toward him down a path through the shrubbery, with a dark, youngish woman in an advanced stage of pregnancy on one side of her, and the fair youth who had originally admitted him to the house on the other. As there seemed to be no way to avoid the encounter he went to meet them.

Five minutes later, having parried an invitation to tea, they were back in the car again. Jenny said, as she stretched out a hand to the ignition key, "She's pretty, isn't she? Did you like her husband?"

"Is that *Sam* Reade's wife? I thought—"

"His second wife. I got muddled, too, because she couldn't possibly be David's mother—that's the boy you saw. But all the rest of the children are hers, and much younger than he is."

So it was the first Mrs. Reade who had felt so possessively about her niece, so bitterly about Roger Farrell. Or were the emotions which her husband imputed to her a mere echo of his own? It didn't seem to matter much either way, except that the relationship between the two partners wasn't quite so simple as Roger had implied.

Jenny wasn't waiting for his comments. The car started smoothly and then bumped its way down the rutted drive toward the gate. "If you were a Napoleon of Crime, how would you live?" he asked her. "In a place like this, or in the height of luxury?"

"Luxury, I suppose . . . if I could choose my own extravagances. But . . . this place, Antony—"

"What about it, love?"

"There's quite a lot of land with it, and it goes right down to the river. But at least," she added, slowing as she reached the gate and beginning to edge out cautiously into the roadway, "I'd have something done about the drive."

Antony was following what he hoped was her train of thought. "You mean, the Reades might have a valuable property but not be particularly concerned with spit and polish," he said.

"Some people aren't. And I'll tell you something: Mrs. Reade isn't interested in clothes a bit, but she was wearing emeralds that must have cost the earth."

"Was she, indeed?"

"If you can't tell the difference—! And the boy has a new Jaguar," Jenny went on. "He looked at this as if it was some sort of an antique, but, of course, he was too polite to say so. So you see—"

"They may be 'choosing their luxuries,'" Antony agreed. "I'm

118

beginning to think I made a mistake . . . I should have gone on the Stock Exchange."

"You weren't talking about being a stockbroker, you were talking about crime," Jenny pointed out. "And I wouldn't mind betting if you *had* gone in for finance, we'd be even harder up than we are now."

Antony sighed and slid down a little farther in his seat. "Sam Reade said you needed judgment if you were going to get anywhere," he assented.

They were going back to Kempenfeldt Square for tea, because Antony's appointment with the Wilsons wasn't until six-thirty. He had spoken to Isabel Wilson that morning, and she had told him they were going to a matinée; and he couldn't decide whether she didn't understand the urgency of Roger's predicament, or whether she didn't care.

Because Meg Hamilton was in his mind too, he wasn't surprised to find Jenny following a route that would take them past the house in Bayswater where she lived. He alighted without comment when they arrived there and made his way up to Meg's apartment on the first floor. Just for the moment, when she let him in, her eagerness turned to a look of heart-rending disappointment. Then she said with an almost breathless haste, "I'm so glad you came, darling. Another five minutes and I'd have been screaming mad."

"Don't chatter at me, Meg." He followed her into the little drawing room, which usually amused him because it should have been an exquisitely neat example of modern *décor* (that was how it had been planned for her by a well-known stage designer), only somehow Meg's personality *would* intrude, in a bewildering variety of ways: from the bookcase with its rather shabby contents (*Wuthering Heights* and *Alice in Wonderland* and a battered copy of Bentley's *Jacobean and Caroline Stage*) to the riot of flowers in one corner (a higgledy-piggledy arrangement with no sort of relation to gracious living) and the quiet tones of the water color over the fireplace, a fishing village at dawn. "I think I'm jealous

119

of Roger," he added, lightly, but with a serious look.

Meg grinned up at him. "Well, I did think it might be him," she admitted. "You see, he wasn't at the theater last night; or, at least, he didn't come round to see me."

"He's gone down to Grunning's Hole."

"I suppose that means he's being noble, as you said," remarked Meg. "But we aren't trying to hide anything, I can't see that it matters—"

"You'll have to leave us a few of our illusions," Antony told her. But he shook his head when she looked at him inquiringly. "Jenny's downstairs," he said. "Come along." She went away to find her coat and handbag without another word.

Jenny gave her a doubtful look when she scrambled into the car. "Have you got everything you need for the theater?"

"Yes, but—"

"I'll feed you," said Jenny, "so you won't need to come back here again." She wasn't looking at her friend now, her attention was on the car again, but Antony saw Meg's expression of distaste and said roughly:

"You can't stop eating altogether."

"Why shouldn't I, then?" She turned to look at him over her shoulder, and with one of her lightning changes of mood her face was animated again, her tone cheerful. "Did you see the papers?" she asked. "They hated the play."

"All except the *Clarion*," said Jenny. "They said it was significant." Her husband wondered briefly when she had found time for this research. "And they all liked you," she added firmly. She knew quite well that Meg, perhaps for the first time in her life, wasn't interested in the notices of the new play, but she didn't want the subject of their own adventures the previous night to be mentioned until they were home again. But the death of the two policemen had been in the forefront of her mind all day, and she wasn't particularly adept at dissimulation. Already Meg was looking at her thoughtfully.

"Something's happened," she said. And when there was no immediate answer, "You may as well tell me," she added. " 'Ye'll no fickle Tammas Yownie.' "

"Well, you see—" said Antony, and:

"You'll have to tell her," said Jenny; both at the same time. Antony embarked reluctantly on his recital. He told her what had happened during the night, but he didn't mention his talk with Sykes, or the later interview at which Briggs also had been present. And he wondered again just where his duty lay.

He had only just finished when they turned into Kempenfeldt Square. Meg had a puzzled frown between her eyes and he wondered uneasily what sort of unanswerable questions she was about to produce for his undoing. Then he saw her stiffen. "You told me he'd gone away," she said; her tone was accusing, but she didn't look back at him.

The Jensen was drawn up outside Number Five, and Roger Farrell, who seemed to have been strolling aimlessly, came hurrying along the pavement to meet them. He looked a little taken aback when he saw Meg, and greeted her with a formality that had never been evident before in his manner toward her. Then he went to the door of the Maitlands' car and held it open for Jenny. "I've got to talk to Antony," he told her, with an urgency that robbed the words of rudeness, despite their obvious meaning.

Jenny, who had meant to take the car straight round to the garage, got out obediently. "Come on, Meg. We'll go and put the kettle on." She paused to smile at Roger, but his eyes were already fixed on Antony's face, so she took Meg's arm and urged her up the steps. And at that precise moment Sir Nicholas Harding came around the corner of the garden in the center of the square and began to cross the road toward them.

Antony was in two minds whether to make the introduction; there was so obviously something on Roger's mind that he wouldn't be able to contain for much longer. But any evasion might well be condemned later by his uncle as secrecy; and it seemed only too likely that the two would have to meet sooner or later. Even so, if he had foreseen the effect of his words he might well have decided on silence. Roger looked at Sir Nicholas and said, with an air of relief:

"Then you may as well know why I've come, sir. You see, I didn't know what to do about this." He tugged for a moment at the canvas which covered the back seats of the open car and threw it back to reveal the body of a man . . . a little man who lay in an oddly relaxed position, considering that *rigor* was obviously well set in. There was blood on his shirt, but as he lay on his side the wound that had killed him was not immediately visible. "He's been shot," added Roger helpfully.

Antony knew himself to be staring, with the one thought going stupidly through his head that this time the man wasn't in uniform. Sir Nicholas raised his head and looked at Roger, and said in his mildest voice, "Perhaps you have been misled about the convention in these matters, Mr. Farrell. It is not really normal procedure to deliver the corpse to counsel's own front door."

9

ANTONY COULD NEVER LOOK BACK ON THE EVENTS OF the next two hours without a feeling of unreality. This was partly due to his uncle's presence, because Sir Nicholas took charge with angry efficiency and he had no real need to exert himself; no opportunity, in fact, to do anything but what he was told. The only initiative he took was in the matter of the conversation which followed his asking Roger, "Who is it?"

They were standing together on the pavement and the tonneau cover was in place again, and Sir Nicholas had gone into the house to telephone. Roger shook his head and said, "I don't know." And paused a moment before he volunteered the additional information, "I found him this morning."

"Found him?"

"In the car. Outside the cottage." He sounded impatient, as though his meaning should have been obvious. "And when I say this morning, it was nearer lunch time. I'd put some books in the back, and when I went to look—"

"There he was!" Antony was merely bewildered, but the tone of his voice, he realized, was sharply satirical. "I only meant," he added, "was that the first you'd seen of him?" And this time he succeeded in sounding apologetic.

"Yes, of course. I told you—" But for no reason he could have explained, Maitland was suddenly convinced that Roger was lying. And again he was shaken by indecision. *If I say to him now, there's one way of keeping Meg out of this; well, not out of it altogether, but on the sidelines . . .*

"If you knew him," he said, "it doesn't follow that you shot him." *But why should Farrell be lying; he'd been frank enough up to now, or was that just an illusion.*

"I tell you—"

"Never mind. Could he have been there when you left town? When did you put the books in the car?"

"Just before I came to meet you last night. And when I dropped you here I drove straight down to the cottage. So it could only have been during the night—"

"Who knew you were going down to Grunning's Hole? Besides myself?"

"I know I told Isabel, she was annoyed their weekend at Petersfield was put off. And the doorman knew, and the chap at the garage . . . I don't really remember." He hesitated and then added awkwardly, "I realize it was stupid, driving back here."

"I suppose it was one way of solving the problem," said Antony, with a gleam of reluctant humor.

"I didn't know what to do. And I could only think . . . the local bobby . . . I'd never have made him understand."

"Well, if my uncle didn't seem particularly sympathetic, I'd better explain what happened here last night. Your arrival, you see, was something in the nature of the last straw. . . ." But he knew the tale almost by heart now, and he watched Roger's expression as he told it, and he could have sworn that his surprise was genuine, as well as his look of horror.

After that, the police arrived, and they both went into the house to wait. The car was fingerprinted and driven away, and a more senior policeman arrived, full of questions, followed by Geoffrey Horton, rather out of breath. At which point Sir Nicholas relaxed a little, which was just as well, because Roger was already completely unnerved by a vigilance which had almost forbidden him to breathe until his solicitor was present. It was only later that Antony realized his uncle wasn't certain what he himself might have said to Farrell.

But at last they all went away together in a police car, and Maitland—left alone with Sir Nicholas and disliking his expression—said hurriedly, "I'll have to tell Jenny . . . and Meg."

"If Jenny has succeeded in keeping Meg quiet as long as this," said Sir Nicholas, with a remarkably accurate estimate of the situation, "she can manage a little longer." He was in one of his rare moods of restlessness this evening, and Antony stood with his back to the empty grate in the study and watched him move aimlessly from desk to window and back again. "This man Farrell . . . is he mad?" he inquired abruptly.

Antony considered. "No," he said, at length. "I think it's just that things have sort of caught up with him."

Sir Nicholas breathed deeply, in an overwrought way. "There's no question *now* he'll be arrested," he said. "What's this nonsense you were talking earlier about his thinking it would be justice?"

"It's just—" he sought for the word—"a scruple, Uncle Nick. You see," he added, after another pause, "he had a great regard for his father." He realized as he spoke that he was echoing Sam Reade's phrase and faintly apologetic tone.

"That, I suppose, explains everything," said Sir Nicholas. And back he went to the window again, returning to the desk only to glare at his nephew.

"His mother killed herself," said Antony, "and now he thinks it was his father's fault." He watched his companion's expression, and added carefully, "I didn't say it was sensible, but that's how he feels."

Sir Nicholas continued to stare at him stonily. "Are you trying to elicit my sympathy?" he demanded.

"Of course not, sir." The innocent tone was a little overdone, but not without intention. He looked at his watch. "I've got to go," he said. "The Wilsons are expecting me, and I must talk to Jenny—"

"You'd much better leave that to me," Sir Nicholas told him. And added testily, seeing Antony's startled look, "I'll tell Meg

125

what has happened, and see that she gets to the theater on time."

"Yes, Uncle Nick, but—"

"I think my diplomacy is equal to the occasion," said Sir Nicholas with finality. *"I,* after all, have never been known to reduce a witness to hysterics." And having thus silenced his nephew, though he'd had to go back several years to do so, he preceded him into the hall, and by the time Antony pulled the front door shut behind him was already halfway up the first flight of stairs.

Antony found a taxi quickly, but even that piece of luck couldn't get him to the Wilsons' on time. They had what is usually advertised as a bijou residence, and the only fault Antony could find with it was that it looked, somehow, too correct; so much like an interior decorator's dream as to appear, paradoxically, not quite the thing.

His first impression of Isabel Wilson was that she was quite fantastically like Roger; his second, that the setting was all wrong for her. He had been shown into a small, impersonal room, and she swept in on him almost immediately with an unfriendly look and the obvious intention of making his lateness an excuse for cutting short their talk. She was a tall woman, and as sturdily built as her brother, and you'd have to admit she was handsome, Antony thought, if you weren't too scared to do so. He made up his mind right away that if once he let her take the initiative all was lost. If it wasn't already.

"I'm afraid I have very little time, Mr. Maitland." She had a deep voice and the assurance of a much older woman. She was, he supposed, no more than in her middle thirties. She had not offered him a chair or taken one herself, so that his mind presented him with a sudden incongruous picture of the Israelites standing to eat their paschal feast, with their loins girt and staffs in their hands, and—presumably—one eye on the clock. And if anything was calculated to give you indigestion, surely that was it. He said, with no attempt at all to sound ingratiating, "Roger told me he'd explained the position to you."

"He told me a lot of things, a lot of nonsense." She laughed angrily. "I understand you're a lawyer of some sort, Mr. Maitland. Surely *you* don't take him seriously."

"I'm a friend of your brother's. He's at the police station now, and his solicitor is with him. If you like we can defer our conversation until after his arrest. Perhaps that may convince you—"

"His arrest?" For a moment he thought he had shaken her. Then, "I don't believe you," she told him.

"That's a pity. The situation has become more complicated since he spoke to you yesterday, but no less serious."

"I'm not interested in generalizations."

"Very well, I'll try to make myself clear. Several things happened last night. For instance, a man was murdered—so far as I know he hasn't been identified. But Roger drove up to town from Grunning's Hole with the body in the back of the car, and naturally the police—did you say something?"

"No . . . no. It's incredible!"

"In addition, there was a shooting affray last night in which two policemen were killed and a third seriously wounded. The police believe this to be connected in some way with Martin Grainger's death; and there is a clear link between Grainger and your brother." He paused, looking for some sign that his words were going home. "The link is your mother's suicide," he added deliberately, "and the fact that Grainger had been blackmailing her, and your father too."

The calm, almost scornful look couldn't be natural. She said, still coldly, "It isn't the sort of thing that can happen to us," but for the first time he thought there was doubt in her voice and did his best to press the advantage.

"It's happening to Roger," he assured her. "And you'll be involved in the publicity, you know. I don't see how you can help it."

"Did he do it? Did he kill this man, Grainger?"

"Grainger was a blackmailer," said Antony, his eyes on her face.

"You mean . . . he deserved to die? But he could have been punished—couldn't he?—without Roger doing that. It's so . . . so inconsiderate of him," she said, "so unconventional." And Antony stared at her until he realized suddenly that she wasn't joking, she was speaking in all seriousness. But perhaps it wasn't so unreasonable, after all, from her point of view. To be unconventional was a deadly sin, while murder probably never entered into her calculations at all. He began to wonder what sort of a man Leonard Wilson was, and then he realized that she was eyeing him in a considering way.

"If I talk to you," she said, "will it help avoid a scandal?" Her tone was no more friendly than it had been before.

"Is that all you care about? It *may* help Roger; that's the best I can do."

"I see." She stood a moment, weighing the matter up, and then turned abruptly and went out into the hall. For an instant he thought she had chosen this way of closing the interview, then he heard her voice, raised a little, but still peremptory. "Leonard! Please come here." She came back into the room again, and this time she seated herself, very upright, on one of the chairs. Whatever the real purpose of the room, it wasn't designed for lounging.

Leonard Wilson was an inch shorter than his wife; a slender little man, very neat in his appearance, with dark hair rather overlong, and a carefully trimmed imperial. He looked less like a bank manager than anything Antony felt he could have dreamed up, even after a late supper of cheese and onions, and his voice did nothing to alter this impression. It was light, and very pleasant, and had a curious quality of tone which gave a sarcastic flavor to his mildest remarks. Isabel Wilson ignored this inflection completely, treating everything he said at exactly face value.

"It seems the situation Roger described to me is more serious than I had supposed," she told him as he came into the room. "I think we should find out what Mr. Maitland wants to know."

"But that's just what Roger asked us, isn't it?" said Wilson, opening his eyes very wide. By implication, any other course would have been unthinkable. He turned to Antony, studying him for a moment with open interest. "We'd better sit down," he suggested.

For some reason, this apparent helpfulness irritated Maitland as Isabel's show of heartlessness had failed to do. He seated himself and returned Leonard's look with a direct one of his own, and asked the one question he was pretty sure would annoy—and perhaps embarrass—him. "The firm's bank account is at your branch, isn't it? Reade and Farrell. How does it stand?"

Again Wilson's eyes opened wide, and this time the effect was one of shocked surprise. "I hardly think I could tell you that," he said. "I hardly think it's a proper question."

"I'm here at Roger Farrell's request. You can phone Reade if you like, before you tell me."

"I think I won't bother him. In any event, I couldn't recall the exact balance. The account is running at about its usual level . . . will that satisfy you? There have been no improprieties in its conduct." He paused. "No discernible improprieties," he added.

This was all that Antony had wanted on the subject, and more than he had expected. "Did you know James Farrell was being blackmailed?" he asked, and let his eyes travel from Leonard, who said "No" gently and did not attempt to elaborate, to Isabel, who replied energetically:

"I still think it was some of Roger's nonsense."

"Could you convince the police of that? It would help him a good deal if you could do so."

"It's never easy," said Leonard, "to prove a negative."

"Particularly when the positive statement happens to be true." Antony's tone was dry. "Perhaps if I ask you if you know of any reason—"

"If my dear wife knew of any," said Wilson quickly, "I am sure that filial piety would—er—effectively seal her lips. As for me, I know nothing to the point . . . how should I? It is hardly likely that he would make any such admission, either to his bank manager or his son-in-law."

"You're talking a great deal of nonsense, Leonard," said Isabel curtly.

"Do you think so, my dear? But Maitland, I am sure, sees the point of what I say. Even if he is becoming a little annoyed with me."

"Knowledge can often be obtained indirectly," said Antony, whose annoyance, in fact, was rapidly giving way to a rather grim amusement. Now, of this odd pair, which was the dominant partner? He thought suddenly that Isabel was playing a part—"wife of a successful banker"—and that it was this alter ego of hers who had bought and furnished the house, purchased her dress, and dictated the intolerant self-respect which showed so clearly in every word she uttered. And in these respects, Leonard deferred to her. But if you could get down to fundamentals . . .

That, it seemed, was not to be permitted. "Oh, I'm sure you're right," said Wilson. "By someone with an alert, penetrating mind. Now, ask anybody if they'd have made me a branch manager if I'd been that sort of person. Head Office, perhaps; they've room for one or two brains there. But much more likely a branch accountant . . . they're the chaps who do all the work, you know, and when *I* did that job everything was in a quite appalling muddle and we worked until eleven o'clock every night."

"So they promoted you, I suppose?"

"But, of course!" Leonard told him. "After six months," he added complacently. And then, perhaps softened by the success of his diversion, he went back without prompting to the original question. "I should have thought Reade would be a better source of information concerning my revered father-in-law's activities. Unless, of course, he had a reason for keeping quiet."

"I saw him this afternoon—" Antony began, but before he could get any further Isabel interrupted him.

"Are you saying my father was a criminal?" she asked her husband angrily.

"Oh, no. It might easily have been some other type of indiscretion," said Leonard in his misleadingly gentle way; and, surprisingly, she flushed and was silent. "I wonder why it should interest you, Maitland," Wilson went on. "I should have thought it would have been a point of academic interest only, to the defense."

"We have to know what to expect," said Antony. "Besides, there was someone else concerned—"

"A woman?"

"No. Another man who had a motive."

"But if Grainger was a blackmailer, a hundred people may have had a motive for killing him. The question—surely?—is one of opportunity."

That brought it straight back to Roger Farrell and, incidentally, annoyed Antony again, even though he knew the statement to be a true one. "A note was made of the time and place where payment was to be made," he said deliberately, "and the nature of the appointment could easily have been recognized by a man who had himself been the subject of one of Grainger's demands."

"Does that affect the issue?"

"I think it does. The note was left in Roger Farrell's room on the afternoon of his mother's funeral, and three people had the chance to see it. Hubert Denning, Sam Reade and yourself."

Isabel Wilson started to say, "Really, Mr. Maitland—" but both men ignored her, and the protest trailed into silence. Leonard's eyes were opened very wide again; brown eyes, with a mildness as deceiving as the affability of his tone.

"So one of us," he said quietly, "has been elected proxy? Are you sincere about that, I wonder? Or is it just a trick?"

"No deception at all," said Antony. But the suggestion was too near what Superintendent Briggs had said for him to relish it overmuch.

"Well, that raises quite a new train of thought. Doesn't it?" he added, glancing at his wife.

"If you mean Roger may be innocent after all—"

"I haven't quite reached that point yet," her husband told her, frowning, and looked back at Maitland again. "I still don't know why James was being blackmailed," he said.

"Or anything about the threats that were made to Mrs. Winifred Farrell?"

"Obviously not." But the denial didn't satisfy Isabel, who said with all her usual energy:

"Poor Mother. Even she wouldn't have been so silly," and for a moment Antony was diverted by the choice of words, or perhaps it was her tone that suggested a lack of sympathy. He put the thought aside for future consideration and said reflectively:

"A diamond worth a thousand pounds. She wouldn't have given it to him for love." And again Isabel flushed, and again he didn't know whether it was anger or embarrassment.

131

"Come, my dear." Leonard sounded amused. "Mr. Maitland isn't suggesting anything improper." He turned to look at Antony again. "To get back to your thesis—" he said.

"You mean, to the fact that Roger didn't shoot Grainger." Now, why had he put it like that, as if he were sure?

"You implied that you thought . . . someone else might have done it." It was the first time that Leonard had sounded hesitant, and it seemed altogether an insufficient reason for Antony to lose his temper again.

"It f-follows—doesn't it?—on my p-premise?"

"One of the three men you named?"

Anger was a luxury, and just now he couldn't afford it. "I was merely demonstrating a possibility. There may well be others."

"Anyone in London." The sarcasm in his voice was even more marked now; but oddly, considering the suggestion that had been made, he did not sound altogether unfriendly. "So far," he said, "our answers to your questions don't seem to have been particularly helpful."

"We'll try again then. Can you remember the summer months, five years ago?"

"Five years?" asked Isabel. She sounded suspicious, as though there might be some trick about the question.

"1958. Your parents took their holiday in May. They went to Teneriffe, I'm told."

"Oh, that summer. What about it?"

"Was there any change in their routine?"

"How could I possibly remember that? Unless it was that they took their holidays so early. That was unusual."

"Was there any special reason?"

"Mother felt like it, that's all. She said they enjoyed themselves thoroughly," said Isabel, and somehow the very triteness of the phrase convinced Antony that further questions on this subject would be futile. He remarked instead, "A man named Cooper," and looked vaguely from one of his companions to the other as he spoke.

"I don't know anyone . . . do you, Leonard?"

"I think he means your parents' friends. Don't you?" Wilson asked.

"Yes." There was a pause, and then he prompted gently, "His name was in your father's diary. He lunched with him at the Savoy in August that year."

Again there was the doubtful look. "I think you should tell me why—" but Wilson interrupted impatiently:

"The other man who might have had a motive? You'd better tell him, Isabel, if you really remember."

"He had a peculiar name."

"Vaughan," said Antony helpfully.

"Yes, but he called himself 'Von.' I remember that very well, because before Mother met him he telephoned, and she assumed he was a German—von Kuyper, or something like that—and she thought how well he spoke English but he must have learned it in America. It wasn't until Dad phoned the number he had left that he found who he really was."

"And who was he, really?"

"A Canadian."

"Oh, that one," said Wilson, in a tone of enlightenment. "Mr. Farrell didn't know him, and didn't want to, I gather."

"No, but that was because he didn't like being thanked. Dad never said . . . even Mother didn't know until this Mr. Cooper told her . . . but he had a brother who was drowned and Dad had nearly died himself trying to rescue him."

"When was this?"

"A long time ago. Long before the war."

Antony found himself frowning.

"Does that upset your calculations?" asked Leonard. He didn't sound as if this would cause him any great distress.

"Don't worry, I haven't any. Cooper was here on business, then?"

"No, he'd come to live in England. I think Mother said he'd retired."

"That makes sense," said Wilson. "Dollars!"

"Yes, I see." Antony paused, undecided; but Isabel was going on with her explanation. She seemed to have taken her husband's request surprisingly to heart. "It seems an odd thing to do, after all that time. But someone had written to tell him about his brother's death, and how Dad tried to save him; and I suppose he wrote then, though Mother didn't remember it—it was the year we moved to Wimbledon Common, and I expect she was busy—but when he was coming over he thought he'd like to look Dad up."

"Had the brother been a friend of your father's?" There was a sudden sharpness in Maitland's tone, as though a thought had struck him, and Leonard looked at him curiously.

"No. From what Mother said he wasn't living in England. It might have been a holiday, or business."

"Do you know where the accident happened?" Maitland asked.

"I wasn't very interested, I'm afraid."

"Well, which year did you move to Wimbledon?"

"That was in 1933. I can hardly remember the house we had before."

And that seemed to be that, and probably the only interesting thing about it was the fact that Wilson had wanted his wife to continue; whenever they exchanged looks there had been encouragement in his. Most likely he saw in the story a distraction from more awkward questions.

"Would you say Roger got on well with his partner?" Antony asked abruptly. Isabel looked as though she saw a personal affront in the change of subject.

"I've never heard of any dissension."

"But the Reades disapproved of his marriage, did they not?"

"Oh, *that,*" said Wilson. "I thought you were talking of business policy."

"But in any case," Isabel put in, "it was just because they were so young."

"And the bitterness passed?"

"Not altogether, and I don't think it's quite reasonable, you know. I'm not trying to uphold Roger's actions, but during the war, I believe, people were more than usually inclined to act on impulse."

"And the girl died while he was abroad?"

"Yes." She paused and looked at her husband. "I didn't see him again until two years later. By that time, he'd got over it."

"I wonder—" said Antony. Leonard Wilson was looking at him quizzically.

"I hadn't the pleasure of Roger's acquaintance at that time," he said. "But I don't imagine he was ever particularly communicative."

"Perhaps not. How does he get on with Mr. Denning?"

"Well enough, I think." But Isabel shook her head.

"Uncle Hubert likes his own way," she said positively. "And so does Roger."

"That's true enough," her husband agreed.

"The day of Winifred Farrell's funeral—"

"Are we getting back to this mysterious note again? In Roger's bedroom, you said? I didn't see one, or notice anybody pick anything up to read."

"Were you all three in the room together?" Antony asked.

"When we first arrived at the flat. We were all dressed up to the nines, you know, and we'd been to Paddington after we came away from the cemetery, and were feeling rather hot and grimy. Afterward, we were chatting and having a drink. I don't remember anyone's movements."

"Not even your own?"

"Certainly not my own."

"Do you remember, Mrs. Wilson?"

"Of course I don't."

"Then my remaining questions are for you," Antony said, turning to Leonard again. "Did you know Martin Grainger?"

"I know Galloway's Chop House." He paused; the precise wording seemed to be important. "I've seen a man there whom I take to be Grainger, but I can't recall that I've ever done more than pass the time of day with him."

"I see. Did you go there with James Farrell?"

"Now and then."

"And during the past year?"

"Once or twice a month, I should say."

"Thank you." Antony got up as he spoke. "You've been very

kind," he said and was immediately annoyed with himself for this concession to formality. He looked down at Isabel and said with a faint smile, "Need I tell you not to worry?"

Leonard followed him out into the hall and closed the door carefully behind him. "You mustn't misjudge her, you know," he said gently.

Maitland swung round. He couldn't have said what quality it was in Wilson that affected him so strongly, but when he spoke his bluntness was deliberate. "She's more concerned for the proprieties than for her brother, don't you think?"

Wilson smiled, and his voice was amused. "I wouldn't say you aren't right, but—in all the circumstances, you know—I must say I approve her choice of priorities."

"D-do you, indeed?"

"I think so. But don't get me wrong. I don't like Roger, but I'd much prefer to see him free of suspicion, even apart from the fact that his arrest might prove an embarrassment."

"Should I admire your magnanimity?" Antony pulled open the front door, but paused on the threshold and turned for a final word. "I'm sorry if I misled Mrs. Wilson. This scandal she's so afraid of: short of a confession from the murderer within the next couple of hours, there isn't a hope of avoiding it."

And that, he reflected savagely as he walked down the mews, ought to hold the pair of them for a while.

He found Jenny hovering solicitously over his dinner, persuaded her that ten more minutes wouldn't quite reduce it to a cinder, and went into the living room to find himself a drink. "Meg wouldn't believe me," he said, collapsing onto the sofa and stretching out his legs, "but if marrying Roger means seeing much of her in-laws she'd much better call the whole thing off."

"Does he want to marry her?" said Jenny. "Meg seems to think—"

"That's your department, love, but I should imagine he does." He paused, staring down at the hearth where Jenny had fixed the electric fire from the bedroom because the evening had turned so cold. "I wonder, did Geoffrey ring up."

"Yes, he did. He said they had a frightful time at Scotland Yard, but Roger hadn't been arrested," said Jenny, paraphrasing freely.

"They haven't—? They must have done!"

"Geoffrey was surprised, too. If it meant they'd changed their minds . . . but he was sure it wasn't that."

"I'm sure, too."

"At least, it's a respite." Her gray eyes were fixed on him hopefully. "Can you do anything, Antony? I've said this before, but . . . it's different when it's someone you know."

"I'm sorry, Jenny."

"You see, it's Meg. I don't want her to be hurt." She saw his expression and added urgently, "Antony, what is it?"

"I'm afraid . . . you can't live other people's lives for them, love," he said, and saw her look of surprise at the roughness of his tone. But he couldn't say, "she'll be arrested, too." He couldn't tell Jenny that, and watch the light fade in her eyes and know that he was hurting her. She had always loved Meg, ever since the first time she had come to Kempenfeldt Square in the skimpy navy-blue coat with rabbit fur at the neck, and a navy beret worn at the most unfashionable angle. And, of course, Jenny was right . . . it's different when it's someone you know.

"What did Geoffrey say?" he inquired.

"Just what I told you. And he's coming tomorrow morning at eleven, and would you tell Uncle Nick—"

Antony grimaced. "What jolly fun!" he remarked bitterly. "What happened to him, by the way? I rather expected—"

"He went to the theater with Meg, and he promised to take her home afterwards," she explained.

"Yes, of course, I'm glad about that. Though his fondness for her isn't doing anything to improve his temper." He paused and then said abruptly, as if he had reached a decision, "She thinks Roger's guilty, you know."

"Don't you, Antony? Don't you really?"

"Not any more." He was surprised by his own certainty, and even a little distrustful of it, because just now at the Wilsons' he hadn't been sure at all. "I thought you liked him," he said.

"I do. But that doesn't mean—"

"Don't *you* start being sensible, Jenny. I don't think I could bear it."

"The man who was killed was a blackmailer," she pointed out.

"And the constables last night? And the man in the car?" And as he spoke, as though on a cue, the telephone rang. And they both sat and looked at it for a moment in a hostile way, before Antony got up and walked across to the desk in the corner.

"Mr. Maitland?" Of all the people who might have been phoning him, Inspector Sykes would have been a long way down any list of probabilities he might have made out. Antony mastered an impulse to put the receiver down again . . . or to say he was dead . . . or the Czechoslovakian Embassy . . . or just the wrong number.

"Good evening, Inspector," he said, and heard his own voice stiff and unfriendly. There came an unmistakable chuckle from the other end of the line.

"I thought you'd 'appen be feeling like that," said Sykes indulgently. "And seeing as how you do, I'd like to say I appreciated your discretion this morning. Though not, perhaps, your self-control," he added in a ruminative tone.

"Is that what you rang up to tell me?" asked Antony, diverted . . . as much perhaps by Sykes's deliberate lapse into his native broadness of speech as by what he said.

"Not only that," the detective told him, declining to be hurried.

"Well, then?"

"It's just something I thought you might like to know. You'll remember I told you we were looking for a particular person in connection with the breaking and entering job at Grainger's office," Sykes went on.

"Yes, of course. Have you found him?"

"You might put it that way, Mr. Maitland. But I'm afraid he isn't in a position to help us, except perhaps in a negative sort of way. You saw him yourself this afternoon, for that matter, in the back of Mr. Farrell's car."

Antony uttered a brief malediction. "Then why the hell didn't you arrest Roger Farrell?" he asked. But, of course, Sykes wasn't going to give him a reply to that. "By the way, is Briggs still hoping to catch me faking evidence?"

If he'd hoped to throw the detective off his stride he was disappointed. "He wouldn't have been so blunt, you know, if he hadn't been so angry," Sykes told him. He paused and added, "Bates is still alive," as though the thought followed naturally on what he had just said, as indeed it did.

"That's one thing to be thankful for, at least."

"And as for the superintendent—"

"Don't tell me he didn't mean what he said, Inspector. We both know him better than that."

Sykes made no attempt to deny this. Instead he remarked, "There might be something you forgot to tell us, Mr. Maitland, being out of temper yourself this morning," and the amused note was back in his voice again.

"If I could tell you anything about last night I would, and gladly. Did you find the diaries helpful?"

"Not a bit."

"Well, what I've learned about Roger Farrell's affairs is . . . for the defense," said Antony.

"Just as I expected." Sykes heaved a sigh.

"But as you've already given me one piece of information—"

"The reward of virtue, Mr. Maitland."

"Well, I'll be discreet about this too, if you'll tell me. About this gang—"

"The men who've been specializing in shipments of bullion?"

"Yes, what about them, Inspector? How long have they been operating? And where? And how many of them are there? And—"

"Wait a bit, wait a bit. We know very little really. The present series of robberies," said Sykes slowly, "has gone on for at least eight years, and not very frequently. I say 'series' because of the similarity in technique, which couldn't be coincidental. One or two hauls a year, well planned, well organized . . . and shoot your way out if there's anyone in the way."

"Have there been many deaths?"

"Too many. I think the total is seven with the guard this week."

"Any arrests?"

"No. Two years ago, near Southampton, the getaway car was smashed up and we got back the 'takings.' We made out there must have been just the driver, and he was injured, or why leave the gold behind? Anyway, we never found him, and though all the prints on the car are on record, we've never been able to match them up."

"The car?"

"Stolen. No help there," said Sykes sadly.

"I see. But do you think . . . an organization with one man running it?"

"For what my ideas are worth, Mr. Maitland, I think so. Up and down the country they've worked it, and never a clue that didn't fizzle out before it got halfway to anywhere. And not a hint to be had of where they're holed up between jobs, or how they get the stuff out of the country. I'd take my oath they're not even known to us, and there's been enough pressure on our usual informers, too. Might be a gang of ghosts," grumbled Sykes, obviously with a sense of grievance. "And what's more, if the same chap hasn't been operating one kind of racket or another for twenty-five years now, I'm much mistaken."

"Twenty-five years!"

"Since the war, anyway. The black market offered great rewards, you know. And great temptations. And afterwards . . . there are always opportunities, when you know where to look for them."

"Yes, but—"

"At one time it was the post office," said Sykes, ignoring the note of protest. "Registered mail and the like. And there were a few hauls of diamonds, but that's not so easy to keep up, you know. Like snatching the week's wages—the precautions catch up with you after a while."

"Yes, I suppose—"

"It's just an idea," said Sykes. "But it's as if he left his signature, Mr. Maitland. You get a feeling about things like that."

"I can see you do," said Antony. He sounded a little breathless. "Any more questions?"

"No . . . nothing else. I'm grateful, Inspector."

"Roger Farrell couldn't have been involved all that time ago, but his father could," Sykes pointed out. He seemed to find Antony's tone puzzling, and in some way unsatisfactory.

"Yes. Yes, I know that." All he wanted was to get away and think this over. "Give my love to the superintendent," he said. "And thanks again."

When he had eaten he phoned Roger Farrell. It was half-past ten by that time, and after the events of the day he thought perhaps the other man might be showing some evidence of fatigue. But there was nothing to be learned from his voice; he sounded a little surly, but as energetic as ever.

"I'm still here, you see."

"So Horton told me. Roger—"

"Well?"

"Had your mother an address book?"

"What the—?"

"Had she?"

"There's a Christmas card list in the drawer of her writing table," said Roger grudgingly. "If I haven't thrown it away."

"I want the address of a chap called Cooper, Vaughan Cooper. Your parents met him in 1958."

"His name was in the diary, wasn't it? But I don't see—"

"If you're not tired, Roger, I am." This time the message seemed to get through. Farrell said:

"Right," in a businesslike way and put down the receiver with a regrettable lack of gentleness. There was a long pause before he came back to the phone again, and Antony had time to ponder again the chances of success. If Mrs. Farrell had been the kind of woman he imagined, careful, perhaps even over-punctilious in the most casual relationships . . . "He lives at Virginia Water," said Roger's voice in his ear.

Antony wrote down the address. "I'll see you tomorrow," he promised.

"Wait a bit. Meg was with you . . . is she all right?"

"There are times when I could wring her neck," said Antony sourly. "But she isn't a coward." He heard Roger laugh.

"She isn't, is she? I won't keep you then . . ."

Antony cradled the receiver and sat looking down at the address scrawled across the blotting pad. He could get in touch with the chap now, if he hadn't moved, and with luck he'd be able to arrange a meeting; and when he'd seen him he'd know . . . everything . . . or nothing? He realized suddenly that he was afraid of pushing the matter further. There was a question he should have asked Roger, but perhaps he hadn't wanted to remember. He turned and met Jenny's eyes, and got up stiffly.

"Will you do something for me, while I take another look at my notes? Get on to Directory Inquiries. . . ."

THE DEAD MAN'S NAME WAS ELLIS. IT WAS IN ALL THE papers next morning, together with the fact that he had been found "by the police" in the back of a sports car which was parked in a London square. This reticence might have been expected to do something to pacify Sir Nicholas, but if Antony anticipated any relaxation of his uncle's hostile attitude he was to be disappointed.

Sir Nicholas was growling to himself when Horton arrived and Antony went downstairs to join them in the study, but at least he had tidied the papers relating to the arson case so far as to heap them together on one corner of the desk . . . a rather shaky-looking Tower of Babel, which was obviously going to take the first excuse to fall down again.

Geoffrey Horton was a solicitor, and well known to both Sir Nicholas and his nephew. He was several years younger than Maitland, had red hair and a cheerful disposition, and the extent of his criminal practice, which he had been carefully cultivating for some time, had made it natural for his partner to pass the conduct of the case over to him. Mr. Armstrong had done so with relief; his own experience was extensive, but not in the courts. And he had a strong feeling that if he had to depart from custom and defend a client accused of murder, Roger Farrell was the last man he would choose for the experiment. Geoffrey was more confident, but this morning there was something a little half-hearted about his smile; he was eyeing Sir Nicholas rather as a nervous recruit to a bomb-disposal unit might eye the first mechanism entrusted to him. And inevitably Antony was amused by the sight, and his spirits lifted a little.

"As there has been no arrest," Sir Nicholas was saying when he went into the study, "I cannot see why you wish to involve me in your discussions." This was extremely unfair; he'd have had plenty to say later if he'd been excluded at this stage. But his nephew's arrival seemed to distract him from his grievance. "Why hasn't Farrell been arrested?" he asked sharply, without allowing any time to greet the visitor.

"I asked Sykes last night. He wouldn't tell me."

"Surely you're not going to let a little thing like that discourage you."

"You don't like guesses, sir." The Tower of Babel tilted dangerously as Sir Nicholas brought his hand down heavily on the desk. "Making the connection between Farrell and the man who was suspected of opening Grainger's safe ought to have removed their last doubt—"

"So much is obvious," said his uncle.

"—so I can only suppose they're becoming ambitious and want to establish Roger's connection with the bullion robberies too. Or, more likely, they hope he'll lead them to his accomplices." He picked up the pile of papers as he spoke and dumped them out of harm's way in a corner of the room. Sir Nicholas waited until he came back to stand between desk and window before he said:

"You don't believe that such a connection exists." He sounded accusing.

"No, I don't, though the police may be right about James Farrell. What I don't like is the general assumption that whatever he was up to, he'd have been more likely to confide in Roger than in anyone else." His casual tone might have argued a lack of interest; now he looked down at Horton and gave him an encouraging grin. "I'm sorry, Geoffrey, that doesn't make it any easier, does it?"

"At least it will stop me lamenting the fact that my client refuses to consider anything but a straight 'not guilty' plea. We can hardly plead justification with the whole countryside strewn with superfluous corpses," said Horton sadly.

"But I don't think he's responsible for any of them," Antony protested.

Sir Nicholas was looking at him oddly. "You sound very positive," he said.

"Yes, sir, I am."

"And that means—"

"It means we've got to prove it. And what I'm afraid of at the moment is that some more evidence will turn up . . . for the prosecution, you know."

Sir Nicholas picked up a pencil and began to sketch on the blotting pad. "What do you mean?" he asked, not looking up.

"If you'll bear with the assumption that the murderer saw Meg's note—"

"I am already subscribing to the unlikely premise that Roger Farrell is innocent," said Sir Nicholas tartly.

"Well, then . . . I think the murderer felt this was too good a chance to miss, to catch Grainger unawares, and I don't suppose he cared that Roger might be suspected. But I don't think there was a deliberate attempt at a frame-up."

"Probably not." There was a dryness in his tone that Antony didn't like.

"It's different now," he said. "There could be no other reason for leaving Ellis's body in the back of the Jensen than a deliberate attempt to implicate Roger. Either from malice or to ensure his own safety, the person concerned has decided on a course of action. It could lead anywhere."

"It could lead to our being laughed out of court," said his uncle. He sat back to admire his sketch. "Such a convenient argument," he added. "I wonder how many times it's been tried."

Antony ignored this deliberate attempt to depress his spirits still further. "Did you learn anything from Farrell's interview with the police?" he asked his friend.

Geoffrey looked at him warily. "Don't jump to conclusions," he warned, "but this new evidence you're talking about may already have turned up."

"Don't be cryptic, Geoffrey. Has it or hasn't it?"

"The police have taken a heavy-caliber rifle from the cottage at Grunning's Hole for testing. A .470 double rifle, to be exact. Farrell professes not to know whether it belonged to his father or not."

"He would," said Antony, rather more irritably than the point seemed to warrant.

"There was another rifle there, and the local police took that when they searched the place on Thursday, but it wasn't the right size. The thing is, it's no use our saying this one is a plant if it turns out to be the one that shot Grainger. They know damn well it wasn't there before, but they think—of course—that Farrell took it down with him on Friday night."

"Of course," echoed Antony. Sir Nicholas broke his pencil point and muttered something but made no more open comment.

"They didn't say that in so many words," Geoffrey said, "but it's fairly obvious—"

"And not particularly helpful," said Sir Nicholas, abandoning his search for another pencil and clasping his hands on the desk in front of him.

"Not at all helpful," agreed Geoffrey amiably. He seemed to feel happier now the discussion was under way. "Perhaps you'll like this better. Ellis was shot at close range with a .38 automatic. They haven't found the gun."

"It seems we have still something to be thankful for. When did this happen?"

"Most likely between midnight and six o'clock on Saturday morning, and probably not more than an hour before he was bundled into the back of the Jensen."

"Well, that's vague enough," said Antony ungratefully.

"There's one other thing. He'd been knocked about before he was shot. Probably some hours before."

"Now, why—?"

"Search me. There was a good deal of bruising on his arms and a particularly heavy one on his jaw." He hesitated and then added in an expressionless voice, "You'd notice, I dare say—"

"That Farrell's hand was grazed." In his turn, Antony spoke

evenly. "Yes, I noticed that." And he added, with a sudden spurt of anger, "What d-difference does it m-make? You don't b-believe him anyway, do you?"

"I'm trying to keep an open mind," said Geoffrey with dignity.

"Yes, I'm sorry." And I'm not playing fair, he thought, but I don't *know* Roger lied to me.

"He says he grazed his knuckles on the car door, where the lock sticks out," said Horton. His tone did not quite conceal a sense of grievance at being offered this unlikely story.

Sir Nicholas had been watching his nephew's face. "It could be true," he remarked, and drew his own conclusions when he saw the look—half relieved, half guilty—with which Antony received this surprising comment. Then he turned back to Horton again. "Where did Ellis die?" he asked.

"They think at Grunning's Hole. Nobody heard the shot, but that doesn't help Farrell either; the cottage is well away from the village."

"I suppose it's unlikely that *our* gunman rushed down there and shot him," said Antony. "Well, one thing's certain, it's no use asking anyone for an alibi. Our man has the resources of a big organization at his command. I don't suppose he even shot Grainger himself," he added in an aggrieved tone.

"A master criminal," said Sir Nicholas consideringly. "I might have known, my dear boy," he added with an air of cordiality that was utterly misleading, "that I could rely on you sooner or later to broaden my education in this way."

Antony grinned. But, "the situation isn't of my making," he protested.

"You think not? Well, I'll concede your 'gang,'" said his uncle with an air of distaste, "because *our* burglar was certainly one of them and I can't think of any other reason for his taking an interest in us. But what if you follow the trail and it leads you back to Farrell?"

"It won't." He moved a little to stand at the corner of the desk. "Sykes got the diaries from Jenny. Did I tell you that, sir?"

"You did." He sounded indifferent, but Geoffrey's tone betrayed a greater interest.

"Did you learn anything from them?" he asked.

"I don't know. How can I know? A certain amount of background information about James Farrell's acquaintance, and it ought to mean something . . . if we're right, it's cost enough." He turned his head, and for a moment his eyes met his uncle's. "He's still alive . . . the third policeman, I mean. But they don't feel he's out of danger."

"I know," said Sir Nicholas. "I phoned the hospital too." He paused and then added deliberately, "Why mention the diaries, if you're so vague about their meaning?"

"There's one thing I wondered about." Antony had pulled a rather ragged envelope from his pocket and was scowling at it. "If the diamonds really denote blackmail payments, the first one was made in September, 1958." He glanced up and saw his uncle's expression, and a rather dogged note crept into his voice. "Farrell might have given himself away to Grainger by talking with any of the three men we're interested in . . . all right, sir, *I'm* interested in," he added irritably. "But what prompted the conversation? That's what I'd like to know."

"If they were laying plans—" said Geoffrey.

"I know, but that's some more of the guesswork you both dislike so much . . . that James Farrell was involved with the gang," Antony pointed out. "If he wasn't . . . well, that's guessing too, but at least it might lead somewhere."

"Well . . . where?"

"I don't know. I've nothing to go on but a couple of dates, things that might tie-in together, you know. And a man who's coming to see me at noon today."

"Who?" snapped Geoffrey. He found this vagueness unnerving.

"A man named Cooper, a retired accountant from Nova Scotia."

"Oh, for heaven's sake!" said Horton, losing patience. "Say what you mean."

"But I don't know what I mean," Antony pointed out, with a misleadingly lucid air.

Sir Nicholas, in desperation, picked up the blunted pencil and went back to his drawing. He knew the signs, and if Antony hadn't some idea in his head . . . and most likely something foolish . . .

Meg had spent a restless night, so it was no penance to get up early. She went down to the corner and came back with a number of papers, each of a rather more sensational character than the ones that would later be delivered to her door. By the time the kettle had boiled she was pretty sure there was no news in any of them of Roger's arrest. Sir Nicholas and Jenny had both promised faithfully to let her know, and she believed them but she wanted to be sure.

She wondered for a moment whether there was some new evidence; perhaps the police had changed their minds after all. But she didn't really believe that, she had no facility at all for self-deception. She didn't really understand what was happening, so much seemed to have grown out of Martin Grainger's death, as if that one act had been the catalyst that set all the other events in motion. But that had nothing to do with Roger; she wasn't even sure any more that he had shot Grainger, though once it had seemed so obvious. She had gone over it so many times, how he had looked when he spoke of his mother's death, and then that Tuesday evening when he had told her that the blackmailer was dead too.

But it was too late to worry about that now; she blamed herself for having helped him, and if he hadn't killed Grainger after all it would be a relief to her conscience as well as to her heart. Antony would have been appalled if he had realized the clarity with which she viewed the situation. As a public figure for many years, there was nothing she could have learned from him about the results of adverse publicity, and she had no illusions as to how her story was going to sound in court. She thought she would be telling it as a witness, not as one of the accused; but it is to be doubted whether she would have found even this latter prospect more daunting than the one she foresaw.

She made tea and drank two cups slowly; and thought it would be sensible to have some toast as well, only she couldn't face it. From habit she rinsed the cup and tidied the kitchen before she left it. As she went back into the bedroom she recognized suddenly the emotion that was gripping her, and smiled a little wryly at her own expense. Stage fright! Well, at least, she knew how to deal with that. You ignored it, and after a while it went away.

Because she was so early she made her preparations slowly, and it was nearly half-past ten when she arrived at Leinster Court. The doorman obviously knew her from her previous visit; she thought suddenly there wasn't much he'd miss. She smiled and said "Good morning" brightly, and went past him to the lift with a confident air.

There was a longish pause after she rang the bell of the Farrells' flat. (She had never met Mrs. Farrell, but—like Antony—she had a clear picture in her mind, and thought of this as the place she had lived, rather than as Roger's home.) And then the door opened and Roger stood on the threshold blinking at her, and suddenly the stage fright vanished, to be replaced by a sort of bubbling self-confidence that was quite unlike anything she had ever experienced before.

Roger, meanwhile, was eyeing her doubtfully. It might have been no more than dissatisfaction with his own appearance: he was tousled and unshaven, and though he had put on a dressing gown his feet were still bare. Meg's chin went up. "I want to talk to you," she said.

He gave one look at the door across the landing and backed rather hurriedly into his own hall. "Come in then," he invited. Meg stalked past him into the sitting room.

"The place is a pig sty," she announced.

Roger looked round a little wildly. "It's quite clean," he protested, ignoring the note of tragedy she had managed to infuse even into the hackneyed phrase.

"And a fine chore 'twill have been to the lass who had the cleaning of it," she told him severely and marched across the room to fling open the window. "You could at least have emptied the ash trays," she went on, and as she turned her militant eye came to rest on her companion. "As for you, Roger Farrell—" she said.

"I overslept."

"Then you'd better go and get dressed while I make you some breakfast."

"But, Meg, you shouldn't be here."

It was as if the words broke a spell. He saw her flush, and

watched—with a quite painful awareness—the crumbling of the pathetic wall of make-believe she had built about herself. But her head remained high and her eyes never dropped from his own. "I came," she said, "to find out if that's true."

"My dear—"

"Don't cozen me, Roger," she flashed at him, and the unlikeliness of the word momentarily distracted his attention from what she was saying. "If you don't want me, that's all right. But you've got to tell me so."

"It's just . . . you've got to understand, Meg . . . it isn't fair to you."

"What isn't fair?"

"You're involved in this mess. I know that. I'm sorry. But you needn't come in any deeper."

"Don't be a fool, Roger. It's too late to try to protect me."

He shook his head at her. "It's too late," he repeated. But now the words meant something different. To Meg—but admittedly her thoughts inclined to extravagance—they sounded like a knell.

"You were lying to me then? When you said you loved me . . . that was a lie? Say it, Roger, say it!"

"Things are different now," he told her desperately.

"Things? Or you?"

"I don't know . . . I don't know, Meg." He took a step toward her, and against her will she put her hands into his. "My father loved my mother . . . and broke her heart in the end."

"I'm really very tough, Roger."

"Are you, indeed?" He laughed and pulled her toward him. "There was a song," he said, "before your time, Meg, you wouldn't remember—" He broke off and stood looking down at her for a moment, and then said in a changed voice, "That's another thing, you're not the first love of my life, you know."

"If you think I'm a fool—" said Meg, and began to struggle futilely against the strength of his grip on her wrists.

"You are, my dear, if you think I'm about to edify you with the story of my life. Stop fighting me, Meg, and listen. Did you know I'd been married?"

"You never told me."

"To tell you the truth, I never thought about it. It's so long ago it seems like a dream. We were both nineteen, and I told Maitland the other day I'd never regretted it, but I don't know whether that's altogether true. If she'd stayed at home, as her parents wanted, she wouldn't have been in Putney when that bomb fell. So you see—"

"You're thinking of yourself as a sort of jinx," said Meg accusingly.

"Do you think I'm so far wrong?"

"I was in love with a man once," said Meg. "And you might say that was a tragedy, because he married someone else, and he put on weight, and had five children—"

"What does that prove?"

"Nothing. I'm telling you, what's past doesn't matter. Not what happened to you, or to me, or to anyone."

"I don't think logic's your strong point, my dear."

"Isn't it? I'm just trying to tell you, I've been hurt twice, and I'm not afraid."

"Twice?" As he spoke, his hands tightened.

"The other was . . . nothing. He never knew."

"And did he . . . marry . . . and grow fat?"

"He was married already."

"Well . . . the cad!" He sounded indignant, but when she looked up at him his eyes were laughing.

"Don't you see?" she said desperately. "Don't you see? If you say again that I don't belong here you'll just be proving it's true—"

" 'For each man kills the thing he loves'? Is that what you mean, Meg?"

"I only know . . . you'll be hurting me *now*." He wasn't laughing any longer. She added urgently, "Roger, was that the song?"

"Nothing quite so poetical, I'm afraid." He stood looking down at her for a moment with a rather quizzical expression. "If I let go your hands, will you hit me?" he asked.

"It all depends," said Meg crossly.

"Well, I'll have to risk it." His hands moved to her shoulders; he held her a little away from him, rather as though he were admiring a portrait. "A silly song, Meg, and I don't think you'd approve of the words."

"What are they, then?"

He didn't answer immediately, but pulled her toward him again and put his arms round her. " 'Kiss me, my dear, and so let us part,' " he quoted, and the mockery in his voice might have been for both of them, or only for himself.

"The worst kind of sentimentality," said Meg breathlessly, but she didn't have time for any more. Roger laughed again and kissed her.

GEOFFREY WAS STILL AT KEMPENFELDT SQUARE WHEN
Vaughan Cooper arrived, but he disclaimed—rather more forcefully than was necessary—any desire to be present at the interview. Antony did not press the matter and saw him to the front
door before he went to rescue the visitor from solitary confinement
in the little-used drawing room. "You'd better come upstairs," he
invited, "before you freeze to death."

"Now, don't you be worrying about me. I've lived here five
years, and I guess I've gotten acclimatized," Cooper protested, but
he showed some alacrity in obeying the summons. He was a small,
wiry man, with a lined brown face, a lively eye, and a quick way of
moving, and he looked, to Antony's secret dismay, less like *deus
ex machina* than anyone he was putting so much trust in had a
right to do.

"It was good of you to come," he said again when they were
settled by the fire upstairs, and Cooper had accepted Scotch as a
substitute for the rye that had been his first, though tentative,
choice. Jenny was curled up in her favorite corner of the sofa; she
prided herself on being able to produce a meal without a great
deal of last-minute fussing, and besides that, she was curious. She
wasn't quite sure what Antony wanted to hear, but she thought
she'd be able to tell from his expression whether the story pleased

him. The visitor relaxed and beamed at her in a friendly way before replying.

"I'm not too clear what I can do for you," he said. "But you surely made it sound urgent."

"That's why I asked you to come here, wasting your time, rather than my own." Antony grinned at him disarmingly.

"This problem you spoke of, just what's the trouble?"

"Murder," said Antony. "And a man I think is going to be wrongly accused. And a girl . . . who's fond of him." He kept his eyes fixed on Cooper as he spoke, but he wondered if Jenny guessed how nearly the last sentence had come out differently.

Vaughan Cooper looked startled but also a little skeptical. "I've said I'll do what I can, no need to spin me a yarn," he said.

"I'm not . . . it's deadly serious—"

"I don't know anything about a murder, that's for sure."

"No, of course. It's motive I'm looking for, and I think it may go back a good many years. The trouble is, I can't explain *how* you can help me. It's the wildest of guesses on my part to think you can." He was talking earnestly now, trying to get over his own sense of urgency, but afterward he wondered if Cooper had even heard the last part of what he said.

"A good many years . . . how many?" he asked.

"Thirty." Antony sounded apologetic. Put into words, the wildness of his ideas seemed more apparent than ever.

"And the name of the man you spoke of? The man who may be accused."

"Farrell. Not the man you met five years ago, his son."

"You seem to know a good deal about my affairs." This brought no reply, except for a rather vague gesture, and after a moment he added in a thoughtful tone, "I owe James Farrell some gratitude."

"He died last year."

"And that very fine lady, his wife?"

"She's dead, too . . . a couple of weeks ago."

"It isn't her death—?"

"Nothing like that. You wouldn't know the man who was killed. Neither did Roger Farrell, for that matter. But—"

"Then how can I help you?"

"By telling me what you know of your brother's visit to England . . . why he was here, and how he died."

"Thirty years, you said. And that's right, my dear man, thirty years. But I don't understand."

His bewilderment was evident enough. And what was the use of trying to persuade him? "I've told you, I can't explain," Antony said and kept the irritation out of his voice well enough, but there was a frown between his eyes.

Perhaps Cooper noted the signs of strain. He smiled suddenly and said in a formal but friendly tone, "I said I'd help you, and I won't go back on that."

"Then—" But the eagerness died out of Antony's voice. He broke off and added, "I don't even know your brother's name," as though this were an insuperable obstacle.

"Roy. He was thirty-four when he died."

"And how did that happen?"

"An accident . . . didn't you know that?"

"Yes, but how soon after he came here?"

"The first weekend. He came over by sea, there wasn't all this flying in those days, and he wrote when he got settled in his hotel; but that letter didn't reach me till after the news of his death. He'd arrived safely, he said, and the weather was fine. There were a lot of exclamation points after that; it was June, but from all he'd heard he didn't expect to see the sun while he was over here. And he'd gotten himself fixed up with a weekend's sailing, which suited him fine. But before that, as I said, there was the cable. And there was a letter from this Mr. Denning."

"Hubert Denning . . . was he the owner?"

"That's right. A gaff-rigged cutter, Roy said. They went out early Saturday morning—I'm quoting Mr. Denning's letter now— and it came up rough overnight, but nothing to worry about. Early on Sunday Denning was in the galley, and the other two were on deck. He felt the lurch when they jibed, but he didn't know then it had happened accidentally. But then he heard Farrell yelling for him, and the boat was being put hard about; and when he got on deck there was no sign of Roy. He'd been steering, and the boom had swept him overboard. By what they made out he must have been knocked out, because he went down immediately. They went back to what Farrell reckoned was the place, but there was nothing to be seen. Farrell, who was a strong swimmer, went over the side and dived till he was exhausted, while Denning swept a wider area with the cutter, in case they'd been wrong about the place. He said by the time he persuaded Farrell to give up he was almost at the last gasp himself; a brave man, that was how it struck me, and quite careless of his own safety. But they never saw Roy again. Weeks later he was washed ashore. I had a communication from the coroner's office about identification—dental records, and so on. They were very emphatic it was no use my making the trip, and as Mrs. Cooper was ill at the time I was glad enough to be spared. But they established it was Roy all right, from what I heard later."

"And returned a verdict of 'accidental death'?"

"So I was told. But to go back to Mr. Denning's original letter, when I'd gotten over the shock a bit I acknowledged it, of course; and naturally enough, I wrote to James Farrell too."

"Did he reply?"

"Oh, yes. A stiff sort of letter, it was, but I could understand that. He didn't like being thanked."

"No, I suppose—" There seemed to be a bitter taste to the words. He no longer wanted to hear the rest of Cooper's story, but he'd asked for it, after all. "You met him . . . later?" he asked.

"Yes, I thought . . . I could tell from Roy's letter he was the right sort, and there are some things you don't forget. He'd moved, of course, but Mr. Denning hadn't; I got the address from him. And we met a few times, but I got the feeling he was always afraid I'd say something to embarrass him. I wouldn't, of course, I'd got his measure by then."

"He never seemed at ease with you?"

"Just that. Well, I found a place that suited me, and settled in. And that was that, really. I didn't see any more of them, but we'd exchange a card at Christmas. Until this last year, and then I didn't think of him being dead—just that they thought it was long enough."

"Yes, I see." And the other thing that had to be asked, though now he felt he knew the answer already. "Was it a business trip your brother made? Or was he on holiday?"

"Business. But, knowing Roy," he added, smiling, "he'd have managed to get the most out of it, one way and another."

"What was his business?"

"A mining engineer." The reminiscent mood seemed to have taken hold of Cooper now; for the first time he needed no prompting. "That was a job that took him about a bit, as you can imagine, though mostly in Canada. That's how he came to make his headquarters with my wife and me; being a bachelor, and liking it that way, he'd come home to us between jobs. This time he'd been asked for a report on a mine in Northern Quebec—iron ore, as far as I remember. It was being made rather a big thing of over here, from what he told me, and just before he left he said to me, 'They're not going to like it, Vaughan, they're not going to like it at all.'"

"Why was that?"

"Not the mine itself, where it was. 'A lot of greenhorns,' he said. 'A mile's a mile to them in England, and never mind what sort of ground it covers. So I'd better go over myself and put them straight,' he said. He was only home long enough to pack his things."

"And the name of the mine?"

"Abukcheech. An Indian word meaning 'mouse,' he told me, which was something I didn't know. But I remember because he made a joke of it; all that promotion, and that's what it turned out to be, a mouse."

A joke . . . yes. A rather sour joke James Farrell must have thought it. "Where was the report to be delivered?" he asked, but this time Cooper shook his head.

"That's something I don't remember, the name of the firm concerned." But easy enough to find out, Antony thought, and did it really matter? The report would have ruined Farrell, and presumably it had reached the city eventually; but by that time the stock had been sold at the height of its value. What had Reade said? Farrell's luck!

"I'm more grateful than I can say, Mr. Cooper." Jenny heard

the note of finality in his tone and went away to the kitchen. It wasn't very long before Antony joined her. "He's gone to a great deal of trouble, and I can't walk out on our luncheon party . . . but hurry things up, love, as much as you can."

"It's all ready." She pulled open the oven door and then paused for a moment, looking at him over her shoulder. "Do you know, now?" she asked.

He didn't answer directly. "I can't prove anything," he said, and sounded disconsolate.

"Then what's the rush?"

"Because I've got to try. And it's such an ugly story, Jenny." He shook his head. "Do you think Roger will thank me for telling him his father's a murderer?"

Jenny took a dish of potatoes from the oven and set them down very carefully on the tray. "Must you tell him?" she asked and looked up, her gray eyes troubled.

"It looks like a choice between that and letting him be convicted." He sighed. "But first," he said, "I've got to make him tell me the truth."

"Make him?" said Jenny doubtfully. She seemed to be giving the possibility serious consideration, and Antony laughed aloud and sounded really amused.

But after he'd had a talk with the doorman at Leinster Court that afternoon he stopped seeing anything at all funny in the situation.

In the end, Meg had provided an odd sort of combination of breakfast and lunch, and they ate in the kitchen and sat for a long time over the meal, in spite of the cramped quarters. Meg poured a third cup of coffee, which was more than she usually allowed herself. She watched Roger lighting a cigarette, and found that she was translating his actions back into mood, as she might have done in the case of a fellow actor if she was trying to assess his performance. All his movements were naturally decisive, but she thought there was a hint of nervousness too. And nothing's really settled, she thought forlornly, but perhaps that doesn't matter. The moment is good, and it may be all we'll have . . . ever. And as if he knew what was in her mind Roger put out his hand to cover hers. He was thinking how absurdly right she looked, sitting there with a tablecloth pinned round her for an apron, and a few wisps of dark hair escaping from the confining plait.

The chime of the door-bell didn't sound at all melodious to either of them. Roger swore and ground out his cigarette. Meg followed him as far as the kitchen door and only went out into the hall when she heard Antony's voice. "I want to talk to you, Farrell." She was so far in her own dream that it didn't occur to her immediately that as a greeting it was a little abrupt. But when he stopped short at the sight of her and added, even more curtly, "I'm s-sorry to interrupt, but it h-happens to be important," there was no mistaking the fact that he was in a blazing temper and didn't care who knew it.

Antony didn't wait for a reply, but went on into the sitting room. He turned and waited for the other two to follow him, and saw with a quite reprehensible satisfaction that his tone, if not his words, had angered Roger too. He came into the room with Meg at his heels and demanded resentfully, "Just what do you mean?"

Well, he hadn't meant anything, of course . . . except, perhaps, to annoy. And the chap was at the touchy stage, ready to flare up at any real or fancied slight, but Maitland was far too furious himself to care about that.

"It's n-nothing to me," he said, "if you want to f-fiddle while Rome b-burns. But isn't it time you told me the truth about your f-friend, Ellis?"

"Ellis? I don't—"

"It was in the papers," said Meg. She moved a little closer to Roger as she spoke, and she was staring at Antony as if she had never seen him before. "The *other* man who was shot."

"Oh, him!" said Roger. "I didn't know him." His tone was almost contemptuous.

"For God's sake, Roger, d-don't lie to me again!"

Perhaps the suggestion of appeal in his voice helped to cool Farrell's anger. He said, much less stiffly, "Don't you think you'd better explain?"

"I've been talking to the d-doorman."

"I see."

"So I know quite well that Ellis visited you on Friday afternoon; you t-told me yourself you weren't at the office that day. He wasn't seen to leave."

There was a silence. Roger crossed to the table by the window and took a cigarette from the box there. "You'd better sit down, Meg. This may take some time." But his eyes were on Antony as he added challengingly, "Are you suggesting I killed him?"

"It's difficult to see how you'd have got his b-body down to the car," said Antony. "But there's nothing to preclude a later meeting."

"Down at Grunning's Hole, for instance?"

"That's what the police will say."

Meg had seated herself on the Empire sofa, which had been restored to its original place. She said now in a distant tone, rather as if she were discussing something that couldn't possibly—not possibly—be any concern of hers, "Did the man come here, Roger?"

"It would be rude to contradict so positive a statement, my dear."

"But what did he want?"

He did not look at her, his eyes were fixed on Maitland's face. "I'm damned if I'll tell you that," he said deliberately.

Antony returned his look steadily. He wasn't angry any longer, it wasn't an emotion he could ever sustain for long, and now he saw, with uncomfortable clarity, how things might look from Roger's side of the fence. "I imagine he came to sell you a tape recording," he said.

"You know it all, don't you?"

"I can guess . . . quite a lot. You split your knuckles when you knocked him down; I imagine that was your first, instinctive reaction, wasn't it?"

Farrell's right hand was thrust into his pocket. "I don't like threats," he said. There was something uncanny about his coolness now.

"He wanted money, I suppose."

"Of course he did. He said—" He broke off and looked at Meg and then back at Antony again. "He said he'd been paid to burgle

161

Grainger's place, and he'd taken a file and given that to his employer and told him it was all there was."

"Did you ask him who—"

"He didn't know. A tall, red-haired man; the description meant nothing to me."

"And his terms of reference?"

Roger's lips tightened. Then, "Just what you'd expect: anything to do with my father," he said. "So he offered me the tape. He told me it was the record of a 'most interesting conversation.'"

"And was he right?"

"I don't know yet. He told me where I could find it, but I didn't pay him for the information."

"I suppose," said Antony, looking about him in a vague way, "these flats are pretty well soundproof."

"At any rate, nobody seems to have overheard us."

"I'm afraid the police are as good at guessing games as I am. Did you fetch the tape?" he added casually.

"No. It's safe where it is for the moment." And then with sudden heat, "D'you think I want the thing? Do you think I want to know—?"

"I understand that. I'm sorry. But it records a conversation."

"I know that, don't I? My father wasn't given to soliloquizing."

"I must find out who he was talking to."

"So there is something you don't know," said Roger with a sort of gloomy satisfaction.

"Well, I do, as a matter of fact, but I can't see any other way of being sure."

"That's a pity."

"I think it is. On the evidence as it stands," said Antony with calculated brutality, "you haven't a hope of being acquitted."

"I'll take my chance on that."

"Oh, what's the use!" Antony had been picking his words carefully, but now his temper flared again. *"You'll* take your chance, will you? What about M-meg?" And before Farrell could reply he had whirled round to face her and added furiously, "D-don't interrupt. This has n-nothing to d-do with you."

If Meg realized the irrationality of this remark she made no

162

sign. She stuck her chin in the air and glared at the two men impartially. "You're both being very childish," she said.

"Wait a bit!" As Roger spoke Antony turned to look at him again. "Is that true? Could you keep Meg out of this?"

"I don't think there's any way of doing that. What I'm trying to tell you is that it's not just a case of her evidence any longer; there's every likelihood she'll be arrested."

"They can't do that!"

"Don't be silly, darling," said Meg. "Haven't you heard of being an accessory before the fact?" She got up from the sofa and came across to stand at Roger's side, and slipped her hand under his arm. "I do think you ought to listen to Antony," she told him. "I daresay they won't convict me after all, but if they think you—"

Roger wasn't looking at her, and for a moment Antony wondered whether she realized just what she was asking him to do. But then he met her eyes, and saw in them something he recognized: all the pain of waiting, of standing by and being powerless to help. He knew then that she wasn't even thinking of the murder charge, or what might happen to either of them when it came into court. This attitude of Roger's was something that had to be dealt with before they could look to the future, and she wasn't under any illusion that it was going to be easy. Grainger's statement came into his mind, and the reiterated catch phrase "Knowledge itself is power"; the trouble was, it could also be so very painful.

So their eyes held for a long moment, and he thought—and did not realize how incongruous it was—"I can understand her as he never will." And then she smiled at him and said lightly, " 'To win or lose it all,' darling," echoing what had been in his mind. But her hand tightened, a small, involuntary gesture, on the sleeve of Roger's jacket.

Farrell did not seem to have noticed the silence. "You're right, of course," he said, but his voice sounded uncertain. Then he looked down at Meg and said with something of his usual assurance, "It's in the left luggage office at Victoria."

"You've got the ticket?"

"Yes." He paused again and then added steadily, "We've got a machine at the office. I don't know if this tape will fit."

163

"We'll have to see." He didn't want to look so far ahead, and he began to wonder whether he'd been quite fair in the arguments he had used to bring Roger to this point. After all . . . "It won't be legal proof of anything, you know," he said, making up his mind. "Just something we can base the defense on . . . I hope. And even then, it may not be successful."

Roger was looking at him rather oddly. "You're not thinking of using it as an excuse?"

"I'm interested in the other man's identity, not in the subject of the conversation. And in case you still don't trust me," he added with surprising mildness, "how would that help Meg?"

"No, I see. But when you came storming in here just now—"

"I'm sorry about that."

"You might have regretted it even more," said Farrell with a rather grim humor, "if I'd lost my temper too."

"Oh, but you did," said Meg. She wriggled her hand out of his and moved away a little, as though she were seeking a place from which she could view the scene dispassionately. "And it wasn't very sensible, because it was obvious *then* that he believed you about the rest of it . . . or why be so angry, just about Ellis?"

"Why indeed? Is that right?" Roger demanded.

"Near enough." He frowned at Meg. "My uncle has been known to talk for hours about my credulity."

"If you ask me, darling," she told him, a little tartly, "you haven't exactly been overflowing with it the last few days." She saw from his smile that he'd a pretty good idea what her own feelings had been, but there was reassurance too; he wouldn't give her away.

"Never mind that." Roger spoke with his usual decisive energy, though the look of strain was still about him. "It won't take me very long to get to Victoria—"

"I'd better go. Don't you realize they'll have a tail on you, at least since yesterday?"

"Does that matter?"

"If you're arrested with the tape in your possession it will matter a good deal."

"Well, anyway, I have my methods. The police have still got the

Jensen, so they'll expect me to be leaving on foot. But I can get down to the garage without being seen; the janitor's a good friend of mine, he won't mind my taking his Austin, and even if they're watching that exit they won't be expecting that."

"I still think—"

"You can come along, if you like," Roger flung at him, "if you can't trust me to bring the tape back with me."

In some obscure way, this seemed to be a challenge. "Have it your own way," said Antony. "I'll take Meg home with me, shall I? You can join us there." But even then he felt uneasy.

12

By five o'clock Meg was growing anxious, and Jenny and Antony were running out of reasons why Roger might have been delayed. By six o'clock it seemed obvious that he wasn't coming to Kempenfeldt Square, and Antony rang the Leinster Court flat to see if the arrangement had been somehow misunderstood. The phone shrilled unanswered, and he tried again in case he'd got the wrong number; but still there was no reply, though he let the ringing go on for a long time.

He was wondering what to say to Meg when his own phone rang, and he snatched off the receiver again in a hurry and heard Inspector Sykes's placid voice greeting him. And that was the answer, of course . . . that Roger had been picked up by the police, in spite of taking the janitor's car; he only hoped it had happened before he reached Victoria. So when he asked, "Is Roger Farrell with you, Inspector?" he wasn't in any doubt what the answer would be.

But it seemed he'd been wrong in his assumption. There was a pause, which somehow conveyed the effect of surprise, as though Sykes was there in the room with him and had raised his eyebrows; but when he replied the detective's voice was as calm as ever. "I was hoping you'd be able to tell me where to find him, Mr. Maitland."

"No. No, I can't."

"I've just got back from Leinster Court. Seems he wasn't seen to leave, but he isn't in the flat. Odd, isn't it?"

"Negligence somewhere, Inspector, I should say."

Sykes ignored the comment. "I understand you were there yourself, Mr. Maitland, earlier on."

"Mr. Farrell left before I did. I don't know where he is now." And that was true enough, but he hoped Sykes wouldn't press the question. "Does that mean—?" He broke off, because he didn't want to add "that the warrant's been issued" . . . not with Meg listening to every word he said.

"It means there'll be a call out for him, if we don't locate him soon."

"I see." And they must know he'd brought Meg here, though Sykes had carefully not mentioned it. The chances were they wanted to pick up Roger first . . . or was that wishful thinking? He said, on an impulse, "Look here, Inspector, I may be able to help. Where can I call you?"

Again there was a pause, a tribute to the unexpected. "I'll be here at the Yard for another hour at least," said Sykes at last, and Antony heard the click that meant the connection was broken. He turned and met an accusing look from Meg.

"I should have gone myself," he said, "only I thought . . . oh, well!" He got up and went across to stand in his favorite place on the hearthrug and looked down and said in a worried tone, "Meg . . . he meant it, didn't he? He wouldn't have destroyed the tape?"

"No," said Meg. She thought, if his word means anything at all . . . "No," she repeated more firmly.

"Then—"

"You said you didn't want the police to find him with it."

"I don't."

"But you told the inspector—"

"You asked me to take a hand, Meg."

"But not to sacrifice Roger for me, Antony. You wouldn't do that?"

"I might be tempted," said Antony with reluctant honesty, "if I thought it would help." He couldn't tell her, even now, how strong

167

the temptation had been. "But at the moment—can't you see?—it's Roger I'm worried about."

"So am I," said Meg simply.

"Then keep quiet and let me think." He turned his head and looked at Jenny, and said as if he were giving her a valuable piece of information, "Whoever killed Ellis could have talked to him before he died."

"I suppose he could."

"So he may have known where Ellis put the tape, and that Roger had the cloakroom ticket. I don't much like that idea, do you, love?"

"You mean . . . there could have been an ambush?"

"Something of the sort." His eyes met Meg's again, and his tone was bitter with self-reproach. "I should have thought of that," he said. "Still trust me?"

"Yes, of course. Can I do anything?"

"The worst thing of all . . . wait." He started back toward the desk, but added, over his shoulder, "Jenny can tell you all about that."

There seemed to be an awful lot of Wilsons in the telephone book. He found the number at last, and heard Leonard's voice with a confused murmur of conversation in the background. "Is Roger there?" he asked.

"What? Oh, it's you, Maitland. We have a few friends—"

"I can hear them." He paused. "Not Roger?"

"That's just what I meant," said Leonard, with the odd inflection of sarcasm that Antony found so annoying.

He was tempted to say, "Make the most of it, they may not be such good friends of yours tomorrow." Instead he muttered, "Thank you," and put down the receiver, and had recourse again to the phone book. It took longer to get Sam Reade. It was a child's voice that answered, the elder of the two little girls, at a guess, and he heard her calling "Daddy! Daddy!" as she gradually went out of earshot. And after a long time Reade said gruffly, "Hallo!"

"I want to get hold of Roger. It's rather urgent."

"Who's that?" His voice was sharply suspicious. "Oh, Maitland. Well, I don't quite know why you should think—"

"He isn't there?"

"Bella could have told you that."

"I'm sorry to have bothered you." He sat and stared at the telephone for some moments after he had cradled the receiver, and then said without looking round, "Roger seems to have the most damnable trick of making himself unpopular."

"Who were you talking to?"

"Mr. Reade, then. Leonard Wilson before that."

"Roger wouldn't go to them," said Meg positively.

"That wasn't exactly what I had in mind." But he hadn't expected anything from those two calls, they'd been a tribute to an uncertainty he didn't feel. "We'll try again," he said. This time it was a man's voice that answered his first query.

"I'm sorry, sir, Mr. Denning is not at home."

"I'm trying to find Mr. Roger Farrell . . . an urgent matter. I suppose you don't happen to know—?"

"Mr. Farrell hasn't been here today, sir. But I believe Mr. Denning is spending the evening on board the *Susannah,* so it's quite possible that Mr. Farrell is with him."

"For God's sake, man, where is she?"

"The boat, sir?" The smooth voice was faintly huffy now. "She's moored at Chelsea, near the Cheyne Walk pier."

As far as he could remember afterward, the conversation finished there. He got up and asked Jenny, "Is Uncle Nick in, do you know?"

"He said he was going to see Mr. Halloran."

"Never mind." He thought for a moment of seeking him there; it would be a help to have his backing, but was there time? "I'm going over to the Yard to have a word with Sykes," he said, and met Jenny's eye and realized she knew he was lying.

"That's a good idea," she told him steadily. "Meg will stay here with me, so you'll let us know—won't you?—as soon as there's any news."

"Of course I will. Don't worry," he said, and felt like a hypocrite. But she'd understand he couldn't leave things there.

Downstairs in the study he took up the phone again, and this time he didn't need to look up the number he wanted. "Hallo, Inspector," he said, when finally he heard Sykes's voice; and paused because, even now, he hadn't quite made up his mind how to play the hand. He could say, "Roger Farrell's on board the *Susannah*," and they'd send there to look for him; but they'd get no further if Denning simply denied he was on board. Or there might be trouble, and the police unprepared for it; he couldn't risk that. He'd be frank with Sykes, and see where that got him, but he wasn't very hopeful of the result.

"Care to come ghost hunting, Inspector?" he asked.

But he was alone when he reached Chelsea, and it was already dusk; he followed the directions that had been given him, and came to the jetty, and saw the dark bulk of the *Susannah* beyond, majestic among a huddle of smaller craft. There were people aboard, if the lights were anything to go on, but he hesitated a moment, listening to the water slapping against the wooden piers, and—farther away—the sound of a small boat chugging its way upstream.

He hadn't got any change out of Sykes, and now he thought he'd been a fool to waste time trying, when he couldn't offer him anything like proof. He also thought, what if I'm wrong, and strangely it was the first time the idea had occurred to him. If he was wrong, there'd be trouble of a different kind from that he was expecting, and Superintendent Briggs would undoubtedly see in his actions a confirmation of every suspicion he'd ever had; it might even be that Sykes would agree with him. But if he was right, that was the thing to hold on to . . . if he was right, and it wasn't already too late. . . .

Even allowing this, no amount of argument would make his present course seem sensible. He was coldly aware of the chances of failure, the very small chance of success. He couldn't even make a plan, because it all depended how he was received on board.

So he called, "Ahoy, *Susannah!*" and felt a fool as he did so; and called again, more loudly.

His hail wasn't answered from the yacht, but by a man in a frieze jacket who materialized from the shadows at his elbow, startling him half out of his wits. "What did you want, sir?" he inquired.

"To get aboard the *Susannah*."

"Have you business on board, sir?"

"I shouldn't be surprised if Mr. Denning's expecting me." This seemed to produce no reaction, so he added, "In any case, I want to see Mr. Farrell."

"I think you must be mistaken, sir." There was a harsher note in the man's voice now. "Mr. Denning is alone."

"Then perhaps he'll be glad of company." He wondered, suddenly, what would have happened if, instead, he had offered to leave. His companion was out to get all the information he could, but he didn't think that would be a popular move. "My name's Maitland," he said. "How do I get on board?"

"I'll give them a hail, sir." He went to the edge of the jetty to do so, cupping his hands, but turned back sharply when Antony kicked at a pebble and set it rolling across the boards. "They'll be right across with the dinghy," he said. "The steps are over here, sir." He stood very close to Antony's side while they were waiting.

It wasn't often he was able to forget that he couldn't lift his right arm very far and that he had little strength in it; there was all too often an ache in his shoulder to remind him. Tonight he was very conscious of it as he clambered down into the dinghy, and then suddenly he was aware only of the stillness. The faintest murmur of traffic; a radio, decently muted, from the cabin cruiser they were leaving on their right; the quiet dip of the oars in the dark water. The man in the frieze jacket was watching them from the jetty, his face a pale blur, featureless, expressionless. And then the *Susannah* loomed above them, and there were surprisingly solid steps to climb, but not so solid that he couldn't feel the weight of the oarsman, who must have tied up quickly and be coming up close behind him.

He had been expecting a reception committee on deck and was surprised to find only one man awaiting him, until he realized that the sudden light had blinded him to what was in the shadows, and that, in fact, several men were standing there. What, after all, could be more natural? But their silence was, in itself, a menace.

The man at the top of the companionway greeted him with the same rather ironical deference that the man on shore had used.

"Glad to have you aboard, sir." And just for the moment Antony was struck with the sheer humor of the situation, even though there was an eerie quality about the welcome he was being accorded.

"I hope Mr. Denning won't mind my coming," he said, adopting without conscious thought the diffident air of one unsure of his welcome.

"He'll be glad to see you, Mr. Maitland." Antony gave him a questioning look, and he added smoothly, "We were told you might turn up, sir. Jim wouldn't have let anyone else on board."

"Then I take it there's no difficulty about seeing Mr. Denning?"

"None in the world, sir. He's in his own quarters." He turned away as he spoke, and Antony followed him along the deck, and was again uneasily aware of the silent men who watched him. It was all very polite, very decorous; for the time being, it seemed, Hubert Denning was prepared to let him call the tune, and he didn't find the thought reassuring. But then he realized that two of the watchers had fallen into step behind him. They were close at his heels as he followed the first man to the bridge house, through a door and down the companionway steps. The owner's quarters on the *Susannah* had obviously been designed to give the maximum of privacy.

The short passage below had two facing doors but otherwise seemed to be a dead end; here the guide halted and turned with a murmured apology. "You won't object to a search, sir?"

Situation normal, thought Antony to himself, and stood patiently under the inquiring hands of one of the still-silent followers.

"Nothing," said the man at last and stepped back. The left-hand door was open, and Antony got a glimpse of a bedroom beyond before he was ushered through the door on the right. He had been prepared to find the yacht luxurious, but he was conscious of surprise as he went in. Apart from the height of the ceiling, it might have been the bookroom in any house ashore; a brown, leathery place, with a couple of comfortable chairs and a desk that was probably an antique. It was rather dim, admittedly, but perhaps it was because Mr. Denning preferred it that way. He was sitting at the desk, writing, and there was plenty of light falling on to his work from the shaded lamp beside him. He did not look up immediately, nor did Antony's guide announce him in any way, but when he heard the door slide into place he said gently, "Do sit down, Mr. Maitland. I shall be with you in a moment."

Antony stayed where he was, halfway between door and desk, and standing on a carpet which he suspected would have fetched more at a saleroom than the entire contents of his living room at Kempenfeldt Square. He said, "I came to find Roger," and thought that the pen that was traveling so smoothly across the sheet of writing paper checked for an instant before it went on. Denning made no reply and after a moment he added, "You seem to have been expecting me," and made the words a question.

There was a silence. The old man signed his name, blotted the letter, and folded it carefully into its envelope. Then he looked up and said, "No one else was to be admitted. When I give orders, I expect to be obeyed."

"I see."

"You must admit, I did my best to discourage you," Denning added reproachfully. "But I was afraid, in spite of that—"

"You mean, you tried to make me believe Roger was guilty?"

"Yes, of course." He sounded impatient now, and his tone was definitely testy as he got up and came round from behind the desk. "I asked you to sit down, Mr. Maitland. I have the greatest dislike for conducting a conversation standing." He did not speak again until they were both seated, and then he returned to his tone of gentle reproof. "I'm afraid you must have a rather stubborn disposition."

"I wasn't convinced of Roger's innocence at first, you know; that came later."

"Not only stubborn, but contrary," said Denning, shaking his head. "All the same, it seems a pity—" He broke off, and a gleam of malice came into his eyes. "You can't be said really to have helped him, can you? I shouldn't have had to take such drastic action against Roger if I hadn't been afraid your activities would inconvenience me."

"Is he dead?"

"Not yet. And I should much have preferred to leave the matter in the capable hands of the police. He might even have got away with it—who knows?—if it hadn't been for you."

"You couldn't afford to let him keep the record of your conversation with James Farrell," Antony pointed out.

"That's true, but if he had acquired it sooner I need have taken no further action after Friday night. I hadn't expected so much delay before he went to Victoria."

"You don't know Roger very well, do you? He knew when he played the tape back it would tell him why Grainger was blackmailing his father, and that was something he didn't want to know."

"Now, I'd never have thought that he would have been so foolish." Hubert Denning seemed genuinely shocked at the thought. "Not but what his father had some odd scruples," he added, and Antony, watching him, thought how misleading appearances could be: the old man, with his white hair and guileless blue eyes, who yet was capable of complete ruthlessness; while his godson, who could have sat as a model for a pirate any day and no questions asked, had a streak of sensitivity that might well have wrecked both his life and Meg's.

"Can I see Roger?" he asked again.

"All in good time, all in good time, Mr. Maitland. I've got to think first, you know, what on earth's to be done with you." The blue eyes were hard now; it was only too easy to remember the silent men on deck. "Why did you come here?" Denning asked. "And who knows where you are?"

"The police." He put out the statement firmly, but Denning would have none of it.

"Yes, I dare say. You told them a story, no doubt, and they wouldn't believe you. Otherwise, why should you have come alone?" This was too near the truth for comfort, and the old man laughed gently when he saw Antony's expression. "Well, well, I think I have enough ingenuity to deal with their curiosity, even if you have succeeded in arousing it. As for your family, there's no real difficulty there. They can tell the police, no doubt, what you

174

have already told them; and it won't be any more credible at second hearing."

"How depressing it is," said Antony. "to come up against a logical mind."

"So what is your mission here? You had at least sufficient sense not to attempt a clandestine approach—"

"That would have been difficult, wouldn't it?"

"Impossible, I should imagine. But if my crew weren't so loyal—"

"Or so alive to their own best interests," Antony corrected him. Denning looked at him thoughtfully.

"I had no idea your researches had gone so deep," he remarked after a pause. "You must tell me presently how you knew. But first, I asked you a question."

"Why I came here? To see Roger home, and—of course—to get the tape."

"Which is not your property, or his."

"It belongs, I suppose," said Antony, "to Martin Grainger's heirs, executors and assigns. But I imagine the police would feel they had some prior claim—"

"My dear Mr. Maitland! I am sorry to be disobliging, really I am, but how do you propose to carry out this rather ambitious program?"

"I'm not quite sure." This was said with an air of reluctant candor, and Denning laughed.

"And even if all this were possible, what do you think you would have gained?"

"If the police could be induced to take an interest in the *Susannah,* I think they might be . . . surprised, shall we say? . . . at some of the things they found."

"What things, for instance?" Denning's tone remained light, but there was a wariness about him now as he waited for the answer. Antony thought, with a sudden rising excitement, he hasn't destroyed the tape yet. It seemed unutterably foolish that he should have kept it, but still he was sure.

"The rather unlikely nature of your cargo, for one thing," he said. Denning's eyes became fixed as he listened, in an odd, half-mesmerizing stare. "And for another, the presence of the man who broke into my uncle's house on Friday night and shot three policemen as he made his escape."

"Now that," said the old man, "is a deliberate lie. No connection could be proved—"

"Like to bet on it?"

"You would not, after all, be in a position to pay your losses," Denning pointed out, recovering his geniality. "At the risk of being melodramatic, you know too much."

"What do you propose to do about it?"

"One thing is certain, I can't let you interfere with my other arrangements. I shall consider the matter, Mr. Maitland; but meanwhile, you say you wish to see Roger?"

"Very much."

"Then if you will just ring the bell beside you . . . you can reach it without getting up. Ah, thank you—" There was a silence between them until there was a tap on the door and Denning called, "Come in."

This was a man Antony hadn't seen before, tallish, square-built, with red hair and a brown, freckled face. The old man said, "Captain Soames, Mr. Maitland," and waved an introductory hand. And then, "Mr. Maitland wants to see my godson, Soames. I hope you don't mind bringing him here yourself."

"Aye, aye, sir." It ought to have sounded like a charade, but if he was playing a part it was one he was at home in. His eyes turned toward Antony briefly, almost without interest. "He doesn't look dangerous," he remarked, looking back at his principal again, "but are you sure it's wise—"

Denning laughed. "I'm sure you'll be able to control the situation," he said. "He was searched, I suppose."

"Of course. He wasn't armed."

"And Roger, by now, is perhaps a trifle discouraged. Don't worry, Soames, I have a reason for wanting him here." This was said with a smile, and the red-haired man laughed politely, as though at a joke he couldn't see, and backed out of the cabin.

"Foolhardy, Mr. Maitland," said Denning reprovingly.

"I can't think what good a gun would have been, if that's what you mean." He sounded impatient, but a moment later the diffident note was back in his voice again. "Mr. Denning, what's happened to Roger?"

"I'm afraid he was never of a malleable disposition, even as a boy." He paused, shaking his head over the thought. "Of course, it would have been easier to use some sort of sedative in bringing him here, but I couldn't allow that. You see," he added, smiling at Antony as though confident of his understanding, "I wasn't sure how long afterwards a drug could be detected. If there was an autopsy, for instance."

13

Even after this, Antony wasn't quite prepared for Roger's appearance: he had a black eye, and a swollen lip, and a bruise on his cheekbone; his tie was somewhere up behind his ear, and one sleeve had been almost completely ripped from his jacket. He had besides rather a dazed look and offered no resistance when Soames thrust him down in the chair that Denning had vacated, but as there was a gun jammed in his ribs, this was just as well.

Antony was on his feet too by this time, and had backed toward the wall. He didn't look at Roger, after that first, disquieting glance, but kept his eyes fixed instead on Denning's face. The old man had his most unctuous look and said in a concerned tone, "I trust you're feeling better, my boy." Roger swore at him.

"Well," said Denning, ignoring this, "you'll see I have a friend of yours here, and I particularly want you to hear what he has to tell me. You too, Soames, of course; and I think it would be better—if you find it absolutely necessary to shoot somebody, my dear fellow—for you to concentrate on Mr. Maitland."

"Any time you say, sir," said the red-haired man obligingly. He moved from his place behind Farrell's chair and seemed to be measuring the distance with his eye to where Antony was standing.

"Well, preferably, not just yet. Roger, you do understand, don't you, what will happen if you create any disturbance? No, don't start swearing again, you know I have the greatest dislike for intemperate language." He pulled up a chair that was standing near the desk and seated himself, and beamed at each of his companions in turn. "That's better," he said. "Now, Mr. Maitland, if you please."

Antony leaned back against the paneling. "What do you want?" he asked.

"You're going to tell me—aren't you?—just what you know of my affairs."

"I shouldn't like to bore you," said Antony and saw, for a moment, a gleam of anger in Denning's eye. He'd have to be careful, that wasn't the result he was aiming for.

"I think perhaps we could persuade you, if you're really unwilling." The old man was as friendly as ever.

"My dear Mr. Denning, I should be ashamed to put you to so much trouble." That was just the tone he wanted: a bravado that didn't quite ring true, coupled with a distinct suggestion of nervousness.

Hubert Denning smiled delightedly. "I shouldn't stay and watch, you know," he confided. "I find the idea of violence most upsetting."

"Well, you've guessed most of it already," said Antony, worried again.

"I want you to tell me what you know . . . exactly; and how you found out."

"Yes, but—" He looked at Roger and said to him, as though he were making a plea for understanding, "It can't do any harm."

Roger frowned back at him. "Do as you like," he said curtly. Antony couldn't decide whether he was picking up his cue, or whether he really thought . . .

"All right then. Reduced to essentials, it isn't a long story." He wasn't looking at Farrell now. Instead he addressed himself to Hubert Denning, and still with the air of one who, though fearful of the result, was doing his best to brazen out a difficult situation. "Thirty years ago you owned a gaff-rigged cutter, Mr. Denning— have I got that right? And one weekend you went out with your friend James Farrell, and a young Canadian called Roy Cooper,

179

a mining engineer. Cooper had come to England to present a report on a mine in Northern Quebec, but he didn't come back from his weekend's sailing."

"Regrettable . . . really regrettable," said Denning sadly.

"The body was found some time later, and the verdict at the inquest was 'accidental death.' But the coroner didn't know anything about the Abukcheech Mine, and in the city nothing was known of the accident. At least, I imagine that's the case, but even if it wasn't—"

"My association with the mine was not generally known; I have always preferred to work through a third party. James, however, was less cautious—" Denning paused to smile at Roger, and just for a moment his eyes showed an unconcealed hatred—"and would just as surely have been ruined if the report had been tabled too soon."

"Which of you killed him?" asked Antony, and saw from the corner of his eye Roger lean forward and cover his eyes with his hand.

"You know so much, Mr. Maitland, surely you don't need to ask me that?" Denning's tone was mocking; he wasn't even going to the trouble to deny the charge.

"I know your account of the accident, and it doesn't really matter, because it seems that both of you had guilty knowledge. And I don't suppose you'd have welcomed an investigation, but there was no question of that at the time. You continued to prosper, and Farrell . . . I believe that was when he commenced to do so. He moved to Wimbledon Common; I wouldn't mind betting that was a move to a better neighborhood, if not to a larger house. And the following year he bought the cottage at Grunning's Hole. He didn't go sailing with you much after that, though you still continued to be on friendly terms."

"You are now," said Denning, "reaching a part of the story that interests me very much." Antony threw him a quick, apprehensive look.

"If you mean what happened five years ago . . . Roy Cooper's brother retired and came to England. And he got in touch with Farrell, and Farrell got into a panic; because he wasn't a hypocrite, and he didn't care to pose as a hero." He paused and licked his lips, and added irresolutely, "Was it malice that made you give Vaughan Cooper that very highly colored account of his brother's death?"

Denning seemed to consider. "What a very unpleasant portrait you draw of me, Mr. Maitland. I believe it to have been a matter of expediency, nothing else."

"Well, you met Farrell—didn't you?—at the Chop House, and Grainger recorded the conversation between you. I imagine he supplemented the information he got with some inquiries of his own; at any rate, he was then in a position to blackmail Farrell, whom he knew."

"And to threaten Winifred, after James's death. You know, I'm beginning to see why the police wouldn't listen to you; all you seem to have proved so far is the excellence of Roger's motive."

"Unfortunately, that needed no demonstration." Antony broke off, and again there was the quick, appraising look at Hubert Denning. "I say . . . do you really want me to go on?"

"I'm afraid I must insist."

"Oh, well then. Grainger left a sort of diary—"

"Did he, indeed? And the police, I must suppose, have seen it."

"Inspector Sykes showed it to me. It was rather cryptic, though; no names, or anything like that. But he did say that he'd recently discovered the identity of the other party to the original conversation. He was quite pleased with himself to have found another victim, and I think it's ironical that if he'd known of your other activities he'd have left you severely alone."

"What do you know about my other activities, Mr. Maitland?"

"Well, I . . . well, even the police know there's a connection between Martin Grainger's death and the bullion robberies that have worried them for so long."

"How do they know that?"

"The fingerprints . . . I told you," said Antony. Denning frowned, and he hurried on. "They think James Farrell was leading and organizing the gang, and they think Roger took over when he died. I couldn't convince them . . . I mean, they don't believe . . . I mean—"

"Your theory is sufficiently clear. You told them that I—"

"Well, it was true, wasn't it?" Antony demanded. He felt Roger's eyes on his face and wondered what he was thinking. But he hadn't time to worry about that now.

"You mustn't upset yourself," said Hubert Denning soothingly. "So when you spoke of the nature of our cargo—?"

"I meant the proceeds of the robbery at London Airport last Wednesday."

"I see."

"You asked me what I *know,* and this is only guessing. But the rest of it is based on quite reasonable deductions, and this is a—a natural consequence, if you see what I mean. And one or two things, quite innocent in themselves, back up the theory. I mean, your insurance connections would have given you the inside information you needed; and then, there's *Susannah.*"

"A master stroke, don't you think?"

"I do, indeed. And only a coincidence if you just happen to take a cruise soon after one of the robberies . . . to the Mediterranean, perhaps?"

"Tangier," said the old man, "is quite one of my favorite towns. Naturally, it isn't our only port of call."

"And when I came here tonight I began to think there was something in another guess of mine . . . rather a wild one. Sykes spoke of the way the gang seemed to disappear between jobs; like a lot of ghosts, he said. But if your crew were the operatives . . . no going back into the underworld when a job was completed and arousing suspicion because they were unduly flush. They could live quietly on board, and no one the wiser."

"There was another refinement to the plan," said Denning, "that perhaps you haven't thought of. The fact that they were accumulating capital abroad and were at liberty to take time off—a sort of sabbatical year, in fact—turn and turn about. It's an excellent system, isn't it, Soames?"

"Excellent for morale, sir." His tone was as suave as ever, but there was a hint of tension about him, too. Antony looked at him and wondered if, by any chance, it was his fingerprints the police had found.

"A pity, don't you think, that it should all be spoiled by one man's negligence?" he asked.

"I still don't understand how you knew," Soames admitted.

"One of you left your fingerprints on a job . . . twice," said Antony. "Once about six months ago, in a van from which bullion had been stolen, and again at my uncle's house on Friday night. To be exact, he dropped a pocket calendar there, with an advertisement for Galloway's Chop House. Careless, wasn't it?"

Denning clicked his tongue, and said, more in sorrow than in anger, "Who was it, Soames?"

"Jim Bennett, sir, he's got the shore watch tonight."

"You'd better get rid of him, before there's any more trouble." This was said casually, and Roger's eyes widened a little, but Antony was cursing his luck, because it might have been Soames himself and he had a nasty feeling the red-haired man was dangerous. If he could have stirred up dissension in that quarter there might have been something to hope for.

"I'll attend to it as soon as possible, sir," said Soames viciously.

Hubert Denning turned back to Antony again. "Well, Mr. Maitland, since you've been so obliging I may as well finish the story for you. But after that you'll tell me how you knew."

"If that's how you want it."

"I heard from Grainger, as you surmise, and I paid him . . . once. The matter was negligible, but it offended me."

"Yes, I thought it might."

"It wasn't really difficult to find out his identity, he was followed from the rendezvous . . . an A.A. box on the Great West Road. There were several men on that assignment, and I imagine Jim Bennett must have been the one who lunched at the Chop House to make the final inquiries, and that he picked up the pocket calendar there. It was criminally careless; however, that can be taken care of. I shall also wish to know, Soames, who was responsible for recruiting him?" He broke off, frowning. "Is something amusing you, Mr. Maitland?" he asked.

Antony disclaimed hastily. He had a private thought that the choice of the phrase "criminally careless" was a particularly joyful one in the present context, but he didn't think the idea would have any appeal for Hubert Denning. "I thought I was going to sneeze," he apologized. And then, "You were telling us how you tracked down Martin Grainger."

"So I was. Not very difficult, as you see. The actual date of his death was the inspiration of the moment, when I found that note in your room, Roger. It seemed too good a chance to miss—"

"Did you know what would happen?" Farrell put the question in a strangely incurious tone.

"I was afraid they might suspect you, though I can't say I lost any sleep over the possibility. But I wasn't trying to implicate you, my dear boy . . . not then."

"That," said Antony, "came later. After he met me." For a moment he met Denning's look with a sort of defiance, then his eyes dropped away from the hardness of the old man's stare.

"I'd heard your name," Denning explained, "and I made some inquiries. I didn't like what I heard, and I'll grant my informant was right about your ingenuity, Mr. Maitland, though I think he deceived me a little about some of your other qualities. However, I thought you'd lose interest if you became convinced of Roger's guilt." He looked again at his godson. "I wasn't trying to make trouble for you with the authorities," he told him.

"I can't tell you how happy that makes me," said Roger savagely.

Antony spoke hurriedly, before Denning could make any reply to this. "You didn't shoot Grainger yourself, of course."

"Of course not." He sounded shocked by the very idea. "Soames took care of that for me, and of Ellis, of course. Did I tell you I find him invaluable?"

"Did the rifle belong to Roger's father?"

"Did it, Soames?"

"No." He hadn't quite his leader's relish for the situation. "They'll think it did, though; I took it down to the cottage on Friday night."

"Along with Ellis's body? And Ellis told you, before he died, about his talk with Roger that afternoon."

"That's right, he did. Well, he shouldn't have tried to double-cross us, you know."

"He wasn't one of the crew, was he?"

"Nothing like that." Soames sounded scornful. "They're carefully picked, ex-Navy, most of them." He threw a deprecating glance at Denning and subsided into silence again.

"I can see you had to have the tape," said Antony, "but why were James Farrell's diaries so important?"

"A precaution, merely. Perhaps they weren't important at all."

"Perhaps not." He could understand the look on Roger's face, he was feeling a bit nauseated himself. Soames was understandable, a hard man who would kill without a second thought if it seemed to his advantage, but Denning, who professed squeamishness, who didn't like violence, who would order a man's death as casually as he would ask to have the car brought round . . . "I suppose you saw me putting them in my brief case when you called at Leinster Court on Thursday evening."

"I did. And I wondered—"

"It wasn't a very good excuse you gave for that visit," said Antony, pursuing his own train of thought. "When I got to know you better I could hardly imagine you seeking Roger's company for a weekend in the country, and least of all when his brother-in-law was likely to be present."

"What else made you suspect me?"

"I disagreed with the police on two points," said Antony, slipping back again into the faintly apologetic tone that—just for the moment—he had forgotten. "I didn't think Roger had shot Martin Grainger . . . well, I didn't want to think so. And I didn't believe Grainger had knowingly blackmailed a member of a gang so ruthless as the bullion thieves had proved themselves. So there had to be some other reason for his hold over James Farrell, and if I could find that reason it might give me the name of the second party to the conversation, who was now also being blackmailed according to Grainger's own statement. There was admittedly a connection between Grainger's death and the gang, and it seemed to me that this other man was the most likely link . . . *not* Roger. It was just Grainger's bad luck that the financial whale he thought he'd hooked turned out to be a killer shark instead."

"In the interests of accuracy," Denning murmured, "I think you should have said 'harpooned.' "

"There was a parallel train of thought that led from Roger's

185

innocence to one of three men who might have known where Grainger would be the afternoon he died. I explained that to you, didn't I?"

"But you have not explained precisely what led you to me?"

"Cooper's name turned up in Farrell's diary, and I wouldn't have thought twice about it if I hadn't been convinced the bullion robberies were not the reason for the blackmail. So I was looking for something—anything—odd that had happened in 1958, just before the first demand was made. What kept turning up was a series of dates. James Farrell had had a stroke of luck in 1933, that seemed to have set him firmly on his feet so that he was already extremely prosperous when he went into partnership with Reade in 1935. Then I heard about the accident to Roy Cooper, also in 1933; and his brother had turned up in 1958, just before Grainger got busy. Of course, if I hadn't known how Grainger got his information nothing would have made sense at all. But I did know about the other man, and once I'd heard Cooper's story it was obvious who he was."

"How much of this have you told to the police?" The hard blue eyes were expressionless now.

"Most of it."

"I don't think there is anything there that the police will be inclined to credit. If they do ask questions, it's a great comfort to be forewarned," said Denning benevolently. "Nothing to worry about, Soames, we can proceed with our plans with a clear mind."

"That's what I think, sir," Soames agreed.

Denning came to his feet and looked across at Antony. "As you'll have Roger's company, I shall make no apology for leaving you for a while," he said. "I haven't dined, you see, and I imagine they'll have something ready for me by now. I should like to finish my meal before we cast off."

Antony did not speak; he thought now his voice might betray him. Soames asked, "You're leaving them here, sir?"

"As well here as anywhere. There's no lock, of course—I never anticipated just this situation. But the portholes are too small to be of any use as an escape route, and with a guard at the bottom of the companionway . . . you must admit, my dear fellow, this cabin is more easily guarded than any of the others."

"Well, perhaps—" Soames's eyes were busy with the furnishings of the cabin, assessing their possibilities. "At least, let me have them tied," he urged.

"But I don't want any bruises on Maitland's body," Denning told him patiently, as though he were explaining something to a child.

"Shoot him at once, then." No one would hear; the gun was silenced.

"Medical science," said the old man reflectively, "is a very wonderful thing. We won't take any unnecessary risks."

"I suppose it's all right." Soames still sounded uneasy. "I'll put Marlowe on the door," he added more cheerfully.

"You can certainly rely on him." Denning turned again to Antony. "In case you tire of each other's conversation, Mr. Maitland, you may care to play over the recording we spoke of." He said this with deliberation, and Antony was suddenly convinced that here was the reason they were being left alone together, though everything that had been said to Soames was undoubtedly true as well. "I've always been an enemy to every form of ignorance," said Denning, "and it seems only fair to Roger that he should know the truth at last." He walked calmly to the door and stood waiting until Soames backed away to join him.

A moment later the door slid quietly into place behind them.

Antony was across the room in an instant and had his ear to the door. He heard footsteps and Soames' voice raised in a command he couldn't quite make out, and then a clatter of feet on the companionway steps from the bridge house. After a while he relaxed slightly and came back to stand looking down at Roger. *"They*'ve gone," he said, "but keep your voice down, in case the guard moves closer."

Roger looked up at him and grinned slightly, though it looked as if it hurt him. "Be thankful for small mercies," he advised.

"Oh, I am. I thought I'd have to search the whole ship to find you," Antony told him. "I never dreamed they'd leave us together like this."

"After the performance you just put on," said Roger dryly, "I imagine they think you're frightened of your shadow."

"Did I overdo it?"

"Not a bit. It tickled the old boy's vanity, and as for Soames, he'd discounted you as a force to be reckoned with, and had us both dead and buried, long before the end."

"Well, I'll tell you one thing, Roger, I'm scared stiff of your dear Uncle Hubert. I kept expecting him to turn into Captain Bligh under my very eyes."

Roger essayed another smile, grimaced because it hurt him, and abandoned the attempt. He leaned his head against the high back of the chair. "I gather you're unarmed," he said.

"Do you think I'd have been allowed into the presence with a gun on me?"

"And the police—?"

"I told Inspector Sykes where you were," said Antony, "but I couldn't square it with my conscience just to tell him that. I mean, I didn't want a massacre of unsuspecting policemen. Anyway, he wouldn't believe me, he thinks you've made a run for it, you see. So I thought perhaps . . . we may contrive something yet."

"So we may." Roger did not move from his relaxed position, but his voice sounded stronger. "I don't quite understand your relationship with Sykes. On the whole he seems to have been helpful, but you said—"

"Sykes thinks I'm honest, and usually misguided," said Antony carefully. "He's willing to go along with me because—sometimes—I've come up with the right answers; and he has a passion for the old-fashioned virtues . . . justice, and all that. But today . . . I can see his point, you know. He thinks I'm deceiving myself; and how could he start a hue and cry after a man in Denning's position, with nothing to go on but what I had to admit was guesswork?"

"And Superintendent Briggs?"

"That's different. He loathes me *and* he thinks I'm crooked. He said . . . well, never mind that."

"If it's about this business, I do mind rather."

"Just that . . . he thinks I'll go to any lengths for an acquittal." He caught Roger's eye and laughed angrily. "It doesn't matter," he said.

"Not unless we can outwit dear Uncle Hubert," Farrell agreed. "At least, he's left us alone. Like you, I wonder why."

"He wanted his dinner," said Antony literally. "Which, come to think of it," he added in a reflective tone, "is what you might call a refinement of cruelty."

"Are you hungry? For some reason or other, I seem to have lost my appetite. But it should give us a little time."

Antony went again to the door, listened a moment, and then came back to perch on the arm of the chair. "What happened to you?" he asked.

"I suppose I was kidnaped," said Roger, stopping to consider the word as though it was unfamiliar. "I got back into the car at Victoria, and just as I was starting off a chap jumped in at the back, shoved a bloody great revolver against my neck, and told me to drive on. I stalled the car in my agitation—which I'm glad to think annoyed him—but I wasn't in a position to argue; I was sweating, I can tell you, by the time I got her started up again. We drove to a sort of warehouse place, not too far from here, where a couple of his colleagues were waiting; and after it was dark we came on board. I suppose it should have been obvious, but I hadn't realized until then . . . and even when I saw Uncle Hubert it seemed so unlikely, and especially that he should make plans involving his crew. You see, the police asked all sorts of questions on Saturday that didn't seem to make sense, but I didn't know until you were talking just now that these bullion robberies were involved at all."

"They weren't, really. Just a complication," said Antony. "And to go back to what happened, how did you get that black eye?"

"That was at the warehouse. I'm rather ashamed of that episode, really, because it was so completely futile. But I'd have got beaten up anyway, because I'd got the wrong car, and they wouldn't believe me when I told them the police still had the Jensen."

"Not very bright of them."

"That's what Uncle Hubert said, when they told him. And he

took one of my cards—damn him!—and told one of them to hire a car somewhere, in my name."

"What are they going to do with it?"

"The chap will drive down to Grunning's Hole, leave the car, and take out the yawl as soon as it's light enough. He'll rendezvous with the *Susannah* somewhere about mid-morning. I'm not quite sure what sort of an accident I'm going to have," he added, "but I gather it's going to be fatal."

"You have to hand it to him," said Antony gloomily, "it ought to work. They won't know whether it's suicide or accident, but the case will be closed as far as the police are concerned. I wonder how he's going to work me into the story."

"I expect he's going to make it look as if I shot you," said Roger, equally despondently. "That would fit in with what he said to Soames."

"It sounds only too likely. How do you feel now?"

"Ready for anything." This was obviously a lie. "What are we going to do?"

"The main thing is to get away from here. But I can't help feeling, if we could do something to delay the *Susannah* . . . I mean, if we can get that tape to the police—"

"Oh, yes . . . the tape. You've kept on saying it doesn't prove anything."

"I'm sorry, Roger. In court . . . well, I've told you all that, haven't I? But just now, if we could interest them at all in Mr. Denning—"

"How would that help? Perhaps I'm being dim, but—for all Uncle Hubert's solicitude about my ignorance—I haven't really got the whole story yet, you know."

"Did you read about the bullion robbery at London Airport last week?" said Antony. "The proceeds are here, somewhere . . . on the *Susannah*. Well, I'm not absolutely sure about that," he added honestly, "but at least Denning didn't deny it."

"Well, I'll be damned," said Roger blankly.

"So you see why it's important."

"I see that all right. How do you propose to set about it?"

"I thought you'd have some ideas," said Antony vaguely. He

had walked across to one of the portholes, and pulled back the brown velvet curtain that covered it. Beyond, the river was dark except where the *Susannah's* own lights were reflected. A tug was going by with a string of lighters in tow.

"Nice trusting disposition, haven't you?" Roger jeered. "And he was quite right, you know, we can't get out that way."

"I didn't suppose we could." He dropped the curtain into place again. "Well, what about it?" he asked, turning.

"If I could get to the engine room—" Roger broke off, and an odd expression came into his eyes. "If that's the fuse box—" he said, and got up with sudden energy and strode across the room.

"Quiet!" But he had no need to worry. Roger had paused short of the door, and was examining the paneling as silently as anyone could wish.

"I'm not just sure where the engine room is," he muttered, "but with the bridge almost overhead the fuses might easily have been put in here." A section of the panel opened under his hand and he stood contemplating with satisfaction the complex of wires and switches that lay within.

"What are you going to do?"

"Send the whole bloody thing to blazes." He beckoned imperiously, and Antony came up to his side. "Those two cables . . . see! If I join them together it'll put a short circuit right across the electrical system. There won't be any fuses between this point and the storage batteries. Given a bit of luck that should result in a pretty fair holocaust."

"Yes," said Antony. "Yes, I should think it might."

"Would that interfere with your evidence? If there is gold on board I imagine it's being carried as ballast, and by the time the fire float has finished it should be safe enough. Anyway, even if she sinks, it could easily be recovered in this depth of water." A thought seemed to strike him. "Afterwards . . . can you swim?"

In spite of the tension, in spite of the reasonableness of the query, it cost Antony a moment's struggle to stifle his resentment. "I can get along," he said. But then he gave his sudden smile. "Not Olympic standard," he admitted, "and not terribly fast."

"Well, do you think—?"

"I can manage. Could you pack up the tape, Roger? I suppose that really is the one, on the machine there."

Roger picked up the machine and dumped it on the desk. "Do you think that's why he left us here together?" he asked. "Because he really wanted me to play back the conversation?"

"I think it must have been." A sadism too nice for physical violence, but only too ready to inflict mental pain. Roger's mind must have been running on the same lines, because he said thoughtfully:

"I never realized he hated me; I just thought he preferred Isabel because she . . . because she—"

"Had a greater regard for the proprieties," Antony supplied.

"Something like that. Well, there's one way of finding out if this is the tape you want," he added, and put out his hand to the switch. "Shall I?"

Antony didn't attempt to urge the point. There was a moment of silence, and then a whirring sound, a background clatter of crockery, a rumble of voices; and then, clear and agitated, a man saying, "I had to talk to you. Why the devil did you want to give Cooper my address?"

Roger's hand moved again; the tape stopped. "That's Dad, all right," he said in a hard voice. "Do you want any more?"

"Not now . . . no time." He turned to the window again; he didn't want to look at Farrell just then. "Will you take it with you?"

"Yes." The tape was running back now. "I don't think," said Farrell, almost in his normal voice, "it matters if it gets wet."

"Doesn't it?" Antony turned back to face him again and was feeling in his pockets. "I brought this plastic thing with me, anyway," he said, "and I daresay it's waterproof. We may as well be on the safe side."

"I can quite see you may view it differently," Roger said, "but it seems to me Meg knew what she was doing when she brought me to see you that night."

Antony was watching the removal of the tape. "Are you going to marry Meg?" he asked.

"That seems to be the general idea." He tucked the spool into the plastic bag, and put the package into his inner pocket.

"Whatever you hear when we play that thing back?" Antony persisted. It didn't strike either of them that it was hardly the moment for such a discussion; but perhaps, after all, it was, of all times, the only one at which it could have been held.

"Whatever I hear," said Roger steadily. "The thing is, you know, Meg's so confoundedly sensible."

Antony looked at him blankly. Of all the descriptions that might have been applied to Meg Hamilton, this was one that had never occurred to him. "You mean . . . by comparison?" he ventured at last.

"About some things," Roger told him. "I admit she needs someone to look after her."

"I suppose it's all right," said Antony, refraining from comment on the fatuousness of this remark, "so long as you don't want her to give up the stage."

"I don't want her to give up anything. But," added Roger, coming back to the present with a jerk, "the question may never arise."

"Who lives may learn," Antony agreed. He looked round the cabin. "I like your plan, but I suppose you realize we're rather more likely to learn than live."

"I stopped believing in Father Christmas quite a few years ago."

"That's good. Then, listen. The lights will go out, won't they?"

"Yes, of course."

"We'll have to wait a minute by the door, but unless our guard is Casabianca in person—"

"I thought that was the name of the ship."

"What the hell does it matter?" He was shrugging off his jacket as he spoke and kicking off his shoes. Roger started to follow his example and was stopped with a gesture. "Shoes, yes. Not your coat. I put on this dark pullover on purpose, but that white shirt would be much too conspicuous. Button the jacket up . . . that's right . . . and turn up your collar. We've got to keep together once we get into the water, so it won't matter your carrying a handicap. Now! When I think it's safe to move, follow me, and don't start anything unless I give you a sign." Roger was staring at him, and he broke off and demanded: "What's the matter? Is there anything you don't understand?"

"I think I've got it all, so far," said Roger meekly. "But what if the guard's still there?"

"I don't suppose you've ever strangled anybody?" said Antony, rather in the tone of one who deplores the degeneracy of modern youth. "I can probably cope—" he gestured with his left hand, a chopping movement, extraordinarily evocative—"but if not . . . well, it doesn't matter what you do, as long as you knock him out, and as long as you're quiet about it."

"Consider it done."

"The next bit may be tricky, but the darkness will help and there's bound to be a good deal of confusion on deck. We've got to get to the side, and I don't want to be seen going over—or heard, of course—so you'll have to give me a hand. We can go downstream with the current, the tide's running that way, and for goodness sake keep track of me, we don't want to get separated. We'll come ashore as opportunity offers. There's a pier, isn't there, just below Battersea Bridge? After that, it's just a matter of praying we find a phone box not too far away. Right?"

Roger took a deep breath. "On the whole I think it's just as well you didn't express yourself quite so forcefully to Uncle Hubert."

"I daren't," Antony told him with a faint grin. "He'd probably have clapped us both in irons."

"Very likely." Farrell had crossed the room again and was rummaging in the top drawer of the desk. "They took my penknife," he said, "but there's a pair of scissors here, I can use that." He looked questioningly at his companion. Under the stimulus of action all his customary energy seemed to have been restored.

"We'd better get on with it," Antony agreed. "I think it's barratry," he added, as Roger went back to the open fuse box. "Or is that something else?" He watched Roger strip the insulation from the cables, and went on vaguely, "I don't know the penalty, either, but I'm pretty sure it's a felony."

Farrell had wrenched the cables out of position now, so that the bare wires crossed but did not touch each other. "Are you ready?" he asked, and with a sharp movement wound them into contact. As he did so, the lights went out.

There was an agonizing pause while nothing seemed to happen, and the darkness smothered them like the folds of a blanket. Antony had time to remember that Roger had said, "With any luck . . ." Then there was, unmistakably, the acrid smell of burning, and the unceremonious clatter of the fire alarm on the bridge. He put out his hand, and began to slide the door open, very gently.

THE DIVISIONAL INSPECTOR'S OFFICE AT THE LOCAL PO-
lice station was not a large apartment, and with six men in it con-
ditions were definitely overcrowded. Superintendent Briggs had ap-
propriated the desk, and the D.I. didn't attempt to dispute his
control of the situation, but he meant to keep a watchful eye on
what was going on.

"And so the guard obligingly left his post, and the way was
clear for you to leave the cabin?" said Briggs, heavily sarcastic. He
didn't want to believe the story, he'd never had a taste for fantasy,
but he recognized reluctantly that there were at least some elements
of truth in it.

"If he felt as jittery as I did when he heard that damned fire
bell, I'm not surprised he went up on deck." Antony spoke with
surprising mildness, but Inspector Sykes, who was standing by the
window, thought it was probably exhaustion, rather than any sudden access of virtue, that enabled him to keep his temper.

"It doesn't matter why he went," said Roger. "He did go, and
a good thing too. You know all this, Superintendent."

"You forget, we're making a statement," said Antony. He waved
his hand toward the shorthand writer who was sitting in a cramped
position at the corner of the desk, and added irrelevantly, "Scribble, scribble, scribble, Mr. Gibbon," so that the superintendent

196

wondered for a moment if he were becoming light-headed. But he went on soberly enough, "There was one chap in the bridge house, but he was busy with a fire extinguisher and didn't look round. On deck it was lighter, of course, but not light enough to recognize anybody unless you stopped and peered at him . . . and no one was doing that, I can assure you. We went aft, away from the blaze. In fact, it all went better than I expected—"

"There were one or two bad moments," said Roger.

"So there were. And the river . . . this isn't the sort of night I'd choose for bathing. When we phoned the Yard they told us you were here, Inspector. And you sent a car for us, and I suppose you got in touch with the superintendent." His tone was very faintly reproachful.

"Your earlier call left me uneasy," Sykes admitted. "There wasn't much I could do, but I thought I'd take a look round, and Inspector Higgins was kind enough to give me facilities. The report of the fire on the *Susannah* came in, and I was just going down there when your call came through. So I thought maybe it was more important to hear what you had to say."

"Inspector Higgins was also kind enough to give us a change of clothing," said Antony. "And if the superintendent's still doubtful, you can both confirm we were wet when we arrived here."

"Like a couple of drowned rats," agreed Sykes solemnly.

"I can well believe," said Briggs, with an attempt at humor that struck Antony as ghoulish, "that neither of you started out the evening dressed like that." It had to be admitted, however, that their adventures had left both of them the worse for wear, not least in the matter of clothing. Roger, in a sweater and uniform trousers that fitted him well enough, looked more piratical than ever, while Antony, who was feeling the cold, was grateful for the overcoat with which he had been provided, but it was many sizes too large for him, and not precisely elegant. The sight of him was enough to fill the superintendent with irritation, and now he added roughly, "You've admitted responsibility for the fire aboard Mr. Denning's yacht, but how do you propose to prove the rest of the story?"

"I shouldn't have put it quite like that," said Antony. He was conscious of an almost overwhelming desire to go to sleep and was inclined to be resentful of the fact that Roger seemed to have found the evening's events an invigorating experience. "Self-preservation," he added, but it was too much of an effort to explain. . . .

"I've given you the tape-recording," said Roger, all the more belligerently because the idea still troubled him, "and Maitland has told you what this fellow Cooper had to say. Why don't you play it, then? You admit you've got a machine—"

"Of course they have. They played over the other tapes from Grainger's collection, didn't they?"

"And we fully intend to hear this recording." Briggs looked across at the divisional inspector. "If one of your men could fetch the machine from my car—" As he went out, Sykes said in his quiet way:

"Even if it provides an alternative motive for Grainger's murder, Mr. Maitland, as you allege—"

"You're looking too far ahead, Inspector. If it comes to trial the prosecution can say Farrell had motive and opportunity . . . but they can't say now he's the only one that had."

"Would that be enough for the jury?"

"Perhaps . . . perhaps not. Most likely not," he admitted. "But what I'm concerned with *now* . . . if I can just persuade you to take a look at the *Susannah*—"

"What am I supposed to find there?"

"You can take Jim Bennett's fingerprints, for one thing. Wouldn't it mean anything if you could prove his connection with the bullion robberies and with what happened outside our house on Friday night?"

"It would be interesting, certainly," Sykes agreed. "What else, Mr. Maitland?"

"The proceeds of the job at London Airport."

"You admitted yourself that was guesswork. *We* can't take cognizance of the fact that Mr. Denning didn't deny it."

"All right, then, . . . let me offer you the evidence of our crime. You'll have to investigate that."

"There's no hurry," said Sykes placidly. "Inspector Higgins's men are there, and the river police by now, I dare say. No one will be allowed on board except the firemen until we give the word."

"But if Denning and the others leave?"

"At the last report he showed no sign of doing so, and four of the crew are with him."

"Only four?"

"The others are at the Y.M.C.A. Some of them got wet, and that seemed the best place to advise them to go."

"Well, I hope to goodness your people will take care."

"It isn't as bad as that," said Roger suddenly. "He's a cautious old bird. I bet any artillery they had on board went over the side before they came ashore."

"That's all very well, but why are they hanging around?"

"They don't know we got away, and they probably think the fire was accidental. Uncle Hubert thinks he can brazen anything out . . . you heard him; and I expect he wants to keep an eye on his investment. No one would think it strange, in the ordinary way, if he arranged to have the *Susannah* towed away for examination and repair. As for the four crew members, they're sticking around to keep an eye on him. Wouldn't you, in the circumstances?"

Inspector Higgins came in with the tape recorder and put it on the desk. Sykes left the window and came across to fit the tape in place. "In any case," he said, as he made his preparations, "Mr. Denning will be asked to make a statement, before he leaves the scene." He looked up and the amusement deepened in his eyes. Maitland was so very obviously infuriated by his patience and unconvinced by his arguments. Then he pressed the switch and saw Roger Farrell's hands tighten almost convulsively on the arms of his chair. As before there came the whirring sound, the clatter of plates and knives, and the voice said urgently:

"I had to talk to you. Why the devil did you want to give Cooper my address?"

"But, my dear James, how could I do otherwise?" *That was Denning's voice, unctuous and obviously insincere.*

"I don't want to see him. You could have made some excuse."

"He's been in touch with you, I take it."

"He phoned me yesterday, asked me to have lunch with him."

"I hope you accepted." *Denning sounded amused.*

"I wouldn't have done if I'd had time to think. Good God, Hubert, what do you think I'm going to say to the fellow?"

"He will thank you for the efforts you made to save his brother, you will disclaim modestly, and you will then be free to talk of other things."

"I can't do it!"

"Is your conscience troubling you?"

"*My* conscience?"

"You can't deny we were both—shall we say?—much better off without him."

"Better off? That report meant ruin."

"Precisely. You weren't so keen then on the truth being known; and now . . . can you afford it?"

"Because I held my tongue—"

"I can still remember the arguments you used, persuading yourself. What was done was done, and denouncing me wouldn't bring him back to life."

"It was true, wasn't it?"

"It is also true that it was very much to your advantage to keep quiet; and once having done so, so far as the law is concerned—"

"Who said anything about the law?"

"Would you like an investigation? There could be one yet, if anyone knew both sides of the story. Nothing could be proved, I grant you that; but would you like it known that you went sailing with a man who had it in his power to ruin you, and that he didn't come back?"

"Of course I shouldn't, but there's no question of that."

"There'll be no question, unless you raise it yourself, James."

"I'm not proposing to tell Cooper anything."

"I'm glad to hear it. I was beginning to wonder."

"I've kept my mouth shut, haven't I, all these years?"

"And you were wise to do so."

There was a pause, while the tape went whirring on, and the silky menace of Hubert Denning's last words seemed to hang in the air. Roger made a sudden, jerky movement, as though he would have liked to stop the recording there, and as suddenly was still again. Antony looked up, and found Inspector Sykes's eyes fixed speculatively upon him. The superintendent said harshly, "If that's

200

the lot—" and was interrupted by James Farrell's voice, speaking slowly and in bewilderment.

"What do you mean?" *The words were no more than a whisper, and yet somehow, to each man there, it was as if they had been shouted.*

"When I am threatened, I act." *Denning's tone was casual now.* "That's common sense. But Cooper's death showed me that I was in an extremely vulnerable position; I had to remedy that, to insure myself, as it were, against error."

"If you're playing the market, you can never be sure you're safe."

"There are other sources of wealth, James, and since that time I've been exploiting them. If you're careful enough . . . but you have to be very careful. I always was a good judge of men. I've been right about you, haven't I, all along? And so much knowledge came my way, so many odd little items of information, it seemed a pity not to make use of them. Apart from things I knew officially, I've always found that very few men are really discreet, especially among their associates."

"Hubert . . . what are you telling me?"

"You think I'm being indiscreet now? You may be right, but I don't really think so. I told you I'm a good judge of men. We played for small stakes at first, and sometimes we were unlucky; but nobody ever gave me away. It paid them to keep quiet, just as it has paid you to do so, though I've wondered sometimes if it was mainly the thought of Winifred—"

"Leave her out of this."

"It meant a lot to her, didn't it, your changed circumstances? More, perhaps, than it did to you. But I was telling you that gradually, very gradually, the number of my associates grew, and the stakes became really big ones, and it didn't matter any more if some of my speculations turned out badly. I had my insurance, you see."

"I can't believe it."

"Are you really so naïve? I hope I haven't shocked you, because it's really very important that our friendship should continue exactly as before. You do see that, don't you?"

"Why are you telling me this?"

"As a warning. I've learned one thing over these last years: if you're completely ruthless, you can 'get away with murder.' " *There was something horribly like gaiety in his tone now.*

"A threat, in fact."

"If you prefer the word. As long as I can trust you not to put any ideas in Cooper's head, there's no harm done."

"For my own sake, I'm hardly likely to do that."

"The only unpredictable thing about you, James, is your conscience. I'm telling you to keep it within bounds, that's all. I think you will, for one thing because of Winifred. And for another—when you come to think it over—because I've really told you so very little."

Superintendent Briggs came to his feet as Sykes turned off the tape recorder. Antony murmured, "Have at thee!" under his breath, but the inspector, at least, must have heard him for he turned and said:

"Exactly. But we'll have to ask you to wait a while . . . you and Mr. Farrell."

"Yes, of course." He didn't add that, at that point, they'd have had difficulty in getting rid of him.

A few moments later he went out with Roger in the wake of the constable, who had been experiencing a good deal of doubt during the whole of the interview as to how much he was supposed to write down. As the door closed Antony heard the superintendent saying, "You understand the danger involved, Inspector? These men—"

The waiting room was as cheerless as he had expected, but they couldn't complain of neglect. A constable brought them the inevitable tray of tea, and another contributed an electric fire. "It always seems to go cold as soon as the heating's off," he told them, waiting for a moment to see the bars redden before he went away.

"I expect we can thank Sykes for this." Antony hitched his chair a little nearer the warmth and wondered if Roger was ever going to speak again. But it seemed he had come at last to the end of his silence. He got up and poured tea into the two thick cups and pushed one of them across the table.

"You got what you wanted," he said.

"More than I expected," said Antony. "And now, if they find the gold . . . and Bennett . . . that should see you in the clear as far as the gang's activities are concerned."

"Yes, of course. But what about Grainger's death?" He both

looked, and sounded, completely uninterested in the question, and Antony's reply came rather sharply.

"They may not be satisfied that you didn't kill him; but I think they'll realize—now—that we've got a defense."

"You mean, they'll drop the charge?"

"Just that."

"And Meg will be safe?"

"Both of you."

Roger blew on his tea and tried to drink some of it, but it was still too hot. Presently he put down the cup and turned away restlessly. "He isn't a fool," he said. "Why didn't he destroy the tape?"

"He thought he had us safe," said Antony. "And I don't mind telling you, *I* didn't expect that trick of yours to work. Besides, I think you were right . . . he wanted you to know."

Roger halted by the window; there was nothing to be seen beyond, unless it was his own reflection against the darkness. "If he guessed I'd find the truth about my father unpalatable, he was right," he said. "Not that he was a murderer, after all . . . just that he was a coward."

A silence that neither of them seemed able to break spread itself coldly between them. Roger stayed where he was, staring at the windowpane. Antony shivered, and after a moment began to drink his tea.

It seemed a long time before they were called back to the inspector's office again. Nobody could have called Superintendent Briggs cordial, but the result was the same: the charge against Roger was withdrawn.

"But you can't leave us in the dark like this?" Antony protested. Briggs said only:

"Good night, gentlemen," with finality. But Inspector Sykes came out with them to the police car that was going to take them back to Kempenfeldt Square.

"There's a lot of work ahead of us," he told them, shaking his head over the prospect. "Mr. Denning and four of the crew are in custody, a man named Soames among them. And you were quite right about that, Mr. Farrell, they were unarmed, so everything went off quietly. The rest of the crew are safe enough for the moment, it's just a matter of making our arrangements—"

"What about Bennett?"

"Now, that's a different story. There's a body taken from the river with a nasty head wound, and I think—mind you, I say I *think*—it may prove to be Bennett. They said he'd left the *Susannah* a month since; they all said that, and as you saw him tonight there must have been some reason."

"Denning said, 'get rid of him.' I didn't think they'd be so quick about it."

"It doesn't take long to hit a man over the head. No longer than it takes to set a fire, for instance," Sykes pointed out. "They were ready to sail, weren't they? I don't suppose they meant to put him overboard just there, but it was the only thing to do when they had to abandon ship. And lucky for us, or there might have been more difficulty about identification."

"Was he seen to go over?"

"Not exactly. The river patrol picked him up; the fire was going well by then, and they were pretty quick on the scene. But from what they tell me he couldn't have been in the water long; it sometimes happens that the clothes will keep a body floating for a while, so—as I say—we were lucky. We'll know as soon as they've checked his prints, and then I think we'll take some of the other crew members to have a look at him. You never know, they might be persuaded to talk."

"And the *Susannah?*"

"Not in too bad shape, all things considered. And provided no smart lawyer turns up with a writ of habeas corpus before we've had chance to examine her, everything should be quite satisfactory."

"Did they tell you we were on board?"

Sykes allowed himself a prim smile. "There were some crocodile tears over that, Mr. Maitland. And a good deal of consternation when the superintendent told them what had happened. I'll say that for Mr. Denning, his nerve's good, and I don't think he's given up hope even now. His solicitor is with him. But, of course, after hearing what he said to your father, Mr. Farrell . . . well, I expect there'll be more evidence to be found, now that we know where to look for it."

"It's a funny thing," said Antony thoughtfully, "that one of the ideas I thought so reasonable was based on the fact that Grainger didn't know what sort of a tiger he'd got by the tail when he started to blackmail Denning. I admit the conversation was cryptic, but it was perfectly plain he was dangerous."

"I expect Grainger relied on his anonymity," Sykes told him, and embarrassed Roger by shaking his hand firmly before ushering him into the car, and thanking him for his help.

At least this had the advantage of startling Farrell out of his gloom. "Help?" he repeated, rather as if he were fascinated by the word.

"That's changing your tune, isn't it, Inspector?" asked Antony, amused.

"I was about to say, for yours too, Mr. Maitland. If you've forgotten what happened on Friday night, I haven't," said Sykes reprovingly. "Two of our men——" He broke off there to ask, "Won't Mrs. Maitland be worried? You ought to be getting home."

"I phoned her after I spoke to you, while we were waiting to be picked up." He climbed into the back of the car, but Sykes was holding the door and did not slam it immediately.

"I was expecting you to ask for Sir Nicholas to be sent for," he said.

Antony leaned back and grinned at him. "There'd be hell to pay about that if you hadn't been so . . . reasonable, Inspector." Sykes smiled back at him. "As it is, I can tell him Friday night's episode is cleared up—and, like you, that's what he was mainly interested in—and even that I've concluded a sort of truce with the superintendent, which he probably won't believe. And he'll be gratified," he added to Roger, as the car moved away, "that he won't have to defend you . . . or Meg."

"Do you suppose he'd give her away instead?" asked Roger. Antony gave a shout of laughter, and he added huffily, "What's so funny about that?"

"You can't get married with a black eye." He was surprised,

but relieved, to find that Roger's thoughts were taking so proper a course, but he didn't want to say so.

"I can get married just as soon as I can get a special license," said Roger firmly. He turned to look out of the window, and added in so low a voice that Antony was able to pretend he hadn't heard him, "If I wait till it all comes out at the trial I may lose my nerve again."

Obviously the only thing to do about that was to rely on Meg's good sense, which Antony did with some misgiving.

The explanations to his uncle went over more easily than he had expected; in fact, long before they were finished he thought Sir Nicholas's attention had begun to wander. He said, rather severely, "So you needn't have made so much fuss about Meg. I was quite worried." But then he added, confounding his nephew's hopes, "You haven't told me why you went on the *Susannah* last night."

"I was hoping you wouldn't ask me that," said Antony weakly.

"I *have* asked you," Sir Nicholas pointed out.

"I don't see what else I could have done, sir."

"But what did you hope to accomplish?" There was no reply to this, so he added reasonably, "It wouldn't have done any good to get yourself killed as well as Farrell."

"But I couldn't just sit back and fold my hands, Uncle Nick. And I didn't think Sykes was going to do anything." To judge from Sir Nicholas's expression, as an explanation this was getting nowhere. "Besides," he added, "Jenny was worried. She wanted a happy ending for Meg."

"You can't tell me Jenny encouraged you in such a senseless piece of folly," said Sir Nicholas, shocked.

"Well, not exactly." He'd deliberately soft-pedaled his account of the wreck of the *Susannah,* and much good it had done him. What he needed now was something to distract his uncle. "Meg's going to be married," he said.

"Is she, indeed? Do I know the man?"

"To Roger Farrell," said Antony patiently.

"I told you . . . no, you say his part in all this was an innocent one, and I suppose I must believe you. We must hope no harm will come of it," he added doubtfully.

"Jenny's pleased," Antony told him.

"She is a woman, and therefore romantic," said Sir Nicholas. And the interview might have ended on this note of gloom if he hadn't caught sight of one of the papers on his desk and picked it up absent-mindedly. "What could he have wanted with five gallons of paraffin?" he wondered. "He *says* he was going to make the candles himself and that a study of the dictionary will to some degree support his contention. But I can't help feeling . . . do you really think the jury will believe him?"

About the Author

Sara Woods, daughter of a Yorkshire wool merchant, was born in Bradford, England. She was educated at the Convent of the Sacred Heart in Filey Yorks.

Miss Woods worked in a London bank during the Second World War and has even spent some time raising pigs.

Her background as a secretary in a Yorkshire law office has enabled her to write mysteries with an air of authenticity. Her first novel of suspense, entitled *Bloody Instructions,* was published in 1963. Since then she has written a good many more novels, featuring Antony Maitland.

In private life Miss Woods is married to an engineer. At present they live in Nova Scotia, but they travel frequently to England and to the United States.

Format by Morris Karol
Set in Linotype Times Roman
Composed and printed by York Composition Co., Inc.
Bound by Haddon Craftsmen, Inc.
HARPER & ROW, PUBLISHERS, INCORPORATED